METHODS OF
MADNESS

RAY GARTON

Contents

Fat

O ne week after most of the excess fat had been sucked out
of my body through three little holes—and the day after
my mummy-like wrapping had been removed—I woke
up in pain. But I woke up knowing that I would not, as I'd
thought for so long, always be fat. This, in spite of my
discomfort, was an improvement over the previous mornings
of my life, and helped make the pain endurable, even a little
enjoyable. Because it meant the fat was gone.

Finally and forever *gone.*

Actually, it wasn't morning; it was almost two in the
afternoon, because I'd slept late, something Dr. Foster said I
should do for a while.

"Your body," he said, "has been caught by surprise. It'll
take a while for it to adjust to its new condition, and you'll need
plenty of sleep."

To say my body had been caught by surprise was an
understatement; it had been ambushed.

Groaning like Marley's ghost, I crawled out of bed and,
naked, gingerly made the painful trek to the bathroom. I stood
before the full-length mirror on the back of the door, unable to

1

open my eyes for a few moments. I was either savoring the suspense or genuinely afraid to look, I'm not sure which. Dr. Foster had warned me that the transformation would not take place overnight. There would be a lot of swelling and bruising that would linger for weeks, maybe months. But when I opened my eyes, my scrotum shriveled as my testicles crawled up into my stomach. Dr. Foster's warnings did not prepare me for the ravaged body that stood in the mirror before me.

The holes were covered with bandages on the outside of each thigh and the right side of my abdomen. But not the bruises.

They sprawled like rot just beneath the surface of my skin, the color of overripe bananas mottled with purple and yellow.

My head filled with helium and I bowed it, clutching the edge of the sink to keep from staggering.

The bruises alone would have been more than enough, but there was more: stretch marks.

I'd had stretch marks before; you can't lose weight, gain it back, then lose it and gain it again and again without collecting stretch marks on your body like notches on a hillbilly's shotgun. By the time I was thirty, I had as many stretch marks as a mother of four, maybe more. But they weren't like *these.*

These were *trails* carved into my flesh, jagged and interconnecting, some so deep that flaps of puffy loose skin hung down over them. Dr. Foster had warned me of that, too— "After the swelling goes down, you'll have a lot of loose flabby skin; exercise will help that." —but, again, I was not prepared for what I saw. Parts of my body appeared to be melting, the flesh liquifying and running off my bones toward the floor, where it would form a thick puddle at my feet.

I turned away from the mirror, gulping, and leaned over the sink to splash cold water on my face and into my sticky, foul-tasting mouth. As I dried my face, I vowed to avoid mirrors. For a while, at least.

I had been avoiding mirrors all my life; I could do it a while longer…

———————

Remember when you were a little kid first starting school and it was all new and scary, the teachers were tall walking buildings with wise voices and watchful eyes, and you felt small and insignificant and unwanted even by your parents because they'd brought you to this strange place full of strange people and things and they'd *left* you? Remember how scared you were of all those bigger kids in the grades ahead of you who were *not* strangers to this place because they'd been there before and gave you withering, ominous glances on the playground? Remember how that made you feel even *smaller?* And then—*then!*—remember how you—and all the other new kids like you, who were just as scared and small as you—discovered that one classmate—boy or girl, it could have been either—who looked even *more* scared? He or she was different, somehow, ugly, perhaps, but most likely… *fat.* You discovered something: there was someone *less* significant than you. And that made you feel better.

That kid was me.

Oh, it wasn't *specifically* me; I mean, I didn't go to the same school you did, chances are. But that was *me.*

I was fat.

I don't remember *not* being fat. Even before I started school, I vaguely remember my grandmother pinching the nubs of flesh over my chest, scrunching up her face, and saying, "We're gonna have to get you a little bra for your titties, you don't quit getting fatter, Benji." Wonderful woman, my grandma. She was the first person to point out to me that I was fat. She didn't just point it out, she rubbed my face in it. And after rubbing, she would laugh.

I remember one day in the summer before I entered junior high when Grandma came over and I was sitting at the table eating. Dad was working late and Mom was busy doing something or other, so I was at the table alone. Grandma came in and said, "So. Which meal is this, today? Number four? Five?"

I snapped. I stood so fast I knocked my chair over and started screaming at her, using words I'd never used before, words I didn't even know I *knew*. Grandma shrunk back and her lower lip quivered and she whimpered, "I-I-I was just kidding, is all."

That was the last time I ever spoke to my grandma—my parents who normally insisted that I respect my elders, seemed not to mind, perhaps even approved a little—and, unfortunately, it was also the last time I ever stood up for myself, the last time I ever demanded a little respect of my own.

"I *was* fat; I knew it and everyone else knew it. I heard it every day at school, from both my peers and my teachers, and I heard it from my grandma and my cousins and uncles and aunts. After I blew up at my grandma, I changed, I think. Whenever my weight was pointed out to me, cruelly or otherwise, I simply did not respond. The things I said to my grandma, true as they might have been, changed nothing. I was still fat and she was still cruel. So, giving up, I took whatever those around me cared to dish out.

But inside, I reacted. Inside, I hurt. I bled. Inside, I wanted so much to hate them. But I couldn't. *They* weren't fat. *I* was. So I hated myself.

All through grammar school, I had only one friend. I was not lonely. Not as far as I knew, anyway. Does a child born into

4

poverty know that he's poor? No, not until people start *telling* him he's poor. I knew nothing else. I had books to read and movies to see and television to watch and, as far as I was concerned, that was all I needed, that and my best and only friend, a boy named Tommy Fischer. He had a stutter so severe that listening to him comment on the weather was more suspenseful than the best Hitchcock movie.

Sometimes Tommy joined me after school in one of my favorite pastimes: watching television and eating. Tommy was one of those guys who could eat until the sun turned green and never *ever* get fat, so it had no effect on him, but when I think back on those days now and imagine myself sitting in front of the television eating licorice sticks and Pez and peanut butter sandwiches and barbecued potato chips, I can almost *see* myself getting fatter with each bite, with each crunch.

We'd watch *Batman* first; we took it very seriously and would discuss quite heatedly, after each episode, how Batman and Robin the Boy Wonder (whom we both thought was a sissy) would get out of their fix, which would be revealed tomorrow, same Bat-time, same Bat-channel. After a couple more pretty cool shows—*Ultra Man* and *Lost in Space*—we got down to some *serious* television: *Star Trek*. This ritual usually took place at my house, where the food was more accessible: Ho-Ho's and Ding Dongs, pretzels and Cracker Jacks, Ritz crackers and Braunschweiger, and anything else we could find in the 'fridge.

We were inseparable during those early years of our education, until the inevitable happened: we discovered girls.

Actually, Tommy discovered them first. And he discovered that girls had no interest in a guy who took ten minutes to introduce himself. So he started working on his stutter. I'm not sure what he did—read books, listened to tapes, maybe saw a speech therapist, I don't know—but he disappeared during the summer before our freshman year in high school and when we met again that fall, the stutter was gone. Worse yet, Tommy was *cool* He dressed cool, he talked cool, and he acted cool.

Fat was not cool. I was fat. Draw your own conclusions.

The spring of our freshman year, I literally ran into Tommy turning a corner in the hall. Our books went everywhere, but we just stood there staring awkwardly at one another. We'd hardly spoken the entire school year and I think I saw Tommy blush as we stood there. He looked at his shoes a moment, looked at the ceiling, then said, "Huh-huh-hi, B-B-Buh... Buh-Buh-Bennnn... ji. Howzzzzzz... i-i-it g-g-guh... guh-guh-goin'?" I think I flinched; his stutter had been dormant since the previous summer but now he was struggling with his tongue as if it were a piece of raw meat in his mouth. I finally made some dull response and tried to start a conversation, thrilled that he was talking to me after so long, but a gorgeous blonde girl wearing an enticingly snug sweater walked by and cooed hello to him and he immediately said, "Hey, Debbie, how's it goin'? Lookin' *good.*" When she was gone, he glanced at me, swept up his books, then hesitated before giving me a big grin, slapping me on the back and saying quietly, "I'm sh-shuh-showin' 'em Benj. I'm g-guh-gettin' 'em buh... buh-back. F-f-for buh-both of us." Then he turned and disappeared down the hall. I didn't understand what he meant and never found out. We never spoke again.

Suddenly, without even Tommy to pal around with, I was on my own. I didn't handle that well. I discovered I was never truly alone as long as I had food. But even the food let me down; it only made me fatter.

————————

Shopping for clothes was an ordeal, always had been. While browsing through the clothes on the rack, I was invariably approached by an adorable, perky female clerk who smiled and asked, "Can I show you to our Husky Department?" It didn't matter what store I went to, they always wanted to rush me into the Husky Department, like I was going to scare off all the thin guys by poking around in *their* department. And the husky clothes were always the stuff of nightmares. I had the feeling that designers throughout the world were conspiring to keep overweight guys like myself from looking good. I figured they got together late at night and huddled around their drawing boards—a bunch of skinny, limp-wristed, lisping types—and came up with all kinds of goofy outfits with ugly stretch fabrics and horizontal stripes, all the time clapping their hands together and giggling, "Oh, *thith'll* keep thothe doughboyth out of the dithco, *won't* it?"

After Tommy cut me off and I started to balloon even more, something awful happened. I went to the local mall for a pair of jeans and the biggest pair I could find, the *huskiest* pair in the whole *mall*, was too small. That day, that very *afternoon*, I did something drastic… I went on a diet.

After leaving the bathroom—and the two mirrors which lurked there, eager to show me what had been done to my body—I put on my robe, put on some coffee, and turned on the television. It was an October Saturday and wind was blowing against the windows. As a picture formed on the television screen, I was taken back to my childhood afternoons with Tommy Fischer because, on the television, Burgess Meredith was *quacking* with a long black cigarette holder clutched between his teeth, threatening Batman and Robin with a fate worse than death. I checked my TV *Guide* to find that a local station was running a *Batman* marathon: twenty-four hours of continuous *Batman* episodes, back to back. I was in hog heaven.

I sat on the sofa with an idiotic grin on my face, sipping coffee as the day faded into evening. It didn't happen until about an hour later, when Catwoman was taunting Batman in her skintight black suit, tempting him to leave that brat in the green shorts for a life of crime at her side.

The cravings.

My hands felt so *empty*. There was no licorice stick to slip between my lips; no crackling bag of chips in my hand. I wanted to snack.

No, I thought.

"Uh-uh," I said, "absolutely *not*."

The fat was gone, banished, *sucked* out of my body through a tube, disposed of like the trash that it was, and out of my life forever. I was not, under any circumstances, going to let it grow back, let it creep beneath my skin again, swelling me up like a cordless bruise, tightening my clothes, thickening my neck.

No.

I would change the channel, watch something else.

But Julie Newmar was so luscious, so seductive in her black tights and spiked heels. She brought back so many familiar memories, good, pleasant memories. Comforting memories...

... and the hum of the refrigerator in the kitchen was like a lover's bedroom sigh, like a slender, beckoning finger...

But I was determined that I would not—*would not!*—allow myself to give in, as I had so many times before, to those familiar and enticing urges that I knew were no more than destructive habits. I could resist them, and I could do it without changing the channel on my television set. I had never done it before, but I would *this* time. This time, I would not allow the fat to come back and take me in its lover's embrace as it had before. I would fight it. *I would.*

The wind blew outside and there were sounds against the walls of my small house—restless, skittering sounds that grew and faded—and I tried to listen to them instead of that low, almost subliminal call from the kitchen; it sounded not unlike the tuneless humming of a winking, smirking woman as she stepped out of her clothes. But there was something odd about those sounds outside. It took me a moment, but I finally realized what was wrong...

The sounds did not coincide with the angry gusts of wind beating against the walls. I frowned, blinked and stood, facing my front door. The sounds seemed to be coming from the screened in porch that surrounds the front of my house. I went to the door, opened it a crack and peered out as a gust of wind trembled the long rectangular screens. There was nothing out of the ordinary... but I'd heard *something*...

I returned to the television and tried to lose myself again in *Batman*. The sounds outside continued. So did the sound from the kitchen... that steady, monotonous humming...

I decided, as I settled myself again before the television, that I would fight it this time. I would...

———————————

The first diet went very well because I was so determined to reach my goal.

My goal was named Mardee Russo. She was golden-haired with sky-blue eyes and a voice as smooth as baby flesh. She moved like a ballerina and left behind an invisible but oh-so-enticing trail of Ciara perfume—which, to this day, I cannot smell without swooning to thoughts of Mardee—and, for reasons that escape me to this day, she approached me in the school cafeteria one afternoon and asked to speak with me about something very important. We'd spoken before in classroom situations and sometimes we crossed paths walking to school in the morning—we lived only blocks apart; I was always fidgety and clumsy beneath her velvety gaze and said as little as possible for fear of making an idiot of myself, but we *had* spoken. This was different, though, obviously important to her and worthy of privacy because she took me to a corner table and leaned close.

"I know we don't know each other well, Benji," she began, "but you seem... different. More... mature than the others. And... well, I have to talk to *somebody*. It's about... my boyfriend."

And that's how it started, my reputation as a good listener, a confidant, and a source of sound advice in matters of the heart. I'd never had a date and the closest I'd ever come to an actual relationship was having a female lab partner with whom to dissect frogs in biology, but for *some* reason, this girl—this *vision!*—saw in me something she could trust, and poured out her heart on that cafeteria table.

I don't remember what her problem was or what advice I gave—it was simple common sense, I remember that much—but Mardee Russo, the most coveted girl on campus, seemed to think it was the wisdom of the ages, and after that brief conversation in the cafeteria, we became friends. I was honored and I cherished our friendship, but it was simply not enough.

I was in love.

But I was *fat*, and I knew no amount of maturity or friendship could make a girl like Mardee Russo look beneath that fat to see the boy who adored her so.

So I dieted. I ate lots of fruits and vegetables, no junk food— although I craved it like a junkie—and I even exercised, getting up an hour earlier every morning to toss my lumpy body around in the privacy of my bedroom until my skin prickled with sweat.

It worked. It took *months*, but the pounds began to fall away and by spring I found I was no longer being hurried into the

Husky Department by perky clothing store attendants with white Chicklet teeth framed by glossy rictus grins; in fact, some of the very same attendants who had done so several times in the past did not even recognize me. And they treated me *differently*. Their smiles were suddenly genuine and they seemed at ease, almost *relieved*, as if they were thinking, *Oh, thank God he's not another* fat *one*.

If only Mardee Russo would notice the difference, too…

———————————

By the time Batman and Robin were matching wits with Louie the Lilac, the persistent sounds outside were driving me crazy. There was a fat neighborhood cat that sometimes crept through a tear in the front screen and raced up and down the porch diving at moths and flies—and, I suspect, a few creatures of its own imagining—but the cat made a very distinct *ka-flump, ka-flump, ka-flump* as it ran over the wooden floor and more often than not, because it usually lost control of its fat wobbly body, it ran into a wall, or the woodpile, or one of the stacks of junk on my front porch.

These sounds were not like that; they were heavier, quieter, almost as if a dead weight were being dragged over the wooden floor.

I looked out the window a couple times but saw nothing. The wind continued to blow, more furiously than before, and, because I felt too stiff and achy to go out and look around, I settled back onto the sofa and returned my attention to *Batman*, still trying to ignore the siren's call coming from the kitchen: the refrigerator's merciless hum. I knew there were eggs in there… a fried egg sandwich with mustard would sure taste good. There were a couple of shrimp cocktails—you know the kind in the little hourglass-shaped jar, full of ketchup and those little tiny firm shrimp, probably about eight hundred and fifty calories each—and some chocolate Jell-O pudding with vanilla swirls. And there were frozen tater tots in the freezer, right next to the frozen Sara Lee cherry cheesecake. Why hadn't I gotten rid of all those before I went into the hospital? Why hadn't I gutted my kitchen of those caloric bear traps?

The temptation to go to the kitchen for one of those old friends so I wouldn't have to watch *Batman* alone was overwhelming, but then—

———————

—the phone rang.

It was Mardee…

She noticed. It took a while, but she *did* notice. It was in the hall at school. She stepped before me suddenly, her eyes wide, lips parted, and said, "Have you lost *weight?*"

I grinned. "Yeah. Guess so." The weight had been coming off for months and, for months, I'd been hoping she'd notice, but it wasn't until that moment in the hall that it occurred to her that there was less of me.

"You look *great!*"

"Thank you."

"Have you been dieting?"

"Well, I don't know… sort of, I guess."

"Well, you look great. Hey, whattaya doin' tonight? I mean, ylcnow, around six, or so?"

"Oh… nothing."

"You wanna meet?"

"Yeah. Sure. Guess so. Where?"

"Well… how about the Burger Barn?"

I didn't want to go there. No one will ever know how much I *did not* want to go there. But how could I tell her that going to the Burger Barn would undo some of what I'd worked so hard to accomplish? How could I tell her that for me to go to the Burger Barn would be like an alcoholic going to a bar? I mean, you can't meet someone at a place called the Burger Barn and *not eat*, can you? The only reason one would meet a friend at a place called the Burger Barn would be to *eat*, right? But this wasn't just any friend; this was Mardee Russo. "Sure, that's fine," I said, with a plastic smile.

So we met at the Burger Barn. She showed up looking like an adolescent boy's dream and I... well, I looked like *me*. Even though I'd lost a lot of weight—nearly forty pounds—I *still* felt fat and self-consciousness. But I guess I expected some of that self-consciousness to melt away because—and this is *not* to my credit, now that I look back on it—I expected Mardee to look at me differently because I'd lost so much weight. I guess I expected her to fall into my arms and smother me with kisses, or something... I don't know. But whatever I expected, I was disappointed. There was only one reason she met with me; there was only one thing she wanted to talk about: her boyfriend.

His name was Lorne and we talked about him—or, rather, *she* talked about him—for nearly two hours, at which point I administered to her another dose of what appeared to me to be the most *common* sense. She seemed encouraged by my wisdom, took my hand and said breathily, "Oh, Benji, I just don't know what I'd do if I couldn't turn to you. Thank you *so* much. Here," she added, opening her purse, "the burger's on me. You've earned it."

I went home and ate a bowl of ice cream covered with peanut M&M's.

Mardee Russo has always been one of the few constants in my life. We grew up together, went to the same schools, even the same college, and ended up working two buildings apart on the same block in the town of Redding, California, where we'd always lived, and where, for the first nineteen years of our lives, we'd lived only four blocks away from one another. Over the years, of course, I was able to tuck away my affection for Mardee, the way one might tuck away old photographs that are simply too painful to look at anymore. But even now, all these years later, I still get a little dizzy when I catch a whiff of her perfume—still Ciara, she *always* wears Ciara—and when she touches me, even in the most friendly, platonic way, my skin still tingles for several minutes and my mouth becomes dry. I keep telling myself that I'm a big boy and I can take it… but when I decided to have the liposuction done, I still harbored the hope—deep, *deep* inside—that the removal of all that hideous fat and my resulting thinness would finally prompt her to take notice of me in a way she never had before.

She knew I'd gone in for the operation; in fact, she was one of the very few people I'd told. She also knew that my wrapping had been removed the day before and was calling to see how I felt. A few brief telephone conversations—we *always* kept in touch by phone—had been our only contact in a few months, maybe a little more, and I realized, when I heard her voice that day, that I missed her. That was silly, of course, because, although our telephone conversations were always pleasant and upbeat, the only time I ever *saw* her was when she was unhappy—usually because of her current boyfriend, whoever that might be—and I suspected I would be seeing her again soon. She'd been dating a local lawyer for several months, which was longer than I'd expected it to last. When she asked me what I thought of him, as she always did, I told her the truth: I thought he was a materialistic cretin who was so in love with himself—with his good looks, his money and, most of all, his *car*, a Lamborghini—that he would *never* be able to remain faithful to her. She'd smiled then, tossed her head and giggled,

"You just don't see what I see in him." When I asked what that was, she was silent a moment, then shook her head distractedly and said, "Never mind. You wouldn't understand. Just take my word for it, Benji. He's different than all the others and... I'm in love."

Okay, fine.

"Do you feel like company?" she asked as I changed position on the sofa and winced at a few sharp pangs.

"Well, I don't know if I'd *be* good company, but if you don't mind a cripple..."

"Oh, don't be silly. I know you're messed up. I thought maybe I could come over and make you a nice healthy dinner and we could talk."

"Oh. Anything in particular you want to talk about?"

"Well... sort of."

"Your lawyer?"

"My lawyer."

"Sure, come on over."

She said she had to do a load of clothes at the laundromat and she'd be over in an hour or so, then said goodbye. I leaned back my head and sighed, knowing what was coming. Things had changed little between Mardee and myself since high school. Although it hadn't worked—maybe because I hadn't *expected* it to work—I'd tried, the summer after our high school graduation, to change things. Just once...

———————

We were in the park watching the Sacramento River rush by when I decided to do it. I was thin again—well, thin for *me*, anyway—after another of my emergency diets had taken twenty-five pounds off my frame... *back* off my frame, I should say. We had been walking for an hour or so and Mardee's eyes

15

were puffy from crying over the loss of her latest boyfriend, a sophomore at Chico State named Chet… that's right, *Chet;* this was the *second* time Chet had dumped her and, as she had before, she was vowing never to take him back again, never to answer his calls or open his letters again. Hearing this from Mardee was not unlike hearing a presidential candidate vow never to raise taxes. Except for a few sniffles, she was silent as we stood beside the river, waiting, I was sure, for me to pass on another dose of relationship wisdom—something with which I'd *still* had no experience and about which I still knew nothing. But this time, I wasn't going to wing it. *This* time, I knew exactly what I was going to say and how I would say it. I'd rehearsed it down to the smallest facial tic. But somehow, things like that never come out sounding the same if you're not in front of a mirror.

"How long have we been doing this, Mardee?" I asked. My mouth was suddenly gummy as moist tissue paper.

"Doing what?"

"You know… you get hurt by a boyfriend and I try to cheer you up, maybe give you a little advice, make you feel better. That sort of thing."

"Well… years now. All through high school."

"Right. And we're out of high school now, right?"

"Uh-huh." She frowned. "What's the matter, Benji? Are you… tired of it? I mean, if you're sick of hearing about my—"

"No, no, just let me finish, please." I had to stop a moment to regather my thoughts, then: "So, we're out of high school now, and this is *still* happening, right? I mean, here we are, you're crying, and I'm trying to think of something to say that will make you feel better, but… well, I'm afraid that, no matter what I say, it's just gonna happen again. And I hate to see it, Mardee. I hate to watch you go through this over and over. You

16

don't deserve it. *Nobody* does. And I can't figure out why the hell you keep going through it again and again."

"What *choice* do I have?" she asked sadly. "How am I supposed to know if a man's gonna hurt me or not? How do I *tell?* They're all the same, at first. Charming, sexy, sweet... full of promises. Then... bingo, they're with somebody else or just plain *gone.* So how do I know if that's gonna happen or not? I just have to... you know, keep trying."

"Okay, then tell me this. If you knew a guy who wouldn't hurt you —"

"But where am I gonna find a —"

"Just play along for a minute, okay? Let's say there's a guy who would never hurt you, and you *know* he'd never hurt you. In fact, you're so certain of it that you entrust him with your most personal thoughts and problems. This guy, let's say, is concerned about how you feel. He wants the best for you. He... well, he cares a lot about you. In fact... well..." I could see it was dawning on her now, the lights were blinking on, and I stumbled over my words. "... you might even say that... you know, that this guy, um... luh-loves you, because he's seen you go through so many —"

Her face split into an enormous grin and she fell forward, throwing her arms around me and burying her face in my neck. My heart performed feats of acrobatic daring hitherto unseen by human eyes and I lifted my arms reluctantly, almost unable to put them around her and *definitely* unable to believe what was happening. Mardee and I had hugged before; she hugged me a lot, but they were always friendly hugs, buddy hugs. This was different. Her embrace was tight and her lips were pressing against my neck and when I finally put my arms around her, she held me even more tightly and laughed, "Oh, Benji, you are *so* sweet, you know that? I mean, you're one in a million."

I grinned, then, and had to fight back a peal of joyous laughter.

"But really, Benji, you don't have to say that just to make me feel better."

I gulped, pulled back and said, "What makes you think I'm saying it to make you feel better?"

Then—*then*—she looked serious... *really* serious, as if she'd made a horrible mistake... the way you might look when you find out the person to whom you've just told a slanderous Italian joke is Italian.

She whispered, "You mean... you *mean* it?"

I felt my face begin to warm. "Yuh... yeah, I mean it. Is that so bad?"

"Well, no, it's not *bad*, but..." She embraced me again, sighing, and stroked my back. "You're something, you know that? I don't know how long you've felt this way, but it's news to me. You know what you are, Benji?" She pulled back and looked me in the eyes. "You're a catch. I mean you are a *real catch*. You're the kinda guy women dream of finding... well, sooner or later."

"Sooner or later?" I asked in a weak voice.

"Yeah. I mean, you're the kinda guy a woman dreams of settling down with... eventually. I mean, you know, after she's through fooling around and she's *ready* to settle down. After she's... you know, had her fun, sowed her wild oats. Know what I mean?" She put her face to my neck again and whispered, "You're kind... loving... so warm. And you know what?" She pulled back again, smiling. "You're my favorite person in the whole world to *hug*." Again, she pressed herself close to me and said, "You're so sincere ... so giving..." Putting her hands just above my belt, she squeezed the mushy love handles left over from my latest diet. "... so soft and cuddly..."

I wanted to scream from humiliation. I wanted the ground to open up and gulp me down like an aspirin. I wanted to die. But no… that would be too easy. I had to face her.

"Do you understand?" she asked, smiling up at me. "I love you, *too*. I really do. But I love you as a good friend. My *best* friend. In the whole world." She squeezed my waist. "You're my cuddly, chubby teddy bear."

So I was husband material… absolutely out of the question as a *date*, of course, but *perfect* husband material. I had flickering black and white images of myself walking through the door in the evening in a dark suit and tie with a newspaper tucked under my arm, briefcase in hand, kissing my wife—who wore an apron over her gray shirtwaist dress, of course—and saying, "What's for dinner, honey? Are the kids home?" Like Ward Cleaver, or Donna Reed's husband. *See?* I can't even remember *that* poor bastard's *name!*

As we stood there beside the river, still embracing, I paid close attention to the warmth of her body against mine, the graceful curve of her back, the smell of her hair and perfume, the touch of her lips against my neck… because after hearing her little speech, I figured it would probably be the last time I'd ever touch a woman until after I'd walked down the fucking aisle, and I wanted to enjoy it.

But after giving her words a few moments to sink in, I couldn't disagree with her. There I was, eighteen years old, and I was probably more out of touch with my peers, with my entire age group, than anyone could possibly be. I'd never made out in a car parked in the woods or at a drive-in movie. I'd never *been* to a drive- in movie. I'd never attended any of the keggers for which so many of my fellow teenagers seemed to live. I'd never been *invited*, of course, but then, it's really not that hard to crash a kegger if you really want to go. I just couldn't imagine myself attending one… standing around among all those other teenagers who would no doubt be laughing, dancing, getting drunk, getting laid... I just couldn't imagine it. I didn't know how to have that kind of fun; I'd never had any practice. And dance? *Me* dance? Come on. I have a hard enough time keeping a beat by tapping my fingers on a table top, and my fingers have never had all that extra jiggling fat attached to them. The very thought of myself walking onto a dance floor and shaking my booty, even to this day, gives me the chills. That's why I had never attended any of the school dances. That bothered me, too. I'd never even *danced*...

Maybe she's right, I thought. *Maybe I'm just destined to be one of those chubby grinning husbands you see on detergent commercials and sitcoms: cuddly and dependable, but not exactly what you'd call exciting.*

Mardee pulled away and looked up at me cautiously. "Have I hurt your feelings, Benji?"

"No," I lied, smiling...

Between two of the back-to-back episodes of *Batman*, I looked around the living room and realized the place was a mess. Although I wasn't as limber as usual, I knew I could at least pick up a few things before Mardee arrived. But as I leaned down to move a stack of old newspapers—

—something slammed against the front window and I froze. It sounded like something very heavy. Something wet. I stood and faced the window, which was covered by the Venetian blinds. Leaning over the sofa, I parted the blinds and looked out. Everything seemed blurred, as if the window were wet. It *was* wet. Something clear and viscous was dribbling down the outside of the pane. Something with a strange tint to it... a sort of yellowish-pink. And it was fresh. I searched the section of the porch I could see through the blinds, but I saw nothing. Except...

There seemed to be a trail over the wooden floor. A long, broad, wet trail…

I made my cautious way to the front door—cautious because it hurt so much to move—opened it and, as I looked out onto the porch, I heard a loud clatter from the woodpile. My head jerked to the left in time to see a squat chunk of wood tumbling down the side of the sloppy, haphazard stack. It was there that the glistening trail ended: the woodpile. Tiny globs of yellowish-pink clung to the wood. My eyes followed it slowly to the window, then back along the floor… all the way back to the corner where that fat hobo cat was oozing his way through the tear in my porch screen.

"What do *you* want?" I asked, mostly to calm my nerves; I was still buzzing with adrenalin from the crash against the window.

The cat froze, stared at me a moment, then gave a tentative, questioning meow, as if asking my permission to come in and play.

"Oh, all right. Come on."

He flopped onto the porch heavily and looked at me with a curious, bemused expression before curling up to wash himself vigorously.

The screen door was closed and latched; no one had thrown anything onto the porch. As far as I knew, there were no liquids on the porch, nothing to spill.

It looked as if someone had slung something heavy and wet against the window, then dragged it to the woodpile. But there was nothing there. And why did the trail lead back to the corner of the porch and end where the cat still lay, licking himself clean as if he were going on a date?

Then I saw it.

Beads of it clung to the cat's fur and trembled like dew drops on his whiskers. He swiped a paw over his face several times, shook his head furiously and stared up at me with insulted eyes as I approached, limping gingerly over the moist trail in my bare feet.

"So where'd you pick *this* up, huh, kid?" He wasn't too crazy about being touched, but he held still long enough for me to pluck some of the goo off his twitching face.

It was slimy between my fingers... greasy...

When I looked at the tear in the screen, I noticed larger chunks of the substance clinging to its frayed edges. The tear was bigger than when I'd seen it last, too.

It looked almost as if whatever had made that trail had exited through that tear. Or...

"Or," I breathed, "it came *in*... through here."

Have you ever felt like you were suddenly no longer alone in a room? That's how I felt. I'd felt that way before, back when I was a kid. In a decaying, abandoned house in the woods behind our school, Tommy and I had discovered a splintered wooden crate filled with faded, tattered pornographic magazines with pictures of men and women doing things to one another that I did not know were possible, let alone legal. (Come to think of it, they *weren't* legal in some states at the time.) The very afternoon we found them, I went back after Tommy had gone home. I just had to be *alone* with those magazines... you know how it is when you're ten. And right in the middle of *being alone* with those magazines, I felt it. That sense of not... being... alone... *anymore*... It was that feeling of being caught going through your mother's purse, or your dad's wallet, or your sister's diary... I was afraid to turn around, afraid to *breathe*, for fear of seeing my parents—or, God forbid, my *sister*—grinning disgustedly because they'd caught me *being alone* with those magazines.

Once again, I was afraid to turn around. But this time, I wasn't sure why...

Behind me, the cat meowed again, this time firmly, threateningly.

Then he hissed.

I closed my eyes a moment, imagining the cat behind me — and somehow I knew, I just *knew*, that it was standing on top of the woodpile — back arched, hair stiff and ears flat, eyes jet black above those needle-like teeth.

I spun as the cat screamed.

I caught just a glimpse of its tail whipping downward, disappearing into one of the black, jagged openings in the woodpile.

The cat made another sound — an abrupt, final sound, like a sledgehammer falling on a squeak-toy — and then something *else* made a sound. It so resembled a thick wet gulp that I thought it was *me*.

But it wasn't.

It came from the woodpile and, with it, came one more muffled sound from the cat; it seemed to come through a couple of thick feather pillows.

Two more pieces of wood rolled down the side of the pile and thunked to the wooden floor. The entire pile seemed to shift, as if preparing to stand, then I was alone on the porch. Nothing moved. There were no more sounds, except the wind hissing through the screens. I didn't even breathe for what seemed a long time, then I sucked in a sudden breath and staggered against a weathered old bookshelf I'd been meaning to refinish for a couple years.

"Cuh... cat?" My voice sounded like rusty pipes. "Kitty cat? C'mon, boy. C'mon outta there." I knew it would squirm out of the woodpile in a moment, looking around in that embarrassed way cats look when they get caught being clumsy.

It didn't. The longer it didn't, the more I began to expect something *else* to squirm out of the woodpile...

Setting my sights on the front door, I pushed away from the bookcase and moved carefully along the deck, resting my hands on everything I passed in case I needed something to lean on, but as I neared the woodpile, I froze up. I simply could not move. My eyes were locked on that woodpile and I kept listening, waiting to hear something from that damned cat, and when I *didn't* hear anything, all I could think was, *I don't have any shoes on*, and I kept staring at that woodpile—at those big gaps between the pieces, at the darkness inside—knowing I was going to have to walk closely past it to get to the front door.

Run, I thought. But I couldn't run; it was hard enough to walk. Instead, I stood there, staring at the woodpile.

It shifted.

Two more pieces fell to the deck.

And then… it moved. The entire woodpile moved. Toward me.

I tripped over a box of old newspapers as I backed away from it and nearly fell on my face staggering along the deck to the corner, where I made a wide, clumsy turn and stopped outside my bedroom window. The latch hadn't worked since I'd moved in, so it was impossible to lock, but even from the inside, it was a stubborn window to open and from the porch, it was even harder. My weakened condition didn't help any.

In other words, the window wouldn't open.

The thunderous sound of wood tumbling over the porch came from around the corner as I pushed up on the window with trembling, white-knuckled fingers. When the wood was finally still and silent, I heard the sound I'd heard earlier while watching television… but now it was louder. Something heavy was *shooshing* over the deck toward the corner. First, a long ponderous *ssshooosssh…* then a moist gulping sound… then another *ssshooosssh…*

I struggled with the window, struck the frame a few times with my fist, pushed, grunted, and—

—whatever was around the corner moved closer.

The window budged, then budged a bit more, but did not open.

I stopped for just an instant, long enough to suck in a big breath, and glanced toward the corner, just in time to see it crawling—no, no, it didn't crawl… it *poured* itself—into view.

All air seemed to leave the porch as I stared for a long, deadly moment at the thing that jiggled its way around the corner, reflecting the sky's dull light on its glistening yellowish-pink surface, which was covered with what appeared to be bruises—dark, purple-brown bruises—and long puckered scars that cut across its shapeless form, crisscrossing again and again. It was about three feet tall at its peak, but sloped downward into a shivering gelatinous mass with liquidy edges that darkened the wooden deck and tensed suddenly as the thing slurped forward, then relaxed to a breadth of about three or four feet.

And at the end of that seemingly endless instant, the thing rolled forward, straight toward me, and I saw the meandering, pencil-thin veins—no, they were too tiny to be veins—they were miniscule, pink capillaries that covered the creature like a net just beneath its ravaged viscous surface—and my stomach roiled like boiling split pea soup.

The window would open no further.

I looked around my feet frantically until I found a small braided throw rug that had been lying crumpled beneath the window for ages, picked it up, shook it open and wrapped it around my arm. I had begun to perspire and the cobwebs and dust balls on the rug clung to my moist skin and made me itch, but I ignored it as I pulled my arm back and swung it into the windowpane, shattering the glass with a muffled clack.

The thing was a yard away from me as I cleared away the jagged shards around the window's edges and hoisted myself through.

The floor was covered with glass and my feet were bare, so I had to throw myself from the window to the bed, where I landed in a storm of pain that covered my whole body, and then—

—I realized what I had done. I turned to the shattered window and could hear the thing coming closer... *ssshooosssh, buh-gulp... ssshooosssh, buh-gulp...*

I had given it entry.

Trying hard to ignore my pain, I threw myself from the bed to the bedroom door and tumbled, groaning, into the hall, where I slammed the door hard and leaned against it.

It would come in through the window, there was no doubt about that. But... what *was* it?

A part of my brain spoke up; it was the part of my brain that spoke to me—in a sharp, sarcastic tone—whenever I started to overeat after a long bout of dieting. It said, laughingly, *You moron. You know what it is. And you know what it* wants. *It's been torn from its home... it's hurt... it wants to move back in...*

"No," I rasped, pressing my back to the bedroom door. "No, it... it *can't* be that. It's too... too *big*, I was never *that* big..."

No, you *weren't*, the voice chuckled, *but who knows what it's eaten on its way over here? Who knows how many* cats *it's swallowed...*

I clenched my teeth and closed my eyes tightly, groaning, "Noooo..."

Something *thunked* in the bedroom, then it sounded as if someone were in there dragging a bag of sand over the floor...

Running like a penguin because of all my sore spots, I went to the hall's entryway and grabbed the recliner in the living room. It was heavy anyway, but in my weakened condition, moving that chair was a little like moving the whole house. Somehow, with a lot of grunting and groaning, I managed to get it in front of the bedroom door. The door opened inward, but I knew that thing would never be able to operate the knob. In fact, I really don't know why I moved that chair in front of the door; I was scared and it seemed the thing to do.

Leaning against the wall in the hallway, I heaved for breath, exhausted and aching, my eyes locked on the bedroom door.

I heard tires crunch the gravel out front and turned to the open front door. *Dear Lord, she's here*, I thought. But it was only the mailman stopping at my rusty box. I limped to the door, shut and locked it, then returned to the hallway, staring at the bedroom door behind the recliner, and—

—I screamed and fell forward when my bare feet sank into something wet and tepid and so… *squishy*. I landed on the hall floor and, in the second before I began to crawl desperately toward the kitchen, I felt that snot-like substance move around my feet, as if it were being poured around my ankles, slapping against my skin and rising up around my legs.

Pain screamed silently inside me as I clambered on hands and knees into the kitchen, stood and turned to see the thing oozing beneath the bedroom door, pouring out from under the recliner and spreading over the floor.

I babbled something as I struggled to my feet, something that sounded, I suppose, as terrified as I felt, but I can't remember what it was. I slammed the kitchen door and backed away from it, staring at the thin gap between the floor and the bottom of the door.

I could hear it on the other side, swishing over the floor and against the hallway walls, gurgling and slurping…

I felt numb as I looked around the kitchen frantically for something—*anything*—that I could use to…

To *what?* I thought. *To do* what? *What am I gonna do?*

27

Do what you always do, that smartass inner voice sneered. *Feed it*

I laughed out loud. Yes, I was afraid—*terrified*—and that thought didn't make me feel any better—in fact, it made me feel *worse* because it didn't sound all that crazy—but I laughed because it struck me as being very funny, the idea of feeding my own fat; if it had scared me this much when I was a kid, I never would've *gotten* fat!

I didn't know what to feed it.

Feed it the same thing you always *feed it*, that cruel voice said as I turned to the cupboard above the refrigerator.

There was sluggish movement beyond the kitchen door as I opened the cupboard and scanned the selection of junk foods: Twinkies and Ho-Ho's and Ding-Dongs, fruit pies and Slim-Jims and candied nuts… there was even a big bag of Lay's sour cream and onion potato chips.

There they were… all my friends… lined up in the cupboard waiting to be chosen…

For just a moment, I didn't hear that thing outside the kitchen any longer; I heard, instead, the *Batman* theme from the television in the living room, and I looked at all those things in the cupboard, thinking of how very *good* they had always tasted in front of the television… and how good they might taste there again…

Then it slammed against the door.

The slurping sound that followed was thick and slow, but showed no sign of stopping. On tiptoes, I swept my arm through the cupboard and scooped the junk food onto the floor. I bent down and began stuffing the Ho-Ho's and Ding-Dong's and fruit pies into the baggy pockets of my robe, unwrapping the last two I picked up as—

—the thing oozed around the corner of the stove and began pouring itself toward me.

I threw the two Ho-Ho's and they hit the thing with a phlegmy slap. It stopped, seemed to flinch, then folded itself slowly over the two treats and sucked them loudly into its middle as—

—I reached up and grabbed the potato chips as I backed into the sewing room—no, I don't sew, but the old lady I rented the house from called it a sewing room, so I called it a sewing room—ripped the bag open and scattered the chips over the kitchen floor. In the sewing room, I slammed the door and staggered back against the wall nearly tripping over a bucket of nails as I gasped for breath. I could feel my heartbeat in my ankles. My fear was made even worse by the fact that I didn't know what I was *doing* in there! It would no doubt come oozing under the door any minute. *Then* what?

The sewing room opened onto the laundry room, which was small, cramped, and had only a single bare bulb hanging from the ceiling. Besides the door, the only way out of the laundry room was through a small rectangular window above the washer and dryer (the stacked kind, small and compact, with the dryer on top of the washer).

I got an idea.

Lying along the wall on the far side of the laundry room were some old baseboards I'd replaced when I first moved in; there was a bucket of nails at my feet and a hammer hanging on the sewing room wall. If I could get the thing into the laundry room, I could nail a baseboard over the gap below the door and leave it there until after Mardee had gone. Then I could... whatever.

Feeling like a walking bruise, I waddled hurriedly into the laundry room, grabbed one of the boards and took it back into the sewing room, then began emptying my pockets of junk food, unwrapping each one and leaving a trail of Ding-Dongs, Ho-Ho's, fruit pies and Slim-Jims back into the laundry room.

The plastic wrapping was stubborn and I had to pull and bite each one before they tore open.

Then, at the very moment I heard a horrible gushing sound in the sewing room, I realized—in much the same way I realized that I'd created an opening for the thing to get into the house—that I had nowhere to go. I had cornered myself in the laundry room in a pool of meat sticks and packaged desserts and that yellowish mass of quivering fat was just a few feet away from the open doorway sucking up some cherry MoonPies.

I threw myself forward and slammed the door, cursing myself for my stupidity, then backed away from the door, staring at the small gap below it as my mind raced and my heart hammered.

The room was dark except for the fat shaft of dull light coming from the window above the washer and dryer. I stared at that window, thought about my aches and pains a moment, then listened to the sounds coming from beyond the closed door. It didn't take me long to climb on top of the washer, where I stood precariously, hugging the dryer, as I reached up and opened the window.

Not long ago, I wouldn't have fit through that window if I'd been pulled on a chain by a semi, but as I hoisted myself up onto the dryer and clumsily crawled out, feeling as though I were managing to bump each and every sore spot on my entire body, I thought of one of those many clothing store clerks with her plastic grin and perky, bird-like voice and I grunted to myself, "Take *this* to your fucking Husky Department, you *bitch!*"

With a sound like someone overturning a full spittoon, the thing rushed into the laundry room from beneath the door and I glanced back to see it engulfing a row of Ding Dongs.

The world tilted as I squeezed out the window and the ground outside slammed down on top of me like a giant flyswatter. The inside of my head lit up for a moment and the pain was so great that I thought I would be sick. I laid there for a long moment, bathing in my pain, then, after several rapid, desperate gulps, I managed to hold down my gorge and began crawling, slowly at first, then faster and faster until I was on my feet and staggering around to the front screen door like a drunk when I realized that as soon as that glob of fat was through sucking up all that junk food, it would be oozing its way back out of the laundry room to look for… well, for *me.*

My bare feet thumped across the porch, I burst into the house and into the sewing room. I could hear it in the laundry room, slurping and gurgling, as I slammed the door. Dropping to my knees, I grabbed the baseboard and slammed it against the bottom of the laundry room door, dragged the bucket of nails to my side, got up for a moment to grab the hammer and began nailing the board to the door. The slurping on the other side stopped, there was a brief shuffling and, as I drove the last nail in, the thing rushed against the door with a heavy wet slap, and I…

Well, once the last nail was in, I leaned back on my arms, elbows locked, and began to laugh. It was an exhausted, gulping laugh, punctuated by groans of pain, but it was genuine, because the situation seemed funny at the time.

Most people have skeletons in their closets, I thought. *I have my fat in the laundry room…*

I imagined myself a few years in the future, still thin, still in good shape, but with a secret: I only stay that way if I keep feeding junk food to the growing blob of fat locked away in my dark, cramped laundry room.

I laughed some more… until I heard a knock at the door.

"Benji? You in there?"

I swallowed my laughter and stood, realizing that I was a mess. My robe was filthy and my bare legs were scratched from my climb out the laundry room window. My hair was hanging in my eyes and I was trembling all over.

"Benji! It's Mardee!"

"Yeah, yeah," I breathed, scrubbing my face with my hands and sweeping my hair back. "Okay, okay, I'm o… kay."

It slammed against the laundry room door again and so startled me, I fell against the stove, crying out in pain as I bumped one of my incisions.

"*Benji?* You all right in there?" I heard the door open, heard the familiar sound of Mardee tossing her purse onto the sofa, then her footsteps as she hurried into the kitchen. "For crying out loud, Benji, what's—"

"I'm fine, Mardee, just fine, really," I said, speaking too fast.

"Fine? You're a *mess.* What've you been doing?"

"I was… I just… nothing. Really."

"But you look awful! And… and…" She looked down at the film of slime beneath her feet. "… what's *this?*"

I moved toward her, saying, "I just spilled some—" then gasped at the blade of pain in my side.

"You're *hurt!*" Mardee put her arm around my shoulders and started to lead me into the living room, then stopped, looking down at the floor. "What's all this?"

I looked down, saw all the junk food wrappers clinging to the viscous substance and thought, *Oh, shit.*

"Slim Jims? Twinkies? Potato chips?" She looked at me, puzzled. "You shouldn't be eating this stuff, should you?"

I tried to think fast, but I wasn't fast enough because that thing rammed against the laundry room door again.

Mardee's eyes grew and she whispered, "What was that?"

It thumped again.

"Oh… that?"

She nodded, looking toward the sewing room. Pulling away from me, she started to cross the kitchen slowly.

I stammered, "It's-it's a-a-a-a… a *dog*."

She smiled at me over her shoulder. "You got a dog?"

"Yeah. That's it. Except, it's not my dog. It belongs to a neighbor." *Yeah*, I thought, *that's good*. "I'm taking care of it for a couple days. Great big thing. A Dane. A *great* Dane. A great *big* Dane." I laughed and thought I sounded a little like that stoned lunatic who cackles as he pounds on the piano in *Reefer Madness*.

"And you've been feeding it junk food?"

"Had to. He-he got out. Of the house. I nearly—" Another laugh, "—nearly killed myself trying to get him back inside, then… then I sort of, you know… lured him into the laundry room with… Twinkies. Yeah. With Twinkies, and stuff." I panicked, because Mardee was beginning to look less and less convinced.

"Are you sure you're all right, Benji?"

"No, I'm not. Sort of. I mean, you know, I kind of… hurt myself outside." I winced, limped toward the living room, and she followed. That was all I wanted: to get her away from that thing in the back. "C'mon out here and just… well, just try to step over that… stuff."

"What *is* it?"

"You don't want to know."

"Oh. 'Kay."

In some ways, Mardee was *so* easy.

In the living room, I eased onto the sofa with a groan and Mardee dropped beside me, smiling, lifted her hand to slap my thigh as usual, then froze.

"I don't want to touch any sore spots," she said, leaning back and sighing, "Well, now." She folded her arms, commenting on how good I looked considering the shape I was in, then began talking, in that familiar melancholy voice, about her lawyer.

I listened to most of it, but my attention kept wandering back to that thumping sound in the back of the house. I nodded and made the usual sympathetic responses as she went on about how her lawyer was paying more attention to his secretary and clients than to her, but I was imagining that thing sloshing itself against the door, rippling liquidly like a huge mound of mucous. Although I tried to relax and follow Mardee's breathy narrative, her voice seemed to fade and I felt as if I were sinking slowly into the sofa as the thumping grew louder and louder...

"—so he says, I mean, after all this time, he *finally* comes right out and says—"

—*kuh-flump*... slosh—

"—'I don't think I'm prepared to have just one woman in my life on a steady basis, Mardee'—"

—*kuh-flump*... slosh... kuh-*flump*—

"—'I don't think I have the necessary stability.' Can you *believe* it? So, I'm thinking to myself—"

—slosh... *kuh-flump*... slosh...

Mardee's voice was a distant whine, nearly buried by the thoughts trumpeting in my head as it all finally began to sink in. I guess things had just been moving too fast since I'd first discovered the thing in the woodpile, so fast that I'd made a hysterical joke of it rather than giving it serious thought. But those serious thoughts were sinking their teeth into my mind now... teeth as fine and sharp as needles...

The one thought that kept repeating itself over and over was, *It can't be... it's impossible... it just can't be*, punctuated by the sneering, smartass voice of my conscience: *Of course it's possible... it's always come back before... it's just a little upset this time, that's all...*

... *kuh-flump*... slosh... *kuh-flump*... slosh...

34

"—and after all the energy I'd put into that relationship, after all I'd put up with from him, he pops up one day and says he's not pre—"

"Would you like a Diet Pepsi?" I interrupted with a voice full of tremors. My mouth was dry and my hands were trembling and my heart was lodged so high in my throat, I was afraid my tongue was sticking out.

Mardee jerked her head toward me, a little startled, I think, that she'd been interrupted.

"Well… yeah, okay, sure. I could use a break." She took a deep breath and sighed.

Relieved, I said, "Be right back." I got up and headed toward the kitchen, but ducked into the bathroom. I locked the door, splashed cold water on my face and slurped some from the faucet. Even in the bathroom with the water running, I could hear its sloshing and pounding and found myself glancing down at the sliver of space beneath the bathroom door. I was reaching out to turn the water off when there was a knock at the door and my bones turned to rubber; I threw myself aside, knocked the hamper over and spilled dirty clothes on the floor and ended up sitting on the edge of the tub.

"Benji?" Mardee said on the other side of the door. "I'm gonna get my cigarettes from the car, 'kay?"

"Yuh-yeah, shuh-sure." I stood and tried to calm myself but the knock came again and I pressed my back against the wall, looking at the bottom of the door with wide, horrified eyes.

"You sure that's just a dog in there?" she laughed. "Sounds like he's throwing water balloons against the door." Her laughter faded as she went through the living room.

I laughed, too; it was the kind of nervous giggle you'd expect from a fifteen-year-old boy in a whorehouse.

Dirty clothes were pooled around my bare feet. I stared at them for a while, marveling at their size. They seemed enormous, far too big for the Husky Department. JCPenney will *never* have a department that carries clothes as big as the ones that lay on the bathroom floor. My undershorts looked like large sacks; the pair of pants at my feet seemed to have been made from the better part of a parachute; there was even a pea green shirt that looked like it had been cut from a tent. I'd hoped never to wear those clothes again as long as I lived, but as I stood there listening to the thing in the back room, I realized that perhaps I'd been wrong.

So *it* likes *you*, that nasty voice inside me sneered. *Is that so bad? At least it's loyal. That's more than you can say for that bimbo outside. Has she ever done anything to make you believe she's loyal? Or that she even* likes *you? If you weren't always there … if you weren't such a good—and, I might add, tree—therapist… if you did so much as one thing that she didn't like… do you think you'd ever see or hear from her again?*

"No," I whispered to my massive undershorts, surprised by the sound of my own voice.

And what did you *do to it? You had somebody stab a tube into it and suck it out of its home like a milkshake through a straw. And yet, after all that, it still comes home. Is that loyal? Is that a friend? Of course it is. It's more than* she *would ever do for you. So… what's the problem?*

I clenched my eyes shut, pressed my fingertips to my forehead and released a breathy groan. When I opened my eyes again, there they were: all those clothes, so big and bulky and… fat. I felt my face screw up. I couldn't bear the thought of wearing them again. I'd throw them away, all of them. I'd burn them, toss out the ashes and dip into what was left of my money to buy new ones.

Better not, that voice sing-songed. *Just in case it gets back in. You'll need your fat clothes then…*

… *kuh-flump*… slosh… *kuh-flump*… slosh…

36

"Oh, God," I groaned, burying my face in a towel as the front door opened and closed.

She's back. Better get out there. Wouldn't want to make her wait to talk about her lawyer, would *we?*

I was beginning to perspire as I went into the kitchen for her Pepsi and I held the cold can to my face for a moment as the thing continued to move against the laundry room door. I tried to clean some of the slime from the floor with a damp towel, but it didn't help much. I think I was really just trying to stall because I wasn't in the mood to listen to Mardee anymore. My fear and confusion suddenly seemed far more important than Mardee's lawyer. But I went back into the living room anyway, closing the kitchen door behind me.

"I haven't seen this show in... well, since I was in grammar school," Mardee said, smoking her cigarette and smiling at the television, where Egghead was making Batman, Robin and Batgirl cry with exploding onion eggs. She popped her Pepsi open, sipped and said, "I remember you used to talk about this show all the time back then. You and, um... that kid you hung around with. What was his name? He stuttered."

"Tommy Fischer. His stutter was gone by our freshman year." I turned the volume up a little before sitting down, hoping to drown out that dreadful sound...

"Yeah, I remember. He changed so much that summer."

"How would you know?" I was surprised by the bitterness that flared in my voice and turned to her with a casual lift of my brows to cover it.

"What do you mean?"

"Well, you didn't know him, did you?"

"Not very well. No one did, I guess, but—"

"I did."

"Yeah, okay, you did, but it was obvious he'd changed. I mean, he didn't stutter anymore, he dressed differently and...

well, before he at least *seemed* like a nice enough guy, but when he came back, he was an asshole."

That startled me. "An asshole?"

"Yeah. He didn't even hang around with you anymore and you were his only friend. You think *that* was nice?"

I sunk into myself for a moment, digesting that. I'd never thought of it that way before. I'd just figured—

"He was busy with girls, is all," I said suddenly, finishing my thought.

"Yeah," she chuckled, "girls. Ol' fuck 'em and duck 'em Tommy."

Again, I was startled. "What? Really? Tommy *Fischer?*"

"You didn't know that?"

"No. I figured he just dated a lot, that's all."

"Oh, yeah, he dated a lot. But never the same girl twice. He'd tell them anything, and I mean *anything.* Y'know, to get into their pants. And it always seemed to work. He was smooth. But he was an asshole. A prick." She was staring at her cigarette and frowning and her voice was cold and brittle. "One day he was a stuttering geek, the next he was smooth as silk. An *operator.* Like he took a class or read some books, or something. Every girl in school wanted to date him. They were practically *fighting* over him. But that wasn't enough for Tommy. He had to divide and conquer. He got greedy, I guess." She looked at me for a moment. "It was almost like he was on some kind of mission. Like he had a quota, or something."

I'm sh-shuh-showin' 'em, B-Benj, he'd said. *I'm g-guh-gettin' 'em buh... buh-back. F-f-for buh-both of us.*

I found myself smirking. "Did you date him?"

She squirmed, shrugged and stared at the television a moment. "I only went out with him once."

"Well, apparently, so did everyone *else,*" I laughed.

"Oh, you think it's *funny.*"

"Well… maybe a little."

"Then I suppose you think everything else is funny, like the way my lawyer has been treating me. Or like the way every other man I've ever been involved with has treated me."

"No, I don't think that's funny, but—"

"Well, that's what happened with Tommy. It was just… different. On a smaller scale, I mean. He came, he saw, he fucked, he left. That's *funny*?"

"No, no, it's *not* funny. But when you think about Tommy's background, it's a little ironic. I mean, he was—"

"I *know* what he was," she snapped angrily, "and that just makes it worse. You'd think he'd be a little more compassionate, a little more considerate. But *no*. He was just like all the other guys."

"Did it ever occur to you that he had to *become* like all the other guys before any of the girls would pay attention to him?"

"What do you mean?"

"Do you think he would've gotten a single date if he'd remained what he was? A stuttering misfit?"

"Well…"

"No, he *wouldn't* have," I snapped, realizing that I was beginning to sound angry, too. "He had to become one of the guys the girls were always complaining about before they'd notice him. If he'd remained what he was, they would've kept laughing at him. But because he became what they seemed to *want*, they *complained* about him. So who's to blame?"

I could tell by the way she looked at me that she was surprised by the direction the conversation had taken. "You didn't do it," she said. "You were always a nice guy. You never became an asshole. You were always friendly and compassionate and understanding and nobody ever complained about *you*."

"No. They *laughed* at me. And I *never* got a date. Not until I was in college. And even then—*since* then—each woman I took out looked at everybody around us as if she were *apologizing* for being with me. And the couple of women I've actually gotten *involved* with? *Hah!* The first one, every time we made love, she said—" My nose curled and my voice whimpered two octaves higher. "—'I've never done it with a guy, um… your size.' After a while, I got tired of it and said, '*Sure* you have. Last night.' But it never made any difference. It wasn't long before she realized she didn't *want* to do it with a guy, um… *my size*, and she left. And then the next one, oh, *she* was great." I stood, amazed by the energy I was getting from the anger I suddenly felt. "We got together, everything was great, I *thought* we were happy, and then one day she says, 'I thought if I loved you, I'd give you the confidence you needed to lose weight and become a whole person, but I guess I was wrong', and she was gone so fast I couldn't see her fucking *dust*. And the last one—she was my favorite—she left me a note that said, 'I know I said I loved you, but I only said it because I thought you needed to hear it. I thought it would help you become a better person, because you're fat.' Can you believe it? Nice of her, huh? Because I was *fat* So don't tell me about what an asshole Tommy was, because he was just doing what had always been done to him. I know, because we were the same. We were *both* misfits. I just never learned to follow the rules like he did. And if the rules upset you, I'm *sorry*. You made 'em."

Mardee slammed her Pepsi down so hard the end table wobbled, then punched her cigarette into the ashtray with a clatter. She looked at me a moment, her jaw working, then stood. "Well, I'm disappointed in you, Benji. I thought you were different. I didn't think you were one of those guys who goes around thinking that women are just out to make men feel like shit. I thought—"

"I don't think that at *all!* I just think they make men like *me* feel like shit. And maybe it's unintentional. Maybe it's got something to do with upbringing or just plain simple ignorance, I don't know. But they *do* it. Again and again."

Her lower lip quivered and her eyes glistened. "I never did. Did… did I?"

I thought about it a moment, weighed what I wanted to say against what I thought I *should* say. Then I said quietly, "Every day since the first time we spoke."

She sat on the sofa again, let the tears flow and lit another cigarette with clumsy fingers. After a long silence, she said tremulously, "That's not true. I've never done that. I'm not that kind of person. I'm… just *not.*"

I sat beside her and sighed, "You've done it in a million ways, Mardee. The way you speak to me, the way you touch me, or *avoid* touching me. The way you treat me when certain people are around."

"It's… because of what I said. Isn't it?"

"Huh?"

"At the park that day. When you told me, you know, how you felt about me. I always knew you'd hold that against me. I always knew it would come up again."

"Hold that again—I don't hold tha—this has nothing to *do* with that! I didn't bring that up, *you* did!"

"Well, it seems logical to me. You tell me you love me—*years* ago—and now you're holding it against me because I didn't feel the same way."

I rubbed my eyes with my thumb and fingers for a moment, then sighed, "Go ahead. Believe whatever you want. But that's not the case. Not at all."

"Well, it doesn't matter. I didn't come here for this. I don't *need* this. I came here to talk about my lawyer. I needed to talk,

41

that's all. I thought you wanted to hear what I was gonna do about—"

"*See?* You didn't come here to see *me.* You didn't come here to talk with *me.* You came here to talk so I could *listen.* And that's all. That's what I'm *talking* about."

Her lip quivered again. "But we've always talked to each other about our problems. We've always—"

"No, Mardee. *You've* always talked to *me* about *your* problems. Haven't you ever noticed? Your little ongoing soap operas always eclipse *anything* I need to talk about. They're your only reason for ever seeing me. Sometimes, even though we've known each other all these years, I don't think you know me at *all.* You've never stopped talking long enough. And back in high school? I don't know why you talked to me about your boyfriend problems. I was a fat outcast. What did *I* know about relationships? I *still* don't know shit about relationships and I suspect they'll *always* be a mystery to me. Because I'm not one of the beautiful people. I'm not one of *you.* And I never will be, no matter *how* much fat I have sucked out of my body." I was disturbed by my own words and I think it showed on my face. But she didn't notice.

She clenched her eyes and the tears gushed as she swung her arm over to put out her cigarette. Her wrist hit the Pepsi can and it spilled all over her lap. The sight of her covered with Pepsi and sobbing was more than my pushover heart could bear and I scooted toward her, put my arm on her shoulders, wincing at a bite of pain in my side, and held her close. "Don't cry," I whispered.

"I thuh-thought we were f-friends!"

"We *are* friends. But… it's a two-way street… you know?"

She laughed coldly, humorlessly. "I thought you cared about me."

"You *thought?* You mean you don't *know?* I told you I *love* you, for crying out loud!"

"See? I *knew* you held that against me!" she sobbed, pushing me away and standing. "I have to go. I'm a m-mess. I'm sorry I've wasted so much of your time, Buh-Benji. I'm sorry I've treated you so *horribly.*" She reached for her purse and in an instant—

—I was that fat kid again, that fat ugly kid who was lucky enough to be pals with the prettiest girl on campus and I was blowing my one good thing—or, at least what I *saw* to be my one good thing—and the smartass voice in my head hissed, *Yeah, that's it, go ahead and run her off, like you're ever gonna have another woman like this hangin' around in your tubby life,* making me want to scream out "Will you make up your fucking mind!"; suddenly, it was as if all the fat was back, straining at my belt and buttons and filling my pant legs like tree trunks and I grasped Mardee's wrist, stood and said, more than a little pleadingly, "I'm sorry, Mardee. Really. I didn't mean for us to fight like this. I'm just... I'm a little edgy and... well, full of holes." I tried a laugh to break the tension, but with minimal effect. "Please, don't go. Sit down and I'll get you a towel. Okay?"

She thought about it, dropped her purse on the sofa and wiped a few tears, sniffling, "Well... okay. But you... hurt my feelings, Benji."

You've been hurting mine for years, I thought, but pushed it aside and said, "I'm sorry. Really. I'll get a towel." I headed for the kitchen to get the small hand towel hanging from the refrigerator door handle.

Okay, so I wimped out again. I felt good about what I'd said, but I hate confrontation and don't handle tension terribly well; I tend to head straight for the 'fridge and bury my anxiety with a sandwich made of anything I can get my hands

43

on. As I went down the hall, I had to admit to myself that I was disappointed in Tommy. While I understood what he'd done, I couldn't condone it. Anyone who has ever been mistreated should know better than to turn around and mistreat others, even if its done in revenge. Tommy, like myself, had been rejected, picked on and laughed at. How could he do virtually the same thing to all those girls? I was familiar with the *desire* to do it, but that desire was always quelled by the thought of the pain I would be causing by fighting fire with fire. I'd felt that pain too many times—and too deeply—to allow myself to administer it to anyone else. I sometimes hated myself for that, sometimes saw it as a weakness. But my familiarity with that pain had always won out. Apparently, Tommy had found some way to numb it.

———————

In the kitchen, I stepped over the towel-covered goo on the floor and stumbling to a halt when I heard—

—nothing. Absolutely nothing.

I listened. Nothing. I pressed my ear to the sewing room door. Nothing. Trembling, I opened the door a crack and peered in at the laundry room door. It was still intact, but still I heard nothing.

My heart, which had already put forth more than its share of effort that day, began to pound anew against my ribs and my testicles crawled into my abdomen. Even my bowels, which I realized, quite suddenly, were full, threatened to move at any moment.

Why had it stopped its insistent pounding? What was it *doing* in there? Most importantly, and worst of all: was it still *in* there?

I pushed the door open all the way, walked with leaden feet to the laundry room door and pressed my ear to the cold wood. Deadly, empty silence. I tried to open the door, realized it was nailed shut and dropped to one knee, reaching for the hammer.

"Benji? What're you doing?"

I dropped the hammer. "Nuh-nothing. Um, just, I'm, uh…" I sucked in a breath and decided to take care of her first. I got up, grabbed the towel and hurried back into the living room, dropped it in her lap and said, somewhat breathlessly, "Could you excuse me *just* a second?"

She looked up curiously. "Yeah. Sure."

I rushed back to the laundry room, closing the sewing room door behind me and proceeded to pry the nailed baseboard off with the hammer's claw. The nails squalled as they pulled out and the board clunked to the floor. I stared at the bottom of the door, holding my breath, knowing that blob of fat could, at any moment, rush through the pencil thin opening and latch itself onto me…

Nothing happened.

I felt like I weighed a ton as I rose to my feet and my hand felt numb on the doorknob. The door gave a thin squeak as it opened.

The room was empty.

The fat was gone.

A glistening trail of slime ran across the floor and up the front of the washer-dryer, above which the small window I'd crawled through earlier was shattered.

It had escaped.

"Oh, God," I groaned, clutching the doorjambs. "Oh, my God."

I had to get her out. I *had* to get Mardee away from the house before I could deal with it and I had to do it *now*. I rushed into the living room, out of breath, and gasped, "You've gotta go."

"*What?*" She looked shocked.

"You've gotta go."

"So you *are* upset about—"

"No, no, Mardee, really, this has nothing to do with that." I grabbed her arm and lifted her from the sofa, swept her purse up and handed it to her and led her to the door. "Really, this is just a personal problem, nothing I wanna bother you with, *really.* Just go. Okay? Please?"

"Can't I just change my jeans? I've got clean ones in the—"

"Just *go,* Mardee." I got her to the porch screen, opened it and hurried her down the steps.

"W-well, okay, if you're sure you're not ups—"

"No, I'm *not* upset. Really. I swear, I promise. Just go. Call me when you get home. Okay? We'll talk. I promise." I got her on the sidewalk, where she turned to look at me with confused concern. "*Go!*" I shouted. "*Hurry!*"

She frowned, then turned and hurried through the gate to her car, getting in and slamming the door.

I closed and locked the screen door, looking down the porch to the tear in the screen. There was nothing I could do about that, but I could keep it from getting into the house. I rushed inside, closed the door, locked it, then ran for the laundry room where I grabbed the stack of baseboards. Tucking them under my arm, I hurried through the sewing room, grabbing up the hammer and bucket of nails, and staggered to the front door. Falling to my knees with a painful cry, I nailed one of the boards to the bottom of the door, wincing with each fall of the hammer, then stood to rush to the back door in the kitchen to do the same, but I tripped and fell when—

—I heard Mardee's car door slam shut again. Nails spilled over the living room floor and I froze to listen.

The front gate squealed open… clanked shut… footsteps came up the walk…

I felt nailed to the floor. I had to move, but couldn't. It was out there somewhere. With Mardee. Before I could budge, my inner voice spoke: So *what? Let them take care of each other. Get them* both *outta your hair, huh?*

I'm ashamed to admit it, but for just a moment, I actually considered it.

Yeah, just forget about 'em for a few minutes. Go clean the kitchen floor. It's a mess in there, y'know. Later, maybe you can look Tommy Fischer up. Write a letter or give him a call. Tell him all about it. He'd probably love *it, don't you think?*

I felt a chill as I listened to Mardee's footsteps outside and I almost did it, almost went into the kitchen to clean up that mess.

Instead, I heaved myself off the floor, muttering, "No. I can't," clambered to the front door, pulled aside the curtain and looked out the window in the top half. Mardee was coming to the door, a pair of freshly washed jeans tucked under her arm. My eyes darted to the right and—

—I saw it. It oozed across the lawn toward her, slow but determined.

Mardee saw me, smiled halfheartedly and waved, calling, "I just wanna change my jeans, okay?"

I screamed, and I swear to God I sounded like my mother. I clutched the doorknob with both hands, turned it and pulled as hard as I could. The nails pulled out with a groan, the door opened and I threw myself onto the porch, crying, "Go back! Please, *God!* Mardee! Go back! To your car! Go—"

It happened quickly, but in my eyes, it was dream-like... slow motion... underwater...

The yellowish, bruised glob of fat rushed her, wrapping itself around her ankles. Her face was a mask of puzzlement as she fell forward, arms splayed, her folded jeans tumbling through the air before her. It was on her in an instant, covering her like a soggy, grease-soaked blanket and, for the longest time, she lay on the sidewalk, writhing inside that glutinous prison, her scream muffled wetly. Her legs kicked and her arms waved, all four webbed together by the fat that jiggled over her face and back. But then something happened.

It shrunk.

It disappeared.

Quickly.

In an instant, it was gone in a chorus of screams and rips.

Mardee lay on the walk, her legs still kicking, but weakly now, wearily; for a moment, her screams were gurgles, then her voice became whole again, calling my name over and over and over…

I stood on the porch for a long moment, staring open mouthed and breathless, feeling as if my heart had stopped beating.

Her clothes, soggy and discolored, lay around her in tatters. Mardee, mostly naked and jiggling, was a mountain in my front yard. In a matter of seconds, she had tripled—perhaps quadrupled—in size. Her bared flesh folded together in wet, sparkling rolls that shifted and rippled with her sluggish movements.

It took me a moment to realize what had happened, then a moment longer to realize I wasn't having a nightmare.

"Noooo!" I screamed, rushing through the screen door and down the walk to her side. "No, God, *please*… no…"

She was enormous. Gargantuan. Bigger than I had ever been in my entire life. Her hands and feet slapped against the cement like the fins of a grounded fish. I knelt beside her, my vision blurred by tears, and helped her roll over.

Her face was pale as milk, eyes wide, mouth yawning and uttering unintelligible sounds as she clutched the lapels of my robe.

"I'm sorry," I sobbed, helping her into a sitting position. "I'm so suh-sorry, Mardee, my *God,* I'm so sorry."

Her bared breasts were pendulous, her nipples spread over them like small pancakes; her abdomen seemed made of pale gelatin that jiggled and swayed from side to side as she sat up.

"Jesus Christ forgive me," I groaned. "I'm so sorry."

I held her for a moment, squeezed her tightly, running my arms through the residue of fat that clung to her like honey.

"I'm... *so*... sorry," I breathed into her ear.

"Buh-Buh-B-Benji? What's... wrong? What's... *happened*... to me?"

My sobs were uncontrollable. I thought of all those years in school, all that time wasted dodging the poison arrows of my peers... all those years as an adult, when the arrows became invisible but no less deadly. I thought of Mardee as she was back then in those days of painful words and missed dances... as she'd been just moments before...

The guilt I felt then weighed far more than I'd ever weighed in my life.

"Benji?" she whimpered. "What's... happened? To me?"

Crying, I helped her to her feet, my arm around her shoulders—as far as it could go, anyway—holding her close to me as I led her toward the house.

She stopped, looked down at herself and screamed. Her voice echoed up and down the street and cut through my chest like a scalpel. "*Benjiii!*"

"It's okay, Mardee," I whispered, leading her through the screen door. "You're gonna be all right." I led her into the house, patting the mound of her shoulder as I whispered, "I can help you. This is a problem I know something about..."

Active Member

Standing in the doorway of the small apartment, the big detective, puts his hands on his hips and looks around.

"Jesus Horatio Christ," he says quietly. "There's enough blood in here to drown cattle."

He hurried down the wet sidewalk, not wanting to look suspicious, but wanting to be far away from the park as soon as possible. His hands were deep in the baggy pockets of his long green coat, pulled together over the front of his pants. He was crying; his twisted face glistened with tears, his thin chest hitched with sobs.

He had done it again. *They* had done it again. He hadn't wanted to, he really hadn't. But he never realized that until it was too late, until afterward. He never thought about it before, when he could stop it, keep it from happening. How could he think with that voice hissing at him, stabbing upward through the center of his body like a steel barbed spike, up and up, straight to his brain. He could only think afterward, when it was quiet, satisfied, resting. Growing...

He *knew* it was growing. He hadn't thought so at first, but it soon became obvious, impossible to ignore. He wanted, *needed* to tell someone, but he knew he couldn't. After all, even *he* hadn't believed it at first. And if he told someone about the growing, he would have to tell about the voice, too. They'd put him back in that place, give him back to the twitchy-lipped doctors, the stiff-necked nurses. He could almost hear the door locking behind him again. Smell the sterility. The stinging, artificial cleanliness of the halls, the bathrooms. No glass or metal objects. Guarded showers. Jigsaw puzzles and pottery classes. Questions answered with questions. He wouldn't let that happen again. He knew what to do.

He'd known the moment he rolled off that girl in the park. She was tiny. Young. He'd had to beat her to get it inside.

He knew what he had to do, and he was going straight home to do it.

He was surrounded by the city, in the very center of it now. All around him great god-like erections rose toward the dirty night sky. Cars drove by, their tires making moist panting sounds on the wet pavement. A few yards ahead of him a bus, long and fat, grunted to a halt at the curb and he hurried to catch it, his hands still in his coat pockets, his tennis shoes splashing through puddles. Beside the bus, he looked up and through one of the windows. He saw a pretty face, blond, big tired eyes. Looking up and down the length of the bus, he saw that she was alone inside.

The doors opened.

What if it awoke? Told him to follow her, *made* him follow her, forced him with its ugly, insistent pounding?

"Hey, buddy," the driver called. "You coming, or what?"

He backed away, turned, jogged down the walk, away from her.

Never again, he thought, *not after tonight. Tonight it ends.*

The woman in the robe and curlers walks in behind the detective, arms folded over fat, soft breasts. "I knew he'd be trouble," she says.

"You the one that called, ma'am?" the detective asks.

"That's right. I'm the landlady."

He watches her standing there, soaking it all in, ogling the mess. He knows she can't wait to tell her friends. "You received a complaint?"

"I heard the screamin' myself!" she says, pressing a liver-spotted hand to her chest. "Hell, I'm alla way down*stairs* and I heard it myself!" She looks at it some more, all the blood, the knife, and shakes her head. "Yeah, I *knew* he'd be trouble."

He was cold even though he was sweating and gasping from his rush to get home before it stirred, before it spoke.

———

It began years ago. At the boarding academy. His father had sent him there after his mother had shot herself. "Get you some good Christian teaching," the tattooed man had said. But he knew it was *really* to get him out of the way of his father's woman friends. There had been a lot of those.

The dean had caught him one night. He hadn't even heard the keys rattle in the hall. The little man had just walked into the dorm room and found him sitting on the bed with the magazine, masturbating.

"It's evil," the principal had said the next morning. The man had glared at him over the big oak desk, leaning forward, his pockmarked face hard, angry. "It hangs there to remind us of sin and the only good that comes of it are urine and children. It's dirty. Filthy. Why do you think little boys are taught to wash their hands after they *touch* it?" Tiny gems of perspiration had

53

sparkled beneath his razor-like nose. "It must be fought, *trained*, or it will make you do things you have no business doing."

He'd heard it that night for the first time, when he thought he was asleep. Just whispers. Unintelligible. Dream-like.

But over the years it got louder, clearer.

Then they'd put him away, punished him for the things it had made him do. Horrible things. Nasty, wet things that had brought him no pleasure—not *really*, not *afterward*—and had even made him throw up and lose consciousness at times. But they were things that had satisfied *it*, that had quenched its thirst and sated its hunger and, most importantly, silenced its incessant *hissing...*

I'm crazy, he'd thought with giddy relief. *Just crazy, that's all. Now I'll get better and it'll go away.*

And it did. For a while. Long enough for him to feel, to *seem* cured.

Now it did not hiss. It screamed. It scorched the inside of his skull with its hot breath and made his eyes water with a voice that sounded like a nuclear holocaust. It was enraged, perhaps, by the sores that had appeared on it, swollen and running with milky fluids.

And dear sweet merciful Jesus it was *growing!*

His hands, still in his coat pockets, covered it now, pressing over the denim crotch that had grown tight, that would not hold it much longer. The sores, probably draining again, stung. Beneath the pants, he was still wet from its vomiting.

I'm not *crazy*, he thought frantically as he hurried across a street, around a corner. *I never was! I'm not*, no, *I AM NOT CRAZY!*

He thought of that poor girl, limp beneath him, whimpering, and cried some more.

"Why do you say that, ma'am?" the detective asks.

"Huh?" She turns to him jerkily with wide eyes as if torn from deep thought.

"Why do you say you knew he'd be trouble?"

"Oh, he was a nutcase," she says with a wave of her meaty hand. "A week or so ago I come up here for the rent and he answers the door with his pants open, wanger hangin' out, and he's cryin' like a baby."

The detective takes a pad from his overcoat pocket and begins writing. "Did he say anything?"

"Oh, yeah. Blubbered and moaned. Somethin' about it bein' bigger. He was swingin' his thing around like a string of pearls." She chuckles, cold and humorless. "It *was* big, all right. But sick, with big sores."

The detective turns to the young uniformed officer who arrived before him. "Well?"

"The door was bolted on the inside," the officer says quietly. "We had to break in. Eight floors up. Nobody coulda got in."

"Yeah. Figured as much. No surprises here."

"Well, sir. There is one thing…"

———————————

He burst into his little apartment, slammed the door and threw the bolt. Tearing off his coat, letting it fall to the floor, he hurried to the kitchen, his shoulders still quaking with sobs. He pulled out a drawer, almost dropped it, began searching, clanging through the cutlery until he found it. He pushed the drawer back in and held the knife in his hand.

"Oh, God," he breathed, panicking because it was stirring, beginning to whisper before it screamed.

He ripped his jeans open as he left the kitchen and they fell down around his knees. He stopped, kicked his shoes off, stepped out of the pants and hurried into the living room, his fist tight around the deadly knife. He paced back and forth, back and forth, crying, scared because now it was beginning to speak, to *scream*. His eyes clenched and his head tilted back as he fell into a chair. He didn't want to look down because he knew he would see it, knew it had found its way out of the dirty undershorts and was growing, stiffening up even more. Ugly. Diseased.

It told him to put down the knife, but he didn't listen; he tried to ignore the painful voice with tears squeezing from his closed eyes. A scream tore from his chest as he began hacking.

Hacking and hacking…

———————

"What?" the detective wants to know, frowning at the officer. "A guy chops his dick off? No biggie. When I was in San Francisco, there was this guy who took a—"

"Sir." The interruption is respectful. "Like I said, no one could get in. It's obvious he did it. But, um… we can't, uh, find it. We've looked. And, um… it's just not here."

———————

Hacking and screaming, hacking and hacking…

Something Kinky

A s I write this, I am holding a gun in my left hand…
The bar was dark, so I couldn't see his face well, but he seemed nice enough, and I needed some conversation, so when he spoke to me, I responded.

"Well," he said, smiling broadly and toying with his drink, the way strangers at bars tend to do when they try to strike up a conversation with another stranger, "what brings *you* here?"

I shrugged and returned his smile. "Just needed to get out of the house, I guess."

"Ah. Well. Not like everybody else in here, huh?"

"I'm sorry?"

"You know. All these other people. I mean, *they're* not here because they needed to get out of the house."

I looked around. The bar was called Suspenders, and the guy was right; it was the city's biggest upscale meet market and I *hadn't* come just to get out of the house.

"Yeah, well…" I shrugged again.

"So you're not here to get out of the house *either*, are you?"

When I looked at him, his smile was conspiratorial but genuine and I shook my head. "No, I guess not."

He leaned forward on the stool beside me and I got a better look at him. Thin, balding, dark hair and tortoise shell glasses, wearing a dark suit, maybe in his late thirties—about my age—well dressed and… I guess you'd say he looked *smooth*, like he was used to starting conversations and presenting himself to other people.

"That's okay," he said. "Nobody comes here to get out of the house. So what do you do?"

"I'm an assistant vice president at a brokerage firm."

"Really? Would I know the name?" I told him the name and he cocked a brow. "Not bad. Well… you're a pretty good-looking guy. With all that going for you, you shouldn't have a hard time finding what you're looking for. Except…"

I watched him a moment, waiting, then asked, "Except what?"

"Well, I'd lose the wedding ring if I were you. It's not exactly what they look for, you know."

I covered my left hand with my right. "*They?*"

"Come on. Get real."

"Yeah. Okay. You're right, I know." I made a move to take the ring off, but he interrupted me.

"What *are* you looking for, anyway?"

I sipped my drink.

"I mean, if you've got a lady at home, what're you looking for?"

I fidgeted, shrugged, sipped again. "I don't know. Something different, I guess."

"Different? How different?"

"Oh, you know… something interesting… exciting." As I finished my drink the guy gestured for the bartender to get us each another.

"Something kinky?" he asked with a smirk.

"Well… I wouldn't exactly say—"

"Oh, c'mon, don't deny it. What guy doesn't want something a little kinky now and then. You know… getting tied to the bed… having two women at once… even seeing your old lady in some raunchy lingerie is nice once in a while, right?" he laughed. "Always loved lingerie, myself. When I was a kid, those department store catalogs—you know, Sears? Penneys?— those were the closest I got to girlie magazines. Remember the lingerie sections? See, my dad didn't get *Playboy* or *Penthouse* like some of my friends' dads, so those women in their bras and slips and girdles and nightgowns… they were the closest I came to Playmates and Pets. Maybe that's why I get such a charge out of lingerie now. You think? Oh. By the way." He reached out to shake my hand and said, "Larry Ruskin."

"Arnold Kramer. Nice to meet you. And thanks for the drink." The bartender had brought another seven and seven and set it before me.

"Oh, sure, no problem. But, look, I'm not helping you any, monopolizing you like this. I should move on. Nice talking to you, though."

He made moves to leave and I quickly looked around at all the women—all the luscious, smooth skinned women, breasts bouncing beneath silk blouses, firm hips working beneath their skirts as they walked, their eyes and smiles wet and glistening with sexual promise—and something inside me withered. I'd been married too long. I didn't know how to approach them, what to say to them, how to act around them. I couldn't believe I'd even considered it in the first place. But now my only other option was to go back home to Peggy. She would be waiting for me—smiling, soft, warm and… so familiar—and we would watch some television, maybe a movie or two on the VCR, then read for a while and go to sleep. I hurt with guilt to think it, but I didn't want to do that, either.

Grabbing Larry Ruskin's arm as he slid off his stool, I said, "No, really, why don't you just stick around a while. You're not keeping me from anything, *believe* me."

"You sure?"

"Positive." I looked around again, watching the women, then turned to him and smiled. "I'm just not up to it."

"Never know. You might get lucky."

"How? Do you have an instruction manual? A map? Maybe one of those self-help videos that tells you how to pick up women?"

He laughed, tapped the bar with his palm. "Yeah, I think I know what you mean. How long you been married?"

My smile fell away. "Um, almost fifteen years."

"Ah, yeah. I suppose you've never, uh... you know, done anything like this before?"

"No. I haven't."

"Well, that's a long time to be out of circulation. It's hard enough when you're starting out the first time, let alone trying to do it again, am I right?"

I nodded.

"But, hey, like I said, you're not doing too bad for yourself. You're a good-looking guy and—I mean, hey, lookit these other guys, huh? You see them? Lookit that guy over there, huh? I mean, he looks like, what, like one of those mannequins in a department store, right? And how about *him*, this guy over *here?* He's trying really hard to look like he's in a beer commercial, am I right? And you, hell, you've got this terrific job, you're making lotsa money, right? So what've they got that *you* don't?"

"Yeah, but it's not just that. It's, um..." I laughed, waved my hand. "Jeez, I don't even know why I'm here."

"Because you want something different. Something kinky. And we kind of interrupted ourselves when we were talking about that, right? So just what *is* it you want?"

He looked at me with genuine interest. I don't normally tell these things to anyone, especially strangers, but I'd had a few drinks and he was looking at me with that smirk and that cocked brow that suggested camaraderie and… well, I needed to talk to *somebody*.

I sipped my drink. "You know, my wife's father… he's my boss. He owns the brokerage firm I work for. Filthy rich. He's got money shooting out of every orifice in his body. He didn't approve when Peggy started seeing me. See, I didn't have much of anything then, I was just trying to keep my head above water when we fell in love."

"Sounds like an old story."

"Oh, yeah. It is. Like everything *else* about my marriage, I think." Another sip. "See, I'm… I'm looking for some variety," I said uncertainly. "I don't want to be on top all the time."

"Oh, I know what you mean," he said, shaking his head.

I *gulped* my drink and Larry waved for another one. "I'd like a blow job sometimes. Not that I won't reciprocate, you know? There's nothing I love more than going down on *her*."

"Yeah, I hear ya. There's nothing sweeter."

"She doesn't care about that, though. Sometimes—*most* of the time, in fact—I don't think she even *enjoys* it. But I'd like her to go down on *me* once in a while. Without being asked. In fact, I don't always have to actually have *sex*. I mean, *intercourse.* You know, I'd like to just, now and then, suck each other off, or something, or maybe just do it with our hands, then cuddle up. *Different* stuff, you know… a little playing around. And not always in bed just before we go to sleep at night. Maybe another room of the apartment in the middle of the afternoon. Is there something so wrong with that?"

"Hey... not according to Phil Donahue."

"That's what I mean. I watch all those shows—those, you know, those damned *talk* shows—I've read the books and the articles. I keep hearing all these women say their men never want to make love. I keep hearing them say they want their men to be more affectionate, more sensual, more daring and imaginative. But when I try that... what happens? She says, '*That's* not us, *we* don't do that kind of thing.' Or my *favorite:* I'm not that kind of woman and you knew that when you married me.'" I was getting carried away and took a couple fast gulps of my drink, then turned to him and spoke rapidly. "But you know what's funny? I *didn't* know she wasn't that kind of woman when I married her. And you know *why?* Because when we met? While we were going through the whole courting thing? And even *later!* She told me all these stories about this guy she used to see. She showed me *pictures* of them together at parties and stuff. She even told me about his *dick,* for Christ's sake—It was huge,' she said, 'he was *huge'*—like it was a piece of information that was going to make my life *better,* or something. Now, I've heard all the talk... you know, women saying that size really doesn't matter. But they only say that on talk shows and in magazine articles. I think when it really comes down to it, size *does* make a difference. To women, I mean. I think it really *is* important to them. I think that, when they're sitting around talking, with no men in the room, they say things like, 'Well, his cock isn't as big as my *last* boyfriend's... but of course, I don't tell *him* that. I tell *him* that it really doesn't make any difference, but... well, it sure as hell doesn't *feel* as good.'"

I paused to sigh and take a drink, then went on. "It was nothing serious, Peggy and this guy. They weren't in love, or anything. But they'd get together and they'd do all this... *stuff* She'd wear all this sexy lingerie, you know? She'd tie him to the bed and run feather *boas* over his naked *body*, for God's sake! You *name* it, and they *did* it. And she told me all about it in vivid detail. In fact, that was one of the things I found so exciting about her; I figured she was open-minded, she was adventurous, she was imaginative and… *sexual*. But will she do any of that with me? *Hell* no! I'm lucky if we do it in the *missionary* position once every few months! She's still got lingerie tucked away in her dresser drawers that she's had since before we even *met*—stuff she probably wore for *him*—but will she wear it for *me*? *Hell* no! Will she wear any of the stuff *I've* bought her over the years? *Hell* no! In fact, she's never—and I mean *never* in almost fifteen years—looked at *me* the way she looked at him in those pictures… with wide, bright eyes… interested, excited—*happy*… like she couldn't wait to get him home and get his clothes off. But you know what she tells me? She says she didn't *like* all that stuff she did with that guy back then. She says there was too much pressure, that she felt like she was *expected* to perform a certain way with him, to be something she *wasn't*. But it sure as hell didn't sound like that when she was *talking* about him so much!" I shook my head and took a drink. "Sometimes I want to say to Peggy, 'Okay, *don't* like it, then, just *do* it, I don't *care!*' But I… I can't… you know, I just can't *do* that." I stopped, took a breath, wiped my hand over my mouth and finished my drink. Larry waved for the bartender to bring another.

"I don't know," I said, "maybe she's been unhappy, too. Sexually, I mean. If so, I sure as hell haven't heard about it. Maybe she's just told her *girlfriends*. Maybe they sit around talking about—" I chuckled coldly, "—about how small my *cock* is." I shrugged. "Anyway, so I've tried not to put any pressure on Peggy. I bring it *up* once in a while, sure, just to let her know that I'd *like* it if we maybe did that sort of thing now and then, something a little out of the ordinary. *Anything*, really. But I don't *push* her. And still... nothing. I've been waiting... all this time... hoping she'll change her mind and decide that maybe that stuff would be *fun* with me because I wasn't *pushing* her into it, you know? Because I'd like sex to be playful sometimes. I think there should be some *laughter* in bed along with all the panting and moaning. But still... after all these years... nothing. I've thought, a few times, that maybe she's been seeing someone else and she's lost interest in me, but... well, I don't know... maybe I'm being naive, but I just can't imagine it. It just... it seems she's incapable of seeing sex as anything more than some incredible effort she has to put out, something a woman has to do now and then to keep her husband from getting too grouchy. Hell, she gets more enthused and passionate about *housework*—more *involved* in it—than she does when it comes to making love with *me*." My next drink came and I did some damage to it immediately. "And you know how all this makes me feel, Larry?"

"How?"

"It makes me feel like if I hear one... more... woman—just *one more!*—complain about how her husband or boyfriend is insensitive, or how he's ignorant of her sexual needs or how he's unwilling to try anything different in bed... about how he doesn't do what he *used* to do anymore... it makes me feel like I want to just punch her right in the fucking *mouth*. Who*ever* the hell she is." A couple more big swallows. "Because, unless there's something really *wrong* with them, I know how those men *get* that way. Really. I know *why* they don't do those things anymore. Because they stop *trying*, that's all. They just reach a point where it's too embarrassing, too... *demeaning* to put themselves through that kind of rejection... that kind of *high-school-date-humiliation* with their own fucking *wives* and *girlfriends!* Th-they just... they... give *up*."

He pursed his lips and nodded slowly. "I know what you mean. Believe me, Arnold, I know what you mean."

"So," I sighed, "I'm here. Like some shmuck, I come *here*, looking for somebody who'll… well, you know."

"Well, like they say… if you're getting steaks at home, you don't have to go out for hamburgers."

I chuckled. "I've been eating a lot of hamburger helper. Namely my left hand. Or my right. Over the years, I've become masturbatorily ambidextrous."

"Yeah. I know." He chuckled, too, finished his drink and ordered another. After a long pause that was buried by the music and the voices all around us, he looked at me and asked, "So just what is it you want, huh? I mean, you want whips and chains? You talking about oral sex? *Anal* sex? What?"

I was a little surprised; he sounded more serious than before, even *looked* more serious. He watched me a while, then shrugged as if to ask, *Well?* "Um, I… well, look, I, um… what difference does it make?"

"I'll tell you. See, I… *know* somebody."

"Somebody? Somebody *who?*"

"This woman."

"Ah." It seemed clear to me, suddenly: he was a pimp. "Well, that's fine, but I really don't—"

"It's not what you're thinking. I mean, I think I know what you're thinking, and that's not it."

"Well, what *is* it, then?" I was a little annoyed all of a sudden.

"It's, uh… this woman, see. She's… open-minded. Imaginative. Daring. In fact, that's what she *wants*. All that stuff you been talking about here. And I think, uh… that you two would get along. Really well."

"I see. But that's not exactly what I had in mind. I was hoping to just *meet* somebody, you know? I didn't want to do *business* with anybody."

"That's what I meant. It's not what you're thinking. She's not for sale. This is a… a *personal* thing."

That threw me a little, but I hardly skipped a beat. "Well, that sounds great. But I'm just not up to it. I'm not up to *any* of it. I mean… this." I gestured behind us toward all the women. "It's just too scary. For the obvious reasons, of course—I'm out of *practice*—but also because it's just too *dangerous.* All the diseases, all the viruses that're out there now. I'd like some variety, but I'm not willing to *die* for it."

"You're wrong there, too. She's not like that."

"What do you mean, she's not *like* that? It only takes one time to—"

"This woman has only been with one man in over eleven years."

"Oh?" That shut me up for a long moment. "Well… what about this guy? I mean, maybe he's been—"

"This *guy* has only been with one *woman* in over eleven years."

I thought about that a while. I thought *hard*, looking him over carefully. "But how do you know he hasn't—"

"The guy is me. The woman is my wife."

Peggy and I hadn't talked about it in months. *Several* months. In fact, by the time I met Larry Ruskin, it was pushing a year, because the last time we'd talked, it hadn't gone well.

———————————

I'd always heard—mostly on those damned talk shows—that it was a bad idea to talk about sexual problems, no matter how small, in bed. So I waited until we were in the car one evening on the way to our favorite restaurant.

"Not this again," she'd said. She had a very calm, unangry way of saying things like that. Peggy *never* got angry.

"What do you mean? It's been months since we've talked about this."

"That's what I mean. Every once in a while, this comes up. It just gets a little old, that's all."

"Well, why do you think it comes *up* every once in a while?"

"Because you just won't leave it alone."

"But *why* do you think I won't leave it alone?"

"I don't know. I wish you'd tell me."

"I've been *trying* to tell you! For *years!*" I was starting to sound angry, and anger just didn't work with Peggy because, like I said, she didn't *get* angry. So I tried to calm down. "I won't leave it alone because it's important to me. I think it should be important to... *us.*" All she did was nod with a tight-lipped expression. The tightness of her lips was the closest Peggy ever came to real anger. Normally, she had a pretty face—beautiful eyes, smooth skin, full lips... the face I'd fallen in love with—but this one look—this *one look*—made her genuinely ugly.

"Look, Peggy, you know it's not that I think you're a bad lover. You *know* that. You know that I'm—"

"No," she interrupted quietly. "I don't know that. You keep bringing it up, so what do you expect me to think?" Her voice was flat and ungiving.

"Sweetheart, we've been married for nearly fifteen years, so isn't it natural that I'd think you'd—"

"Yes, we've been married for fifteen years, so I would think that we'd understand each other by now. I'd think that we would be comfortable with one another's needs and limitations."

I fought the urge to roll my eyes and dig my fingernails into the steering wheel. But I tried to be understanding; I tried to tell myself that perhaps she was fighting the same urge. "Okay. Let's just not talk about it."

"No. No. If it's bothering you so much, I think we should. You're not happy with us. Sexually, I mean."

"It's not that simple. I just think it'd be nice if, once in a while, we—"

"But that's what you're saying, right? You don't like what we do in bed, so maybe we should—"

"That's *not* what I'm saying. It isn't that I don't *like* what we *do*. I mean... *think* about it. How would you like it if we ate hamburgers every night for fifteen years? Pretty soon, you'd get—"

"But we don't make love every night, it's not like eating. I don't see what eating hamburgers every night has to do with—"

"I don't *expect* us to make love every night, Peggy. Really. I mean, what if we—okay, okay, let's say we only had to eat once a month. Once every *two* months. Okay? Let's say our bodies required us to eat only once every two months. And let's say that when it came time to eat—once every two months, like I said—we ate only hamburgers. *Every time.* You mean to say you wouldn't get tired of that? You wouldn't reach a point where you—"

"I don't know what you're getting at, Arnold, because I am perfectly happy with our love life—our *sex* life—the way it is. If you just want to get laid, then you can probably go out and get any—"

"That's not *it!* Don't you understand that I'm no less attracted to you than I've ever been? You keep saying you've gained weight, that you've gotten *older*, but you still turn me on, Peggy! You! No one else. I want *you!* I-I... Peggy, I *love* you, I *do*, I'm still *in* love with you. I'm just trying to improve what we already *have*, you know? Make it more *fun*. Make it more—"

"Arnold?" She looked at me with that expressionless mask that always seemed to shut me up. "Don't you think we've talked about this enough?"

Yes, we had talked about it enough. That was when I decided we had *definitely* talked about it enough and, if I wanted to get what I was looking for—what I felt I *needed*—I would have to get it from someone other than Peggy.

I nodded. "Yes," I said. "I guess we have."

We had a nice dinner that night, and some nice conversation. We even made love when we went to bed a couple hours after getting home. We laid naked in the dark for a few minutes until I could stand it no longer. As they did every couple of months or so, my needs outweighed my fear of being ignored, which was what *usually* happened. Peggy never came right out and said she didn't feel like it—which would have been a lot easier to take, I think—she never even had an excuse... she just *ignored* me, usually lying there on her side, her back to me, her breathing steady and regular, as if she were asleep, although I knew she wasn't. But that night, when I touched her, she rolled over—probably because of the talk we'd had earlier—and began, immediately, to finger my nipples and press her knee between my legs. That was the most she ever did; she never touched my genitals with her hands... in fact, her hands never made it below my chest unless I *put* them there.

Shortly before we married, Peggy discovered how sensitive my nipples were and, probably because it was the easiest and least messy thing to do, that had been the extent of her sexual aggression ever since: fingering my nipples. Unlike me, she wasn't fond of foreplay; early on in our relationship, she frequently complained that I paid too much attention to it so, after a while, I gave it up almost completely and sort of

69

fantasized about foreplay as we were making love. She lay beneath me as I moved; as we neared the finish, she raised her legs and bent her knees, as usual, clutching my back and shoulders. Peggy reached orgasm easily—she always had—and she usually had a number of them long before I finished; in fact, she sometimes complained that I went on too long, so I usually didn't spend much time enjoying it and just tried to finish as soon as I could.

And that was the last time we'd made love before that night in the bar.

That's the way it had been for years. *Many* years.

Until I met Larry Ruskin.

Larry got a cab and we talked on the way to his place.

"It was her idea," he said. "My wife's, I mean. Julie. She was… bored. I guess I'd never thought about it before, but when I *did*, I realized that, yeah, I was kinda bored, too. Not unhappy, just bored. So we tried a few things. Some we liked, some we didn't. We got some porn tapes from a friend, watched those. Bought some sex toys and played with them. Read a couple books. We had some fun, y'know? Then, after a while, Julie had an idea. I think she maybe got it from one of those tapes or a magazine, or something. Took her a while to get up the guts to suggest it, and I'd be lying if I didn't tell you I felt my teeth loosen when she did. She said she wanted to bring another man into our bed. You know, a threesome. Just a one-time thing. Nothing regular. Like I said, I was shocked."

"It didn't *bother* you?"

"Well… I wasn't crazy about it at first. You know what I mean, right Arnold? After eleven years with her, I wasn't exactly crazy about the idea of watching her roll around in our bed with another guy. It may work in dirty movies and magazines, but in real life, somebody gets hurt. *Somebody's* threatened by it. Anyway, it took a while, but... she talked me into it. I mean, she even managed to turn me *on* with the whole idea. Don't ask me how. I'm still a little flustered by it... the idea of watching my wife fuck some other guy. She kept telling me not to be threatened by it, not to let it bother me, because it would only be once, right? And she said she'd be thinking of me the whole time. And I'd get to *watch* her doing to somebody else all the things she usually did to me—y'know, like watching her suck him while I was inside her and vice-versa—and I'd know *exactly* how it felt."

Larry paused and shook his head slowly and I could tell by the look on his face—the slight smile and distant stare in his narrow eyes—that he was actually looking forward to it; however he'd felt about the idea before, it excited him now.

"Obviously," he continued, "I went along with it. It sounded pretty good. Still does, in fact. And—" He gave me a broad smile, a secret smile, "—I think it will be. And I promise you, Andy—" He lifted his hands in laughing assurance, "—I won't *touch* you."

It was probably the drinks, I don't know, but I started to feel a stir of warmth between my legs.

The cab stopped in front of his apartment building, Larry paid and we went inside, into the elevator and up to the seventh floor. On the way up, he said, "Look, you don't have to do anything tonight if you don't want. Not at *all*, in fact. I mean, maybe Julie's not for you. You can just meet her, we'll talk, have a drink or two, that sort of thing. If you're not interested, you just tell me later. You know... when the time is right. I'll understand, and so will Julie."

The elevator opened, we went down the hall and Larry took out his keys. As he opened the door, he gestured inside and said, "Welcome."

It was dark inside except for a couple lights coming from other rooms. He took my coat and, as he hung it up, called, "Julie?"

"In here," a timid voice called from another room.

He led me across the living room and through a doorway, into the bedroom, where a woman in a long robe lay in bed, her feet covered by a sheet, holding an open book in a pool of lamplight. She looked at me with wide, timid eyes, her mouth partially open, glanced away for a moment, then returned the look slowly, more interested this time—actually *interested!*—examining me, appraising me, one corner of her mouth quivering into a half smile. No woman had looked at me that way since… well, I couldn't *remember* the last time a woman had looked at me that way. In fact, she looked at me in the same way—or so I imagined, and I'm sure now that it was just my imagination—that Peggy looked at her friend in that damned picture she'd showed me.

As I watched her, I knew in an instant that I would be making love with Julie Ruskin that night…

We were clumsy at first, understandably, but our nervousness actually made it more fun, more… *titillating.* I felt like a teenager fooling around with his girlfriend while his parents slept just down the hall.

A while before, Larry had left us alone in the bedroom with a couple drinks, saying we should talk, get to know one another. We didn't talk long, which was odd for me; in the past, it's usually been difficult for me to become sexually involved with a woman I didn't know, let alone one I hadn't at least *talked* with for a while. But this situation was *not* usual.

We sat on the bed and talked nervously for a few minutes—just small talk, nothing substantial—then she touched my hand and stood to remove her robe, saying in a breathy voice, "I really don't, um… you know, I'm not sure what we're waiting for."

I started to say I didn't know, either, but her robe dropped to the floor and my mouth hung open as I stared at her.

Julie was in her early thirties, a little over five feet tall and very shapely—not what you'd call thin, but not overweight—with full reddish-brown hair that fell past her shoulders and eyes like polished copper; she was olive-skinned and beautiful, but seemed unaware of her beauty. I'd expected her to be naked beneath the robe, but she wore a black teddy of rose patterned lace with black garters and stockings; my eyes froze on a tiny red silk rose sewn to the lace between her breasts.

"Well?" she said tremulously, taking my hand. I stood and Julie began to undress me slowly, smiling all the while, but with quivering lips. Once I was naked, she eased me onto the bed gently, her hands on my shoulders, and asked, "What do you want? What would you like me to do?"

Suddenly, after years of entertaining a variety of sexual fantasies, I couldn't think of a single thing I wanted her to do; I was, instead, entranced by the way she was looking at me. She seemed so involved, so… *sincere* about wanting to please me.

I stammered, "Well, I, um, I don't, uh… I really—"

"What about this?" she whispered, reaching down and grasping my erection. "What would you like me to do with this?"

"I-I-I, uuhhh… you can, y'know, you can, uh…" I felt like a fool, an idiot. I remember thinking, at that moment, that if Jerry Lewis had ever done a love scene in any of those old movies, it would have played just like this.

She put a finger to her lips—"Sshhh."—then crawled down my body, holding my cock in her fist, and took it into her mouth, attacking it voraciously, using her mouth and hands, looking up at me the whole time, her eyes smiling as she licked and slurped. Her hand never stopped as she lifted her head a few minutes later and said breathlessly, "Anything you want... I have a vibrator... velvet cords to tie to the bed... you or me, either one... and oils and lotions... anything... anything you want..." She lowered her head again and continued sucking, running her fingers over my balls as I squirmed on the bed, trying to form some kind of response.

"I... I thought we... I thought this was going to be thuh-three, um... y'know, the three of us, um..."

"He'll be here," she slurred. "He's probably outside the door listening. He... he wants... to make sure we're comfortable, thuh-that's all. But he'll buh-be here. This is what... what he's wuh-wanted for a long tuh-time."

That made me flinch. It sounded as if the whole thing had been Larry's idea, although he'd *told* me it had been Julie's. But, as much as I wanted to speak up, to protest, to ask her questions, I couldn't; it felt too good. Instead, I laid back and began thinking about all the things she would do, if only I'd ask...

Larry joined us later, after Julie had taken me to heights of pleasure that, until that night, I had not known existed. She'd tied me to the bed, licked nearly every inch of my body—laughing girlishly half the time, mind you, which just drove me crazier, because she seemed to be having so much *fun*—brought me to the edge of orgasm with her mouth then finished me off by mounting me. After she'd untied me, when my erection didn't go away, she'd grinned and said, "Good, *good*," and that was when Larry joined us. He had come into the room once before, wearing a robe, and gotten something—I wasn't sure

74

what at the time—but the second time he returned, he was naked and smiling as he crawled between the sheets with us.

It was like watching—no, no, *living*—*a* porn film; it was something I'd never expected to happen to me in my entire life, and yet I was experiencing it. I fucked her as she sucked Larry and fondled his balls and, later, we changed places and she sucked me and fondled *my* balls and scraped her nails over my nipples—

—*How did she know?* I thought—

—while Larry fucked her. We changed again and again, experimenting with various geometric possibilities, until neither Larry nor I could take it any longer. He came inside her, clawing the sheets and crying out breathlessly; I came in her mouth with one hand buried in her hair, the other doubled into a fist behind my back.

We were quiet for a long while; none of us spoke or looked at each other. Then, somehow—I'm not sure who started it—we began to do it all over again…

On the way home, fresh from a quick shower at the Ruskins', my hands trembling, I wondered how he could stand it. I knew I could never sit by and watch someone else have sex with Peggy, even if I was involved. It would have hurt too much… in fact, it would have torn my guts out.

That made me think of Peggy. I was going home to her. I looked at my watch; it was after two in the morning. What would I tell her? I'd been coming home late every night for weeks, but never *this* late. Actually, I hadn't been working late any of those nights, I'd been doing exactly what I'd done that evening: wandering around the city restlessly, going to bars, restaurants and nightclubs, searching for a woman who'd be willing to satisfy my dirty little adolescent cravings. There'd never been any danger of Peggy finding out; no one ever answered the phone at the office after hours and she never called if she knew I was going to be late. But tonight I would need *some* kind of explanation.

It wasn't until the cab stopped outside my apartment building that I realized something was wrong, something was *missing*. I'd rushed to leave Larry and Julie, hoping to get home no later than necessary, and I'd left behind... what, my wallet? My... my *necktie*.

Shit, I thought, *something else to explain*. By the time I got home, more than my hands were trembling and my gut was a mess...

I knew something was wrong when I found Peggy on the sofa in the dark living room, smoking as she watched CNN; she'd stopped smoking over two years ago and despised the news. She wore her bathrobe and slippers and—odd for such a late hour—she smelled of perfume. She looked at me over her shoulder and gave a brief, weak smile.

"Home later than usual tonight," she said quietly.

I shrugged out of my coat. "Sorry."

"Oh, well. It's Friday. You can sleep in tomorrow, I suppose." She turned back to the news.

"Yeah, but... I should've called. I'm, uh, sorry, Peg. I should have."

She shrugged one shoulder and I wanted to die. My knees actually felt weak. She looked so pretty there in the glow of the television, her ankles crossed, shiny blond hair pulled back into a little ponytail with corkscrew curls dangling over her ears. Nearly fifteen years... and in a matter of a few hours I had destroyed what had been a perfect record. Maybe not a perfect *marriage*, but certainly a perfect record. And even if it wasn't perfect... well, we'd stuck around this long for *something*, right? And now I'd done *this*... to *her*...

Suddenly all those frustrating conversations about sex didn't seem so important anymore and I felt like crying.

I reached up to remove my tie as I moved toward her, realized once again that I'd left it behind and felt even worse. "Peggy, I'm—"

She turned and there were tears in her eyes.

You're what? I thought. *Sorry? For what?* You gonna tell *her?* Is that *really* necessary? *And why is she crying?*

"—I'm... I'm sorry. Really. I should've called and told you I'd have to work this late. I didn't even know myself. *Really.* I guess I just lost track of time. Didn't even eat. In fact, I'm starv—"

"Please... don't, Arnold," she breathed, standing. She finished her cigarette and stubbed it out in the coffee table ashtray, then her hands fidgeted before her. "Don't lie to me anymore. I know you weren't at work."

My insides froze.

"I drove down to the office and talked to the guard. Sidney. He was very nice. He said he'd seen you leave at six-thirty and that you... hadn't come back all night. That was at... oh, I guess eleven-thirty... midnight." She closed her eyes and rubbed them. She sounded so tired, so afraid and nervous. "Maybe it was wrong. What I did. Maybe it was suspicious and... untrusting, but... I had to know. And you weren't—" Her voice broke, "—*there.*"

I crab-stepped slowly to the chair, groped for the armrest and plopped down, dropping my coat to the floor as I massaged a temple with weak fingertips. It had happened. On the one night that I'd acted, the one night that I'd found what I was looking for and thrown almost fifteen years of jealously guarded vows out the window in exchange for a little sexual variety... she'd discovered my lie. Something moved in my stomach and I knew I would throw up soon.

Peggy stood there, still rubbing her eyes, silent, as if she were alone in the room.

I had to speak, to tell her. Not *all* of it, necessarily, but I owed her some kind of confession. Once I'd worked up enough saliva in my mouth, I whispered, "Okay, Peggy. I'm... I... yeah, I wasn't at work. I went... I was—"

She was at my side in an instant, down on one knee, pressing her palm over my mouth gently, hissing, "No-no-no, Arnold. Just... sh-sshhh. I don't... *want* to know. Really. I've been scared and... God, *terrified*. Sitting here wondering... worrying... going over and over every possibility. Especially the worst ones... the worst *one*... wondering if maybe you hadn't worked late last night, either, or the night before that, or... last week, or last month. And then I realized that I really didn't want to know. Not now. Really. It's better that way, I think. Because if I knew and it *was* one of the worst possibilities... I would have to leave you. And I really don't want that. I could've asked Sidney if you'd been working late recently, but... I don't... want... to know."

"Peggy, please, you don't have to—"

"Sshhh. No. I'm not finished. I've been sitting here for hours thinking and thinking. My mind's been a... *tornado.* I've been thinking, what if... just what *if*... I'm losing him? What could have brought it on? What could I have done to prevent it? And I realized... maybe I've been a little too closed to you. Maybe I've gotten a little too set in my ways. I thought about that a lot, and... well, I..." She stood slowly, opened her robe and let it fall away.

"Oh, my God," I murmured.

She wore a dark purple teddy I'd bought for her almost two years ago, and she looked beautiful. Absolutely beautiful. Part of my heart melted away.

She said, "If that is what's happening—and I *don't* want to know—if I am losing you... I don't want to. I still love you, Arnold. Very much. And I want things to be different."

Peggy took my hand and led me to the bedroom...

We fondled and kissed and caressed and sucked one another for what seemed hours, then made love until dawn, first slowly and deeply, then with a rapid-fire passion I hadn't seen in Peggy since our first few times together. My experience with Julie and Larry Ruskin was completely forgotten, as if it had never happened.

When I slept, I relived the last few hours with Peggy in my dreams. But something was different...

As we rolled on the bed, legs entwined, our mouths occupied with one another's flesh, I saw Larry Ruskin in the room. I saw him again and again. The first time, I didn't notice him until he was passing back out the door. Then I saw him again, crossing the room on his way out. The third time, I saw him hurry in, slightly hunched, glancing toward the bed as if to see if we noticed; he gathered something up in his arms, then hurried out. The next time, I tried to see what was bundled in his arms, but the room was dark, my vision blurry and it was nothing more than a shapeless blob. He came back repeatedly, and each time I tried to see what he carried out; each time I failed.

In my dream, as in his own bedroom, Larry Ruskin never made a sound...

That weekend was like the first weekend after we'd started sleeping together: making love was the only thing on our minds. Rather than sleeping, we napped. Rather than eating meals, we snacked. It was glorious... the stuff of the most secret sexual fantasies... better than anything I'd done during those hours with Julie and Larry because this was *Peggy*... my *wife*... my lover of fifteen years, who had finally opened herself to me, the way I had always imagined a lover should.

Of course... there were a few things I forced myself to ignore...

Peggy suggested no new positions; she left that up to me. She turned none of my suggestions down... *but...*

There was a certain look on her face. I couldn't put my finger on it, exactly—was it in her eyes, in the set of her jaw, or in her lips, maybe?—but I knew one thing: it was not a look of enjoyment. It was more a look of... yes, of acquiescence... of surrender.

With each new suggestion, she would nod her head, perhaps mumble, "Okay," or, "Sure," and assume the position. There was no protest, no disagreement... but neither was there any enthusiasm... any delight.

At first, I thought it was my fault; I thought I wasn't being exciting or imaginative enough. So, on Saturday evening, I told her I was going to step out and get something. A surprise.

I went to the Pleasure Dome, a sex shop that carried porn videos and magazines, lingerie and sex toys. There I bought a vibrating dildo, bBen-Wa balls and some love oils. On the way home, I stopped to pick up a dozen roses.

When I arrived, she was sitting in front of the television again, smoking. At first, I was afraid something was wrong, but she stood, extinguished the cigarette immediately and switched off the television, smiling first at me, then grinning at the roses, then looking at the bag I held with... well, I guess it was a wilting sort of look... the way you might look a man at your door when you discover he's from the IRS. She recovered instantly, coming forward to kiss me. She wore a sheer black negligee I'd bought her a few years ago and when she held the roses to her breast, she was beautiful. But she kept glancing at that plain brown bag...

Later, her displeasure was far less subtle. First we used the love oils, then took a long bath together, then, back in bed... she greeted each new surprise with a brief look of intense apprehension. As I massaged her pubis with the vibrating dildo, the look on her face became unbearable and I sat up, turning off the dildo.

"What's wrong?" I asked.

"Oh, *nothing*," she replied quickly—too quickly—taking my arm and pulling me down beside her.

"No, look, Peggy, if you don't want to do this—I mean if you *really* don't *want* to—just tell me." I tried not to sound frustrated, but probably failed.

She smiled. "I'm doing it, aren't I?"

"That's not an answer."

"What makes you think I don't want to?"

"Your face."

Her smile faltered. "What about my face?"

"You're not enjoying this. At all."

The smile disappeared.

"Are you?"

She turned away and sighed.

"I really want to know, Peggy. I certainly don't want to *force* you into anything. But since you instigated all of this last night, I figured—"

"Because I didn't want to lose you," she whispered into her pillow.

"Lose me?"

"Oh, please don't play dumb, Arnold. You know what I mean. I thought if I gave you what you wanted—what I *thought* you wanted—you wouldn't have to lie to me anymore and go... do whatever it is you *do* at night instead of working late." Her face was withered when she turned to me. "But it's not working. I'm sorry, Arnold, but... it's just not me. I can *do* it... but not *convincingly*."

I sat on the edge of the bed and sighed, putting the vibrator on the floor. "You did it before," I said quietly.

"I didn't like it then, either."

"It sounded like you did when you *talked* about it."

"I know, Arnold, I'm sorry, that was bad judgment and… probably a stab at getting your attention and keeping it. I did it, but I didn't really enjoy it."

"Then *why* did you do it?"

"Because… I didn't want to be alone and that was what he wanted me to do. The same reason I've been doing it for you. I'm afraid if I don't, I'll lose you and… be alone."

Turning away from her, I wanted to say she was being ridiculous, of *course* she wouldn't lose me and I was sorry for putting her through something so uncomfortable and—

—I didn't. I couldn't. I felt angry, foolish, guilty, put upon… you name it. I just sat there for a while, then put on my robe, left the room, made a drink and sat down in front of the television. She didn't follow me out. When I looked in on her a half hour later, she was sound asleep.

———————

As I write this, I am holding a gun in my left hand.

We spoke little the next day and when we did, it was as if nothing unusual had taken place. That evening, we agreed we were both in the mood for a couple of old Thin Man movies, so I walked to the corner video store and got them while she cooked dinner. Peggy went to bed while I stayed up and read; when I followed, she was asleep, as I'd hoped.

Actually, I didn't feel at all bad about the whole thing by Sunday night. She was willing to forget it, so I would, too. We would live our life the way we'd lived it up until Friday night, and—after the brief but intense emotional storm I'd gone through over the weekend—that was fine with me. Everything was normal once again.

Until Larry Ruskin called my office on Monday morning…

"You're a hell of guy to track down, Arnold Kramer," he laughed when I picked up the phone. My secretary had told me a man was on the phone and wouldn't identify himself but insisted he speak to me, so I was thrown for a moment. "Larry Ruskin," he said after a pause. "Remember? Friday night?"

A thick lump of guilt rose in my throat. "Yeah. Yeah, I remember."

"Look, the reason I'm calling is this: you left your tie and, um, let's see… are you missing a pearl handled pocketknife?"

"Yeah, that's mine, too."

"Thought so. Well, I thought you might like to drop by on your lunch hour and pick them up."

I definitely did *not* want to do that. "I'm not sure I can, Larry."

"I'd bring them to you, but I'm waiting for Julie to get home, then we're catching a plane out of town, so I'm kinda stuck here for a while. I'm gonna be gone for about ten days and… or, how about if I send them to you?"

I almost said yes, but realized I'd have to give him my home address or have him send them to my office and neither of those options would work. "Tell you what, Larry. Why don't you just keep them."

"Oh, c'mon. Believe me, we're not trying to push you into anything. Just drop by, have a drink if you want, get your stuff, and you never have to see us again. That was the deal, right? I wouldn't be calling you if it weren't for this."

I decided that dropping by his apartment for a few minutes would be preferable to opening myself up to him, so I agreed.

When I rang the bell, Larry called, "C'mon in!" from somewhere inside; he sounded winded.

The television was on in the living room and what appeared to be a porn movie was playing on the VCR. I looked around but saw no one and my eyes returned to the screen.

Two people. On a bed. A man and a woman. The lighting wasn't very good, but…

I squinted at the television, smirking, because it almost looked like… it looked almost as if…

Slowly, I moved close enough to the television to make out my own face on the screen. My face and Julie's. Naked. In bed.

"What," I breathed, "what in the—"

Something fell and broke in another room and I spun around, my mouth gaping. The bedroom door was open and I could see a pair of legs thrashing on the bed.

"Lar…ry? *Larry?*" I hurried toward the bedroom, but stopped when I saw Larry hunched over the head of the bed struggling with something… no, with some*one*. Julie. Lying on her back. Fighting. Making small pathetic gagging sounds. I staggered toward them and stopped, paralyzed and unbreathing, at the foot of the bed when I saw Julie's face— bloated and purple, eyes bulging, fat tongue stabbing between her teeth stiffly—and the necktie Larry was using to strangle her with black-gloved hands. My necktie.

My paralysis broken by what I was seeing, I dove toward Larry, but he swept something off the nightstand and spun around, shouting, "No!" as he leveled a .45 at my face. "Just get *back* and shut *up*, Goddammit, I'm not *finished* yet!"

I stumbled back against the vanity, knocking over some bottles of perfume and rattling the mirror.

Julie squirmed and coughed on the bed, clawing at the tie that had gnawed the skin off her throat cruelly, but Larry moved fast, taking something else—something small—from the nightstand and swiping it back and forth in front of her face several times.

Julie's head snapped left and right, left and right.

Blood spattered the wall above the bed.

She gurgled and jerked violently when Larry stopped and turned to me, holding up my pearl handled monogrammed pocket-knife.

"A crime of passion," he said quietly, dropping the knife. He aimed the gun at me one more time. "Don't move, or I'll kill you, too." Then he put the gun on the bed and finished strangling his wife.

I slid to the floor, legs splayed before me, back against the vanity, and became numb as I watched her die. I thought, then, that watching Larry kill her—just *watching* and not trying to *do* anything—was probably the worst thing I would ever do in my life. Of course, I was wrong, but at the time, I became sick and dry heaved for a few moments after she was dead. In fact, I was certain that *I* was as good as dead, too, having witnessed the murder. But, of course, I was wrong again.

I was *supposed* to know about the murder.

"Okay, I don't have much time," he said, removing the tie from Julie's throat—it peeled away from her skin with a whisper—and turning to me. "So you'll have to listen carefully." He dropped the tie to the floor and nudged it half way under the bed with his toe.

I felt submerged in water, listening to him speak on the surface. He grabbed my arm and lifted me to my feet, saying, "C'mon, Arnold, let's get a move on." We went into the living room and Larry walked over to a small suitcase against the wall. "You saw what happened, right, Arnold? I strangled Julie. With your tie. The tie that has a little tack with your initials on it. I slashed her with your pocketknife, which *also* has your initials on it. You saw the videotape when you came in?" He gestured toward the television, where snow now hissed on the screen. "It seems I discovered that tape by accident and discovered that my wife was having an affair with a kinky guy who likes to tape himself fucking. We had a big fight, my wife

85

and I. Lots of screaming and shouting. Our neighbors will testify to that. We did a lot of screaming and shouting today. I saw to it. Anyway, I told Julie to break it off with her lover while I was out of town to decide how I wanted to react to all of this. I'm going to—"

The telephone rang and Larry smiled, cupping a hand to his ear.

"Out of town?" I rasped as an answering machine cut the ringing short.

Larry's recorded voice said, "Hello. No one can take your call right now. I'm going to be out of town from Monday afternoon until sometime Tuesday. Julie'll be in and out, though, so if you leave your name and number, maybe she can get back to you."

"See?" Larry grinned. "I'm already gone."

I began to feel dizzy, as if I were about to fall.

"While I was gone," he continued, "Julie called you over to end the affair. You got upset and, in a fit of passionate rage, you murdered her, then hurried out of the apartment in a panic, leaving behind the two murder weapons. I come back from my little trip and find my wife dead. I call the police. They come. They see. They look for you. End of story."

I clutched the back of a recliner to steady myself and spoke in a sandpaper voice: "Whuh… w-whuh-*why*?"

He smiled, slipping into his coat. "Because if it weren't for all of this, you wouldn't be very eager to give me one and a half million dollars."

I backed around the recliner and fell into it, repeating the amount over and over in a breathless stammer.

"Of course, it'll have to be soon. Tomorrow afternoon, in fact. Because I'll have to report this as soon as possible. I can't wait around. If it's absolutely impossible, you don't have to pay all of it at once, but I'll need something. Maybe half. If you cooperate, the murder will be made to look like a break-in and your tie and knife will disappear, along with the tape. Otherwise... well..." He chuckled, picking up the suitcase. "Don't bend over for the soap." Opening the door, he said, "C'mon, let's go."

I couldn't move, could hardly breathe, but forced myself to stand on quaking legs. "I... don't... have it. That much money. I don't *have* it." My heart was beating so rapidly that my chest ached.

"Oh, sure you do. You can come *up* with it, can't you?" What about your wife? Your father-in-law?"

"But I can't—they wouldn't—how could I—"

"Yeah, you're right. Couldn't just come out and ask them for it, could you? Oh, well. You'll think of something. You're a bright guy." He slapped his thigh and sang out, "C'mon, gotta go."

I massaged my chest but didn't move from where I stood. "Whuh-why? Why are you... doing this... to me? How cuh-could you... do that? Kill your wuh-wife? Like thuh-that? Your... your *wife?*"

He rolled his eyes, sighed with impatience and closed the door, dropping the suitcase. "I *have* to, okay? I need the money. Desperately. I mean, I'm in a bind, okay? It's not important what the bind *is*, but it's there. I mean, it's really none of your business." His fists doubled at his sides. "But I am against a fucking *wall*, you know what I mean? This is the only thing I could *think* of to *solve* my problem. Now *you* have a problem, but I can't *worry* about that because I have to take care of my *own* problem. Do you see how it works now?"

I walked toward him, avoiding the urge to look back through the bedroom door at the slashed and strangled corpse that lay on the bed. He locked and closed the door behind us.

"We should take the fire escape," he said. "I don't want anybody to see us."

"You don't think anybody will see us if we take the fire escape?"

"Nobody who matters."

We took the fire escape.

Once on the sidewalk, he said, "Okay, here's the deal. Tomorrow afternoon, you meet me at four o'clock at Jeenie's Weenies on Fourth. You know where it is?"

"I've got an idea, yeah."

"Okay. We meet there. You bring me as much of the money as possible, as long as it's a third of what I'm asking or more. We'll work out everything else later. You got it?"

"But I... I... I can't—"

"Yes you can."

"How? I mean, how do you know that? I can't just come up with one and a half—"

"Sure you can."

I rolled my eyes, trying to ignore my sick stomach. "*How? I* mean, what do you think I'm—"

"Just think about what *I* did." He grinned. Waved. Said, "See you tomorrow." Then he was gone.

I was left standing on the sidewalk, trying not to throw up, thinking, suddenly, of Peggy...

I took the rest of the day off work, claiming illness. My appearance supported my claim. Instead of going home, I went, in a daze, to a bar a few blocks from my apartment and tried to drink myself into a different kind of daze, a more preferable numbness. It didn't work.

Instead, I kept remembering what Larry had said.

Just think about what I did...

... about what I did...

... what I did...

And I got very drunk…

By the time I got home, I had to fight not to stagger. I'd done a lot of thinking—the kind of thinking I could only do while I was drunk, but thinking that I *had* to do, under the circumstances—and I had come to a conclusion.

As I write this, that conclusion is eating a hole in my gut, gnawing its way through my intestines.

Peggy was still up, reading in the living room, when I got home.

"Are you drunk?" she asked.

"Not really. I had a few drinks."

"I… I didn't fix any dinner. I didn't think you'd be ho—"

"That's okay. I'm not hungry." I stood in the middle of the room in my coat, holding my briefcase, waiting for the words to come from my mouth. "How are you?"

"I'm… fine. Are you sure you're all right?"

"Yeah. I'm just…" I shrugged and went down the hall, changed my clothes, washed up and used some mouthwash. Then I went into the bedroom and laid down on the bed, fully clothed, to think.

I still hadn't recovered from what I'd seen and knew I wouldn't for a long time. Having watched Larry murder his wife, several things that I'd been able—perhaps willing?—to ignore on Friday night became clear: what Julie had said about Larry—*This is what he's wanted for a long time*—and the way she'd looked at him while the three of us were together, tentatively, as if searching for his approval; Larry coming into the room to take my clothes out and search them and, most of all, the way he had so carefully learned all he needed to know about me at the bar. Where had the video camera been? In the closet? In plain sight, maybe in a corner of the room?

Well, it didn't matter now. Drunk as I was, I wanted a few more drinks. But more than that, I wanted money.

I was by no means poor, but I couldn't just whip up a million and a half and hand it over to Larry. Not only did I have Peggy to answer to, but her father would step in sooner or later, too; sometimes I think he's kept as close an eye on *our* finances as on his own. Oh, I could come up with some of it tomorrow—stocks, bonds, savings, a couple premature CD's—but the rest of the amount worried me. I'd spent the day going over every imaginable option, only to find them all unacceptable. There was, however, one option… a vile, filthy option that made me ill…

"Is anything wrong?" Peggy asked, standing in the doorway. She wore her robe, but I was sure that, beneath it, she was protectively concealed in her usual throat-to-ankle tan nightgown.

I smiled, shook my head and held out my hand, saying, "Come to bed."

She seemed cautious as she joined me on the bed. I kissed her, softly at first, then firmly, clutching her tightly.

"What's gotten into you?" she asked, laughing nervously. "Besides a lot of booze?"

I said nothing for a while, just looked at her. The lump had returned to my throat and my eyes felt hot, as if they were about to tear up.

"There's something I want you to do for me, Peggy. Just… just one more thing. Like… this past weekend."

She closed her eyes and bowed her head a moment. "I thought we cleared all that up, Arnold. I thought we were through with that."

"Just one more thing. Please. Then… I swear… no more."

Her eyes rose slowly to mine and she said, "What do you want me to do, Arnold?"

She shot to her feet and stalked away from the bed the moment I said it and when she spun to face me, her eyes were narrowed and full of hatred.

"What... is... *wrong* with you, Arnold? What... *made* you this way? How, after all these years, could you even *think* of something like this?" She paced the room, fighting her anger; she was actually *angry*. "How could you *dare* to—asking me to—thinking that I would—"

"I'm sorry, Peggy, but it's... just one time. I... need it."

"You *what*?"

I began to cry so suddenly I surprised myself. "I... need it. Please. Just once."

Her anger was gone as quickly as it had come and she sat on the bed and took my hand. "Arnold, I don't know if I could... I mean, just *thinking* about it makes me—"

"You have to. Just once. Because... if you don't... I'll have to guh-go. Away."

She sat there for the longest time, not looking at me, then stood and went to the door. When she spoke, she didn't face me. "All right," she whispered finally. "But a part of me will always hate you, Arnold. Always."

A few hours later, I was in a part of town unfamiliar to me at a bar I'd never gone to before—my third since I'd left the apartment—staring at a man two stools down from me who wore a very expensive looking necktie.

No, I told myself, *you won't do that, you* can't. *You're not like him... a killer... you'll handle this differently, with no killing...*

The man was handsome, almost *too* handsome, but I didn't have time to look around for a sexually frustrated Woody Allen type and, besides, he looked perfect. He was about my age, in better shape, and his clothes, jewelry and even his manner—although he seemed embarrassed and self-conscious—smelled of a generous income. And best of all, he wore a wedding ring. He sat with his back to the bar, watching the others in the room, and hadn't noticed me yet.

I cleared my throat loudly and caught the man's attention and tried to remember Larry's pleasant smile as I said, "Well… what brings *you* here?"

Biting into a messy chili dog, Larry said, "So, what'd you come up with?"

My hot dog lay untouched before me as I told him the amount.

He chewed, dabbed his lips, frowned, and shook his head. "Sorry. That's not quite enough to begin with."

"Buh-b-but-but it's the best I can *do*."

He shrugged. "Sorry. Hey, you're not eating. The dogs're great here, you know."

"Look, I can get more, that's not a problem, it's just that—"

"Yeah, I know, but there's this: I can't wait around."

"Another day. Just *one more* day." I knew the chance of coming up with much more in another twenty-four hours was slim, but I had to *try*.

"But I'm supposed to be out of town. Remember? My answering machine?"

"So you call and leave a message on your machine. Tell Ju…" The name caught in my throat. "… leave a message that you've been delayed, or you've decided to take another day, *whatever*."

He thought about it a moment.

"Larry, that's the best I can do. What *else* do you want me to do?"

He cocked a brow. "Tell you the truth, I don't care *what* you do. All I care about is the money. Other than that, you can... go to the police and confess?" he chuckled. "Go to Mexico? Kill yourself? I just don't care."

I looked down at the hot dog and couldn't have been more repulsed had it been a fresh glistening turd in a bowl of steaming piss. I was exhausted to the point of illness; after a sleepless night, I had spent the first half of the day rounding up the money. When I was finished with Larry—providing he agreed to another day—I had to rent some video recording equipment, something with which I was very unfamiliar, made even more difficult by the fact that I didn't even know exactly what I needed. Derek, the man at the bar the night before, had been more than eager to get together with Peggy and would be coming to the apartment that evening, so I had to be ready for him; I just wasn't sure *how* to be ready for him. Blackmail was new to me.

"Please," I whispered, eyes closed. "One more day."

He chomped on the chili dog for a while, then asked, smirking, "You going to do it?"

I looked at him. "Do what?"

"What I did?"

My teeth sounded like thunder when I ground them together. "None of your Goddamned business."

He nodded, finished the dog and sucked his teeth between words as he said, "Okay. One more day. No more."

———————

That evening, Derek arrived a few minutes early, but I was ready.

Peggy had been cold since I'd gotten home and, as I'd hoped, she'd excused herself to do some shopping for a couple hours. While she was gone, I set up the camera in the closet and propped the door open just enough; I rigged it to a timer and, once it started, it would record for six hours. When Peggy got home, she was even colder, but I'd expected that. I consoled myself with the thought of it all over with; then I would explain the whole thing to her, tell her why I had to do it, beg her forgiveness. But that seemed so far away...

At the end of the evening, I would have to explain things to Derek and impress upon him the gravity of his situation. Peggy would most likely still be in bed and I would take Derek to my office at the opposite end of the apartment, where I had a loaded .38 which I would use to persuade him. I had no intention of shooting him, of course—I was determined to get through it all without any bloodshed—but I needed the extra leverage, just in case the possibility of his wife and three children seeing the videotape wasn't enough to convince him.

Peggy was in the bedroom when he arrived. Waiting. With a great deal of dread, I'm sure.

I'd had a few drinks—several, actually—to make it all easier to handle. I had some dread of my own.

I offered Derek a drink, too, which he accepted. We sat in the living room for a while, talking. I followed Larry's plan almost exactly. I told Derek to just talk with Peggy at first, just get to know her a little, get comfortable with her. When he'd finished his drink and refused another, I led him to the bedroom and let him in.

As I waited for them to get started so I could go into the bedroom for his clothes, my stomach burned and flames licked the back of my throat. I had some more to drink; it didn't help, but I didn't know what else to do.

Then I heard the first of it.

94

Peggy made a sound. It came from deep in her chest and frightened me at first because I thought he was hurting her. I went to the bedroom door and listened. It came again, louder this time. But it didn't sound like pain. I opened the door carefully and looked in.

From the sound of her, I expected to see them writhing on the bed, but he wasn't even inside her yet. Both bedside lamps were on. Derek was on his knees, straddling Peggy, his back straight, head tilted back, eyes closed; she was on her back, propped up on pillows, holding his cock in both fists, licking and sucking it as she moaned and murmured.

"Huge," she said huskily. "It's *huge.*"

It was. I stood in the doorway, my stomach twisting itself into knots, watching my wife give a blow job to a man with an enormous cock… and enjoying it. She never did it to me unless I asked, and then she did it with great reluctance and both eyes clenched shut. Now she uttered deep laughter, grinning like a child as she licked and sucked him, her eyes staring at his erection with wide amazement.

I wanted to throw up. To scream. To cry.

I remembered Larry's words: *One more day. No more… no more… no more…*

I moved quietly into the room, picked up the heap of clothes on the floor and went back to the door as Peggy gasped, "*Fuck* my *tits.* Stick it between my *tits* and *fuck* them. *Come* on them."

I froze. She *never* used that word. She never used that *voice.* And she never *ever* did anything but roll her eyes when I asked if I could slide my cock between her tits.

I stepped outside the room and dropped the clothes, but turned back and peered through the cracked door.

Peggy squeezed her breasts together as he moved above her. "God, your cock is so big," she slurred, craning her head forward to watch it, "so… fucking… *huge!*"

It was *huge*, Peggy had told me of her friend years ago, her eyes brightening, *he was* huge.

When Derek came, it splattered her face and she grabbed his cock and stuffed it into her mouth as far as she could, slurping the fluid off of it, sliding her mouth up and down the length of it.

Peggy hated semen. Mine, anyway. She always grimaced when she had to touch it and could never bring herself to look at it.

Now she wiped it off her face and licked her hand, staring in awe at the enormous organ in front of her face. She squeezed his cock hard in her fist, looked up at him and, through clenched teeth, growled, "Stick it in me. *Stuff* me with it. *Hurt* my *cunt!*"

He moved down, lifted her legs high and plunged into her. Hard.

She cried out, "Yeah! Oh! Yes! Fuck! Me! *Fuck! Me!*"

The woman on my bed was not my wife. She was a stranger. I had never known her... never met her.

Time is wasting, I thought, backing away from the door and pulling it closed. I bent down to retrieve Derek's clothes so I could take out his wallet, find his driver's license and get his home address—anything that might help him see things my way—when the room tilted and spun around me, throwing me to the floor. My vision blurred. My throat clenched for a moment.

The sounds in the bedroom grew louder; Peggy became more ecstatic, screaming as she'd never screamed for me, not even in our most passionate moments.

I got on my knees, fished for Derek's wallet, but my hands were numb, my fingers stiff and my vision was shattered. I struggled to my feet again, leaned against the wall and eased the bedroom door back open.

Peggy was on her hands and knees now, her head pressed into a pillow as Derek slammed into her from behind. He was grunting. She was screaming incoherently.

I had to get away from the sound, from *them*. I staggered quickly through the apartment to my office at the other end, shut the door and fell into my chair. I realized then that I was crying. Sobbing. And I could hear them still. I could hear the *thump-thump-thump-thump* of the bed and Peggy's muffled cries. With my head in my hands, I blubbered as images flashed through my mind and remembered words were whispered into my ears: our first few times together... so passionate and loving; later—and not *much* later—when the frequency of our lovemaking dropped; all the reassurances she gave me... all the excuses; all the times she brought *him* up, all the things she *said* about him... about that guy... I couldn't even remember his fucking name... and the many times she laughed sweetly and kissed me when I asked her if she missed him because, as she'd told me so many times, he had such a *huge* cock...

You're just tired, I thought as I opened my top desk drawer. *You just need sleep*, I thought as I reached into the drawer. *You've just had too much to drink*, I thought as I brought something cold and heavy from the drawer. *Don't take any of this too seriously and just do what you have to do...*

I flinched when I saw the gun in my hand. I wasn't aware I'd been reaching for it.

The sounds continued... the thumping... the shouting and groaning...

My office faded away around me and, after a moment of darkness, became the living room. I was in the middle of the living room, staring down the hall toward the bedroom.

The living room disappeared and, in a blink, I was standing before the bedroom door. I opened it and went in.

She was rolling over beneath him, onto her back, grabbing his cock and guiding it into her. Her eyes were dark and puffy. She made a sound like a small animal being beaten as he began to move inside her again and the sound became words:

"So... big... so... fucking... big... it *hurts*... so *good*..."

I stood beside the bed staring down at her, at the face that didn't even look vaguely familiar. Her eyes were open wide, but she didn't notice me, was completely unaware of my presence as she clutched her sticky breasts and thrust her pelvis upward to meet his. I moved down to the foot of the bed.

Just put the gun away and do what you have to do, I thought as I lifted it to the back of Derek's head. *You just need some sleep*, I thought as I squeezed the trigger.

Derek's blood and brains splattered onto Peggy's face, much the same way his jizm had. Unfortunately, she had very little time to be aware of what had happened because the bullet went through him and entered her throat.

I looked at them a while, then went back to my office.

As I write this, I am holding a gun in my left hand. I am lifting it to my mouth and biting the barrel so hard that my teeth hurt. Now I am squeezing the tri...

Sinema

B rett Deever had been looking for his dog, Gabby, for half
an hour when he found, instead, a hand.

It lay a couple of yards below him, at the edge of
Vintner Creek, which rushed with muddy waters left over from
unexpectedly heavy summer rains. A tangle of tree branches
were jammed between two large rocks, resisting the flow, and
stuck along the other netted detritus was the hand. From Brett's
vantage atop the creek's three-foot-high embankment, it could
have been a dark, tattered glove, clinging to the branches as if
for life.

Brett's typical nine-year-old curiosity took him down the
embankment and carefully through the mud until he was
within reach of the glove, or doll hand, or—

He stopped when he saw the jut of bone sticking from the
purple mush of wrist.

It did not look like a doll's hand now.

"Gabby?" he called softly, nervously, backing up the bank.
A clump of bushes began to rustle, and when Brett finally
turned his head he saw Gabby's German Shepherd rump half-
out of the brush, tail sweeping back and forth enthusiastically.

The dog was grumbling contentedly, making moist chewing sounds. As Brett drew closer, his stomach began to roil like a cluster of worms.

Gabby was flat on his belly, eyes bright. He lifted his head to smile at Brett around dark, meat-flecked teeth, pink tongue dangling. He had been worrying what looked like the stripped branch of a sapling.

Except it still had a foot.

There was more, and after a sharp, happy bark, Gabby flopped on his back and rolled in it. Flies took to the air in clouds, like specks of soot on a breeze.

Brett stared.

He knew he should be reacting strongly, somehow — screaming or running or vomiting, something like that. The awful smell made him a bit queasy, of course, but what he could see — some stubby fingers and toes, the swollen, blackened half of the face that was visible — elicited no emotions in him.

The walls were up.

He felt numb, detached.

He felt nothing.

Just like in church.

In a town as small as Manning, any death, even one by natural causes, remains the topic of conversation for weeks. A murder is talked about for months on end. When it is one in a series of murders, however, as this was, it is not talked about so much as *felt*. It is conspicuous by the silence it leaves behind.

———————————

But Manning is not just *any* small town. It is located in California's Napa Valley on the St. Helena Highway between St. Helena and Calistoga. It is actually a village more than a town, with a population of only 1,750. Most people in the Valley, however, think of it not as a town or a village, but as a sort of commune.

It is inhabited almost exclusively by Seventh-day Adventists.

Manning was founded in 1897 when the Seventh-day Adventists, led by their "prophet," Ellen G. White, settled in Napa Valley. Another village, Angwin, rose up around the college built by the Adventists atop a hill just above Manning.

Seventh-day Adventists worship on Saturday, the seventh day, rather than Sunday; as with the Jewish faith, their sabbath begins at sunset on Friday and ends at sunset on Saturday. During that time, the only place in town that is open is the church. Weekend mail is delivered on Sunday instead of Saturday (Manning has its own little post office which, of course, employs only Seventh-day Adventist residents). Sometimes Delbert Mundy, manager of the Manning Food Market—which sells no alcoholic beverages, no cigarettes, no meat, and nothing containing caffeine, all of which are condemned in the writings of Ellen White—can be seen on Saturday evenings standing just inside the market's front doors, keys in hand, staring at his wristwatch, waiting for the sun to go down so he can open up.

The thing about Manning that Brett Deever hated most— despised, in fact—was that, unlike its neighboring towns St. Helena and Calistoga, both of which are larger but still quite small, Manning had no movie theater.

It would have done Brett no good if it had.

Along with drinking alcohol and coffee, eating pork and seafood, reading fiction, wearing make-up or jewelry, dancing and playing cards, the Seventh-day Adventist Church's list of condemned activities also includes going to movies.

The summer rains that had hit the Valley with such a vengeance earlier in the month had caused Vintner Creek to disgorge all kinds of garbage onto its muddy banks, none of which was as horrible as the chewy treat Gabby had discovered.

While Brett had found a hand, and Gabby, a foot, the police and their dogs had uncovered a lot more, all of it identifiable with the help of lab techs from San Francisco. Despite massive decay, the body parts were identified as belonging to Jimmy Greenlaw. He was the third such victim in two years.

All three boys had been approximately the same age. The first had been a resident of St. Helena, the second from Angwin, and Jimmy had spent his eight years of life in Manning. All three had been Seventh-day Adventists.

The boys had been sodomized, then dismembered, and their remains cast into the waters of Vintner Creek to find their way into the digestive tracts of various fish and forest animals.

The bone scoring suggested the killer used dull kitchen implements, and that he'd done a sloppy, amateurish job of it. The cut patterns on the bones were a near match; the semen tracks were an *exact* match.

The police claimed there was other linking evidence proving the killings to be the work of a single person or group. They refused, however, to discuss such niceties as chemical proof and tissue damage with the press.

That was just fine with Brett's grandma.

"They'll be back, those reporters," she said a few days after Brett's discovery, seating him at the kitchen table. Grandma was a large gray-haired woman who dressed colorlessly and seldom smiled. She was especially unsmiling now; she'd just chased two more reporters from the front door. As she poured Brett a glass of soy milk, she said sternly, "And you'll not talk to them. Always sticking their microphones into people's faces after something awful's happened. The more awful the *better*, far as they're concerned. That's why I'll not have any newspapers in this house. Rags, all of them." She lowered herself into a chair across from Brett. "No television, either. All those reporters *smiling* while they tell about murders and rapes and homo-seck-shuls spreading AIDS. Course, the television *shows* are just as bad. Nothing but sex and killing..."

Brett sipped the thick sweet milk, wiped off his creamy white mustache and said, "Larry Jackson says *they* have a television, but his parents only let him watch *good* shows. He says—"

"I don't care. A television is Satan's doorway into the home. I know *some* say they can handle it, but if Sister White were still alive, *she'd* tell them differently. Maybe they're watching good shows now—" She spat *good shows* with bitter skepticism, "—but you just *wait*. You watch enough of that stuff and it... it *affects* you." She searched Brett's face for a moment and her eyes clouded with worry. She reached across the table and closed her puffy liver-spotted hand over Brett's small one. "You haven't been thinking about that boy, have you? About those... what you found?"

Brett shook his head, resisting the urge to roll his eyes. "No, Grandma."

"Good. Good. It's not healthy to dwell on that sort of thing. It can... affect you." She watched him a moment longer, as if waiting for a reaction of some sort, then said, "Go study your Sabbath school lesson, Brett, honey. And say a prayer for that poor boy's family. After dinner, you can give me a back rub."

He polished off his milk and Grandma stroked his hair gently, sympathy glistening in her eyes.

The policemen had been the same way. All of a sudden, everyone was treating him as if he were breakable just because he'd found a dead boy. Brett didn't understand what the big deal was. It wasn't as if Jimmy had been a friend of his; Brett had no friends to speak of. They'd had a passing acquaintance in Sabbath school, but that was all. Sure, it was a bad thing that happened and Jimmy's parents were probably crushed, but Brett wouldn't let *his* feelings get involved.

On his way through the living room, Brett glimpsed his Grandpa. Brett seldom got more than a glimpse of him, usually rounding a corner or going through a doorway in his wheelchair, the two stumps of his legs—souvenirs from the Big War—hidden beneath a brown wool blanket. He had his own bedroom downstairs where he ate all of his meals and spent most of his time listening to gospel music on his record player. Brett never heard Grandma talking to him, and he couldn't remember the last time he'd heard Grandpa speak; the only sound he made was the muffled rumble of his chair wheeling over the old wooden floor.

In his room upstairs, Brett locked his door—something Grandma strongly disapproved of—and pulled a fat three-ring binder from under his bed. He flopped onto the mattress and opened the book, searching through the heavy construction paper pages. Pasted to each page were movie advertisements cut out of newspapers. He looked for one in particular and when he found it, he folded his arms beneath his chest, tucked the tip of his tongue into the corner of his mouth, and stared at it, relished it.

The ad took up a quarter of the page and written at the top in letters that appeared to be carved in flesh was the title:

BEDSIDE MANNERS

Below that:

If you sleep in the dark,

he'll find you...
If you sleep with a light on,
he'll find you faster...

Below the words was a picture of a man's blue-jeaned legs from behind; a bloodied axe hung at his side. Between his spread legs, facing him, a woman lay in bed clutching the blankets to her breasts, mouth open in a horrified scream.

The woman was Brett's mother.

The book held nearly sixty ads for all kinds of movies ranging from Academy Award winners complete with quotes of praise from the critics to grade-Z horror films promising lots of bosoms and blood; Brett collected them all. Because Grandma would not allow newspapers into the house, Brett had to fish discarded editions from garbage cans and trash bins, always careful that no one was watching. Once he'd found the entertainment section, he folded the paper up and stuffed it into his book bag, then sneaked it to his room, where it was subjected to scissors and paste. Risky business for a Seventh-day Adventist boy, but even more risky with Grandma around.

Grandma had a nervous tic that wriggled her lower lip now and then, especially when she was upset. At the very mention of movies or theaters, Grandma's lip began to twitch so fast it seemed about to wriggle off her face.

"If you ever go into such a place," she'd say firmly, "your guardian angel does not go with you. It puts a distance between you and the Lord and can be dangerous. Bad things can happen. Your soul is unprotected and if you should die within those walls, you're lost forever."

Brett never understood exactly why it was wrong to go to movies. There were certainly no rules against having a television or watching movies at home on a VCR. There were approved and unapproved movies, of course. The Adventists

Brett knew who owned televisions all claimed to use discretion in choosing programs and movies, but they still *watched* them. Sometimes the church held a "Family Film Night" when they would show *The Wilderness Family* or some Disney movie that was on the Approved List and charge admission to raise money for new carpet in the sanctuary, or something. But going to see a movie in a theater was absolutely forbidden.

Brett had been given several explanations for this law such as, "In a theater you're with a bad crowd, the wrong element," and, "Movies contain unchristian and immoral themes and are a powerful negative influence." None of them satisfied him. *Lost forever* was a pretty strong consequence to pay, but it did not dampen his desire to go to a theater. Brett dreamed of going to movies the way most boys his age dreamed of being a fireman, a secret agent, or an astronaut.

He sometimes met other children his age who were not Seventh-day Adventists and asked them what it was like to go to movies. Puzzled by his urgent questioning, they told him of the warm smell of popcorn in the lobby, the posters on the walls, the way the voices hushed in the auditorium as the lights slowly died, of the coming attractions shown before the movie started, and the *movies...*

He asked them again and again about the movies they saw, wanting to know every detail from beginning to end.

"How come bad things don't happen to the other kids who go to movies?" he asked Grandma once.

"They haven't been shown the truth yet. You *have*. They don't know they're doing wrong, so the Lord won't hold it against them. But someday He'll show them."

There was always a shadow of worry on her face when he asked about movies; Brett suspected she feared he would turn out like his mother.

It had been so long since Brett had seen his mother that he'd forgotten what her voice sounded like. She called him every Christmas and birthday (although she'd forgotten his ninth), but the calls were brief and her voice was fuzzy with distance. He remembered her face only because he had a picture of her tucked in the back of the binder with her letter and postcards.

And now he had a new one: BEDSIDE MANNERS.

A little more than three years ago, Mom had left Brett with Grandma and Grandpa so she could go to Hollywood to become an actress. That's what she'd been doing before he came along, she'd claimed; she hadn't quite made it then, so she wanted to give it another try.

Grandma spoke of Mom only when Brett got a phone call from her. After the call, she would hug Brett to her enormous breasts—she always smelled of mothballs andBengay—and mutter, "Imagine your own mother running off like that. And to *that* town to work with those, those *people*. At least she had the good sense to leave you with me so I could raise you in Christ."

Sometimes it was easy to hate Mom for leaving him with Grandma and Grandpa; he hated Manning, the church, and everything that came with it. But he wouldn't let himself hate her because he always knew she'd come back for him someday. Now he knew he was right.

Brett took his mother's most recent letter from the back of the book. He only got her letters during the summer when he could get to the mailbox first. When he was in school, Grandma burned the letters before he could find them.

Brett honey,
Got my first movie role! It's a cheapie

107

horror flick called *Bedside Manners* and
the part is small—I play a "victim" in the first
ten minutes—but they're using me
on the poster, so it's good exposure...

Brett skipped down to the last paragraph.

I've got a little money now and hope to
come up north and get you soon. Would
you like to live in LA with me? There are
good schools here and lots of things to do...

Brett's chest swelled with the very thought of going away
with Mom.
    ... hope to come up north and get you soon...
    ... get you soon...

                    ... soon...

He heard Grandma in the hall and quickly put the book
away, unlocking the door before she tried the knob, then he lay
back on his bed again.

Brett was so happy that even the thought of having to give
Grandma another of those smelly Bengay backrubs after
dinner could not depress him...

————————

Mr. Moser was the only person in the small Manning church
with whom Brett felt comfortable. The rest of the people there
seemed to be stiff, emotionless machines, programmed to smile
at certain times, frown or look sympathetic at others, set to shed
a tear or say "*A-men!*" during the sermon, and to sing the
designated hymn when the organ began to play. On Friday
afternoons, they washed their cars, cleaned and pressed their

finest clothes; they came to church looking their best but seemed to leave their souls at home…

As Brett sat with his grandparents (Grandpa always parked his wheelchair at the end of a pew) and looked at the empty staring faces around him—some nodding off, others watching the droning pastor but apparently seeing something else—he felt a sadness that was hard to shake. So he didn't watch them anymore. He shut them out along with the whiney organ music and the pastor's level, reverent voice that went on and on. Brett learned how to shut himself off during the hour or so that the service lasted; he heard nothing, saw nothing, and felt nothing. Afterward, instead of feeling agitated and depressed as he normally would, he felt relaxed, as if he'd taken a nap.

He didn't have to do that in Sabbath school, though, because the teacher, Mr. Moser was different than the others. Brett wasn't the only one fond of him; all the kids liked Mr. Moser. There was nothing forced or artificial about him. When he laughed, it was real; his round little belly bounced like a ball and his darkly bearded moon face split into a broad grin.

When he was concerned, as he was that Sabbath after Brett's discovery, his heavy eyebrows lowered over his eyes and his forehead became creased with lines of genuine worry.

He took Brett aside after Sabbath school.

"How are you, Brett?"

"Fine."

"You're sure?"

"Oh. You mean after finding that… boy. Sheesh, everybody's worried about me now."

"Well, that's a pretty awful thing to find."

Brett shrugged.

"A pretty hard thing to forget, too, I'd think," Mr. Moser added.

"I'm okay. Really."

Mr. Moser studied Brett's face thoughtfully for a moment, then smiled.

"How would you like to come out to my place after church, Brett? We could have lunch, then go for a walk and look for lizards."

Brett was thrilled at the opportunity to get out of his grandparents' house for the day and even happier to spend the afternoon with Mr. Moser.

"I'll have to ask Grandma," he said. "She's kinda careful about letting me out of the house because of this… well, you know, the killer. But I'm sure she won't mind if she knows I'm with you…"

Mr. Moser lived at the end of a dirt road about a mile and a half off Glass Mountain Road. His house was small and homey, nestled in the shade of several tall trees. He had no neighbors within sight of his house and plenty of rocky, hilly land around on which to hunt lizards and snakes.

They had a lunch of taco salad and strawberry shortcake for dessert, then went outside for a long walk in the summer sun.

It made Brett feel important to be alone with his teacher; he had Mr. Moser's undivided attention *and* his interest. As they walked, they didn't talk about Sabbath school or church—in fact, Brett completely forgot it was the Sabbath, which would have been impossible had he been with Grandma. Mr. Moser wanted only to talk about Brett.

"What would you like to do, Brett, more than anything in the world?"

"Do? What do you mean?"

"Go to Disneyland? Fly a plane? Ride a rocket to the moon?"

They were walking along a dusty trail and Bret began to thoughtfully kick a rock along ahead of him, wondering if he could confide in Mr. Moser. He decided it was safe to be honest.

"I'd like to go to a movie," he said quietly.

"Pardon?"

"A movie. You know, in a theater."

"Ah. The forbidden fruit." Mr. Moser smiled knowingly.

"Huh?"

"Nothing. Never been to a movie, huh?"

"I've never even *seen* a movie. Not a *real* one, anyway, like *Raiders of the Lost Ark* or *Alien.* Just those stupid movies they show on Family Nights. And sometimes Grandma won't even let me go to *those.*"

Mr. Moser stopped and sat on a fat tree stump, chuckling quietly.

Brett frowned, thinking perhaps he'd said something wrong.

"What's funny?" he asked.

"Well, it's just that… see, I'm chairman of the Entertainment Committee. I'm one of the people who *chooses* those stupid movies."

"Oh." Brett could feel his face growing hot with embarrassment. "I'm sorry."

"No, no, don't apologize, Brett," Mr. Moser laughed. "I know most of those movies aren't very good, but we're kind of limited. It *is* a church function, after all. There aren't many good family-oriented films to choose from. We're always looking for new ones to put on the Approved List, but the committee's standards are pretty rigid. No swearing, no drinking, no smoking. I know what you mean, though; if I have to sit through *Zebra in the Kitchen* one more time, I may be sick." He rubbed his palms up and down his blue-jeaned thighs thoughtfully for a moment, then asked, "If you haven't seen any real movies, then how do you know about *Raiders of the Lost Ark* and *Alien?*"

Hesitantly, Brett told him about his collection of movie ads.

Mr. Moser listened intently, watching Brett with great interest. When he was finished, Mr. Moser said, "Have you ever seen a VCR, Brett?"

"We don't even have a TV."

Mr. Moser winked. "Then let's go back to the house. I've got something to show you."

Back in the house, Mr. Moser opened a tall cabinet in the living room. On the middle shelf was a large television set. Below was a black machine with the time glowing in green numbers on the side. Rows of what appeared to be books filled the top shelf.

"This is a video cassette recorder," Mr. Moser said, "and these—" He gestured at the book-like objects, "—are video cassettes."

Brett stared into the cabinet with awe, his lips parted.

"When a movie is submitted for approval," Mr. Moser said, "I sometimes invite the committee over here and, if it's available on video cassette, we watch it here, then vote on it."

"So you get to see unapproved movies, too?" Brett whispered. "Not just the kid stuff?"

"Well, it's not likely that anyone is going to submit a movie like *Body Heat* or *Tootsie* for approval, but, yes, I get to see all the movies."

"Wow," he breathed, leaning forward to reverently inspect the VCR. "How many videos do you have up there?"

"About sixty movies or so on tape."

"*Sixty?* Sheeesh…"

"All kinds of movies. You name it, and I've probably got it."

Brett stared up at the rows of tapes, imagining what it would be like to sit down and watch all of them—each one, back to back. He glanced at Mr. Moser, thinking there was probably little chance of seeing any of those movies.

But Mr. Moser had a broad grin on his face.

"Would you like to see one, Brett?" he asked.

"But… it's the Sabbath."

"Would that bother you?"

"Wouldn't it bother *you?*"

"Well… why don't we make this our little secret. Just between the two of us. Okay?"

Brett held his breath a moment, expecting him to say he was just joking. It was too much to ask for.

"Okay, Brett?"

Slowly, disbelievingly, Brett nodded, then smiled as he realized Mr. Moser was serious. *Really serious!*

Mr. Moser scanned the tapes and pulled one down, took it from its box, and slipped it into the machine.

"This is a good one," he said. "It's a Disney movie, but don't let that fool you. It's called *Never Cry Wolf.* It wasn't approved because there are a few swear words in it and a shot of Charles Martin Smith in the buff from behind. It's great, though. Sit down. You want some chips?"

Within minutes, Brett was seated wide-eyed in front of the television munching on potato chips and drinking a Crush.

For two hours, he was far away from Manning.

In the following weeks, Brett spent a good deal of his time over at Mr. Moser's watching one movie after another.

Grandma was pleased because Brett had told her he was working with Mr. Moser on some Sabbath school projects. No further explanation was needed; she was glad to know he was investing his time in wholesome activities.

The day after he watched *Never Cry Wolf,* Brett saw *Starman,* a movie that would never even be *considered* for approval; Seventh-day Adventists frown bitterly upon science fiction and fantasy. At the end of the movie, the alien, played by Jeff Bridges, made love with Karen Allen. It was a gentle, tasteful love scene (the movie was only rated PG) with no frantic grunting or moaning, but it was nevertheless startling to Brett. He had neither seen nor imagined people touching each other, with their hands *and* their mouths, the way Jeff Bridges and Karen Allen were on the screen.

He squinted curiously, straightened his posture, and said, "What are they doing?"

Mr. Moser sniffed and fidgeted on the sofa.

"They're, um, making love."

"What?"

"Making love."

"What's that?"

"Well... when a man and woman care very much for one another, they, um... they share their bodies with each other. They kiss and hold each other. Like that." He gestured toward the screen.

"You mean *sex?*"

Mr. Moser nodded slightly, his eyes on the television; he looked embarrassed and uncomfortable.

So that's what Grandma's always complaining about, Brett thought, turning his attention back to the movie.

Nothing but sex and killing...

He could see nothing bad about what the man and woman were doing. In fact, it was pleasant; they seemed to be enjoying themselves.

As the tape was rewinding, Brett turned to Mr. Moser and said, "That didn't look like a bad thing. The sex, I mean. People are always talking about it like it's a bad thing."

"Well, it can be... misused," Mr. Moser said, clearing his throat nervously. "But if it's between a man and a woman who love one another and who are married, it's perfectly natural and... healthy."

"But *they* weren't married," Brett pointed out with a nod toward the television.

"*That* is why the Church doesn't want you to watch movies unless they're approved by a committee."

Brett returned the following day for a showing of *The Color Purple*.

"I think you'll like this, Brett," Mr. Moser said enthusiastically as he put the tape in the VCR. "It's a great movie. In fact, just barely missed the Approved List."

"How come?"

"Oh, some swearing and drinking. But what really did it was the lesbian relationship."

"The what?"

Mr. Moser glanced at Brett with a startled expression and Brett realized that, for a moment, Mr. Moser had forgotten he wasn't talking to another adult.

"Well talk about it after the movie."

It *was* a great movie, although very sad. Brett was surprised at how much the film moved him. By the time it was over, his eyes were puffy and sticky with tears. He didn't want to talk for a while and was silent as the tape rewound. Mr. Moser watched him, waiting for him to speak.

"So what's a... lez-bean?" he finally asked.

"Well, what did you think of the movie?"

"It was good. But I didn't see anything that looked like it might be a lez-bean relationship. Whatever that is. So what is it?"

"It was pretty subtle; I guess you'd have to be looking for it. Remember when Shug and Celie went home after the big fight in the bar?"

Brett nodded.

"And they were alone together? And they started... well, touching each other?"

Another nod.

"That's where, um—" He was fidgeting again, "—where their lesbian relationship began."

Brett waited for him to go on; when he didn't, Brett said, "I still don't know what it is."

Mr. Moser sighed. "A lesbian is... well, it's a woman who would rather make love with... with another woman than with a man."

Brett frowned as he thought that over.

"You mean... *sex*? The women do *sex* together?"

Mr. Moser nodded and said, "Have sex, not do."

Brett pondered the new information, chewing his lip. Something about it bothered him; it didn't fit into his rapidly growing view of things.

"Are there men lesbians, too?" he asked.

Mr. Moser nodded as he turned away from Brett and ejected the tape. "Homosexuals," he muttered, putting the tape in its box.

... and the homo-seck-shuls spreading the AIDS, Grandma had grumbled.

There was another of her mysterious complaints explained.

"Why would anyone want to—" Brett began, but Mr. Moser interrupted him.

"How would you like a popcorn ball? I made some this morning."

Taking that as a hint to change the subject, Brett said, "Okay."

Brett waited for the mail carrier each day, but heard nothing more from his mother. After each disappointing delivery, he would play with Gabby until he knew Mr. Moser was home from work—Mr. Moser was an X-ray technician at the Seventh-

day Adventist hospital in Deer Park and got off at three p.m. —
then hop on his bike and head for his Sabbath school teacher's
house.

A day did not pass without a few warnings from Grandma.

"Don't talk to any strangers," she'd say, "And stay away
from those Mexican hitchhikers, you hear? Probably one of
them who's killing all those poor little boys. Always drinking
their beer and smoking their dope... Course, if you keep saying
your prayers, Jesus'll watch over you and nothing will
happen."

In Brett, Mr. Moser had found a protege; in Moser, Brett had
gained a mentor, and he watched one movie after another, so
many that he would have lost count if he did not list them in a
spiral-bound pocket pad — a new kind of scrapbook. Beneath
the title of each film were notes; Brett learned something new
from each film whether he enjoyed the movie or not.

Sometimes, while sitting on the sofa in front of the TV,
munching snacks, drinking a soda, Brett would glance up and
see Mr. Moser watching him peripherally, usually chewing a
nail or passing a hand up and down his thigh nervously, as if
wiping sweat from his palm. His eyes darted away the moment
Brett spotted him watching, and he always returned his
attention to the movie.

Gremlins, *The Terminator* and *Cujo* defined Brett's next week,
followed by all three *Star Wars* movies in a row. Of the trilogy,
Brett's favorite was the first; he nearly jumped to his feet and
cheered during the final scene in which the heroes were
rewarded for their valor.

At first, Brett found it a bit disconcerting to watch
unapproved movies with the chairman of the entertainment
committee. But Mr. Moser reassured him.

"Remember, Brett," he said, "it's our secret."

One day, Mr. Moser said, "Brett, I think it's time you left behind the little kid stuff." He took down a tape and removed it from its box. "I think you should start learning a little about movies and the people who make them, seeing how you love them so much. Do you know who Alfred Hitchcock was?"

Brett shook his head. He knew Mr. Moser's "teacher voice" by heart; it was the same tone he used in Sabbath school when imparting lessons. Brett was infinitely more interested in the lessons Mr. Moser reserved for him personally, and so paid rapt attention, eager to please. He enjoyed what he was learning, savoring the taste of what Moser had called the forbidden fruit.

Mr. Moser slid a new tape into the VCR. "Hitchcock was a very famous movie director, maybe the most imitated director ever." He saw the puzzlement on Brett's face, and because he was good at teaching, he explained. "The director is the one in charge on a movie set. He tells people what to do, where to stand, how to act. He makes changes in the story; decides how each scene is going to be filmed. He orchestrates everything. Anyway, this movie is Hitchcock's first sound film. The first sound film to come out of England, in fact. It's old—1929—but it's good. I just got it and thought you might like to see it. It's called *Blackmail*."

The title conjured images of letters written on black stationery in Brett's mind. He'd never heard the word "blackmail" before and had no idea what it meant.

As he watched, he learned.

For three weeks, Brett kept their secret and his list of movies grew a little longer each day. From Mr. Moser he learned about movies; from the movies he learned about life.

It was the Friday night of the third week of their secret that things changed.

Friday nights were always gloomy. Grandma never smiled—not that she did much smiling anyway—and was grumpier than usual. The darkness seemed a little darker and the scratchy music from Grandpa's room seemed more mournful than the rest of the week. Grandpa usually sat in the living room on Friday nights, his grave, shiny-bald head hanging heavily from his neck, for which it seemed much too big. He drummed his thick fingers on the armrests of his wheelchair, his eyes blackened by shadow, as Grandma rocked in the squeaky rocking chair, reading Sister White and humming off-key to the music.

Brett was more than eager to get out for the evening.

On that Friday night, Brett arrived to find Mr. Moser on the phone.

"I'm sorry, Jim," he was saying. "I completely forgot about it. I can be there in five minutes... No, no, I have nothing planned. I'll be right there."

When he hung up, Mr. Moser paced before the phone for a moment, chewing a thumbnail, almost as if Brett wasn't there. His eyes finally darted to Brett and his lips curled into a forced smile that was little more than a flash of teeth.

"A Sabbath school committee meeting," he muttered. "Forgot all about it."

"Oh. Do you want me to go?"

"No, no," he replied quickly, turning fully to Brett, holding out his arms and waggling his hands. "No, sit down, have a soda, put in a movie. I shouldn't be gone more than twenty-thirty minutes. I have—" He lowered his voice secretively and smiled. "—I have a surprise for you, Brett. It'll just have to wait a few minutes now, that's all." He took his wallet and keys from the coffee table. "Don't answer the phone, just let the machine get it. Be back in a few."

119

After he was gone, Brett opened the cabinet and, with the help of a chair from the kitchen, pulled *Ghostbusters* down from the shelf. Mr. Moser had showed him how to operate the VCR so he slipped in the tape, turned on the television, and pushed PLAY.

The empty house rang with Brett's laughter as he watched the movie and drank a root beer from the refrigerator. Ten minutes into the tape, he pushed the pause button and headed for the bathroom.

Mr. Moser had given Brett a tour of the house during his first visit. Pointing to the door beyond the bathroom, Mr. Moser had said, "That's my bedroom, and that," he'd added, pointing across the hall, "is the linen closet. If you ever spend the night, there are extra blankets and pillows in there."

"What's this?" Brett had gone to a closed door at the end of the hall.

"Laundry room." He'd taken Brett's arm then and led him back into the living room, saying, "It's a mess."

After he finished in the bathroom, Brett stood at the bedroom door a moment and decided Mr. Moser wouldn't mind if he just took a peek inside to see what his bedroom looked like.

It was dark in the bedroom and Brett reached for a light switch, found it, and flipped it up.

The first thing he saw was the huge screen across the room. He thought it was probably a big-screen TV; he'd heard about them, but had no idea they were *this* big.

Brett stepped over to the television to get a better look and saw that there was another VCR hooked up to it, just like the one in the living room.

He brushed his fingertips lightly around the labeled controls—ON-OFF, VOLUME, COLOR, TINT...

Watching a movie on that big screen would almost be like watching it in a theater…

Maybe this is the surprise, he thought.

Brett hurried into the living room, ejected *Ghostbusters* — returned to the bedroom and turned on the television. When he tried to insert the tape into the VCR, he found another already in the slot. He pushed EJECT and the tape eased out like a tongue from a mouth.

The top of the tape was black as night and the white spools in the casing stared at him like dead eyes.

Looking around, Brett found no box for the tape, but a white label was attached to the tape's edge. In block letters written with a felt-tip marker was written WARNER BROS. CARTOONS #2.

He glanced at the clock beside the bed. Mr. Moser had been gone only fifteen minutes. That left another fifteen; he'd probably be a little longer than he'd said if it was a meeting.

Slipping the tape back into the slot, he pressed PLAY, and sat back against the foot of the bed.

Cheerful music began to play and the words LOONEY TOONS appeared on the large screen.

"Bugs Bunny!" Brett exclaimed happily when the rabbit appeared, munching a carrot. He'd seen pictures of Bugs in a coloring book his mother had sent him. Grandma had taken the book away from him and, in its place, given him a book called *Uncle Arthur's Bible Stories*. No rabbits in *that* book.

After the credits, a short bald man appeared holding a rifle. He was walking through the woods on tiptoe looking right and left.

"Shhh!" he hissed to Brett, looking right out of the screen at him, "I'm hunting wabbits. Heh-heh-heh-heh!"

Bugs suddenly poked his head out of a hole in the ground, took a bite of carrot, smacked his lips a few times, and said, "Aaaaahh, what's up, D—"

The cartoon was gone.

The screen danced with black and white speckles; Mr. Moser called them "ant races".

For a moment, Brett chilled with the fear that he'd done something wrong, something that had perhaps broken the VCR.

He sighed with quiet relief when the picture returned.

But it was not the cartoon of a moment before.

Garbled music played over the television speakers and the screen filled with a square platform surrounded by a fence of ropes. Two huge, sweaty men stood in opposite corners of the square.

"And in *this* corner!" a faceless voice shouted. "Measuring in at ten and three-quarter inches! *Mickey... "the Bone"...* Semen*inski!*"

The men stepped out of their corners as an invisible crowd cheered them on. Their arms were held slightly outward, fingers crooked into threatening claws.

Both men wore tight masks over their faces, one black and one red. Hugging their massive bodies were leather outfits that crisscrossed and zig-zagged; silver spikes and zippers shined all over the costumes.

That was not, however, what shocked Brett.

What made Brett's mouth fall open loosely, what made his breath catch in his throat, was the large triangular opening below each man's waist and the stiff fleshy rod that jutted from thick dark patches of curly hair.

Brett closed his eyes a moment, certain he was not seeing what he *thought* he was seeing. Surely he'd come in on the middle of something—perhaps a recording mistake on Mr.

Moser's part—and had missed an important scene that would explain what he thought he'd seen.

But when he opened his eyes again…

The men were circling one another menacingly, eyeing the exposed sections between their legs.

An odd memory suddenly flashed behind Brett's eyes, vivid in detail. He was sitting in a tub of soapy water bathing on the third night after moving in with his grandparents. The bathroom door opened and Grandma came in—he remembered how overwhelming the smell of Bengay had been—wearing her bathrobe.

"Wash good," she'd said with a smile. Then her eyes had darkened and she'd leaned over the tub. "But when you wash *there*," she'd whispered, pointing to his private area (that's what Mom had called it) hidden beneath the suds, "wash *quickly*. Don't touch it anymore than you have to."

"What?" he'd said, puzzled.

Her lower lip had begun to twitch as she said, "Your pee-pee. Your *penis*. It's… bad. *Dirty*. If you touch it too much, it… wakes *up*. Makes you think bad thoughts. So wash it *quickly*." She'd smiled then and left him to his bath.

Never quite sure what she'd meant, Brett remembered what she'd said each time he bathed and did as he'd been told, not wanting to awaken his penis.

The men on the screen, however, were apparently *trying* to awaken theirs. They were handling themselves, *pulling* on themselves, making their penises grow even larger as they circled one another again and again.

The red man suddenly lunged for his opponent, grabbing unsuccessfully for his penis.

He was not unsuccessful the second time.

The crowd roared.

The garbled music continued, rambling almost tunelessly.

"And the Bone is *down!*" the faceless voice cried.

The red man straddled the Bone, holding his penis in a fist. Reaching up to his masked face, the red man opened a zipper over his mouth, rounded his lips into a large O, and leaned forward.

The invisible crowd went wild.

Brett buried his shock in a forced, familiar numbness until he could watch the film without reacting.

He felt nothing.

Just like in church.

—————

The Sabbath school committee meeting was over in twenty minutes, just as Mr. Moser had suspected it would be. The entire committee was present—eight people in all—and, as usual, they sat around the conference table and socialized after the official business was out of the way.

Mr. Moser excused himself from the chatter, left the room, and headed down the main corridor of the church for the front entrance, walking at a brisk pace, thinking of Brett…

"Ed! What's your hurry?"

He stopped and turned to see Pastor Alexander coming out of his study.

"Well," he began, pushing a smile onto his face, "I'm, uh… I'm in no hurry, really."

"Then step in here for a minute. I want you to meet someone."

Mr. Moser followed the little man with the big walrus mustache into his study where a man, woman, and little boy were seated on a brown leather-upholstered sofa.

"Ed Moser," Pastor Alexander said formally, "I'd like you to meet the Rileys, Jack, Betty, and their son Jason."

Mr. Moser smiled, shook Jack Riley's hand, and said, "Pleased to meet you."

"The Rileys have just moved to Manning," the pastor said. "This is going to be their first Sabbath with us."

"Oh. Well. Welcome. Glad to have you." He glanced at his watch and made note of the time; he'd been gone almost half an hour.

Pastor Alexander moved behind his desk and seated himself in his squeaky chair. "Have a seat, Ed."

Still smiling, Mr. Moser thought of Brett back at the house, sitting in front of the television set watching a movie. What would it be tonight? *Jaws? Stripes?* Maybe *The Wizard of Oz.* He seated himself in a chair facing the Rileys.

"Ed is one of our Sabbath school teachers," Pastor Alexander said. "He works in X-ray at our hospital up the hill—has quite a reputation up there—but I'm happy to say he's very generous with his time. Ed's devoted to our children here at the church." The pastor winked at Jason and said, "You'll be in his class tomorrow, Jason."

The boy smiled hesitantly at Mr. Moser.

"We'll be glad to have you, Jason," Mr. Moser said. "I've got a great bunch of boys in my class. Boys *and* girls, of course."

Jason blushed beneath his freckles and looked away bashfully.

"Fine-looking boy you have there," Mr. Moser said to the proudly beaming Rileys. "Fine-looking boy."

———————————

There was a second movie on the tape and it began as soon as the Bone and the man in red milked one another's penises. That's what it looked like to Brett—milk. Thick, like soy milk.

More of the same.

Brett hit FAST FORWARD, waited a moment, then pushed PLAY.

Still more.

He pushed REWIND and sat watching the ant races, his mind buzzing with questions.

Did Mr. Moser *watch* these movies? He must, or else why would he own them?

But did he *enjoy* them?

He must, or else why would he *watch* them?

Then was Mr. Moser a man lesbian? A—

... and the homo-seck-shuls spreading the AIDS...

—homosexual?

If he liked to *watch* men doing sex together (if that was what those men had been doing, and Brett suspected it was), then...

... then he must like to do it, too, Brett thought.

The tape finished rewinding with a solid *thunk.*

Maybe he was just curious, Brett suggested to himself as he ejected the tape.

Surely Mr. Moser didn't have any *more* of those movies.

Then again, he *had* been very uncomfortable talking about sex.

Maybe even guilty.

Brett stood and dashed down the hall to the living room where he cupped his hands to the pane of the front window and looked for Mr. Moser's headlights in the night.

Nothing.

He hurried back to the bedroom and began his search.

Brett looked through drawers—careful not to disturb anything—under the bed, in the closet.

He found nothing but underwear and clothes, shoes and some dusty boxes and books.

Disappointed, Brett sat on the edge of the bed and slowly looked around him for a place he might have missed.

To his left, at the head of the bed, there were two rectangular sliding doors, each with a round brass knob in the center. Brett slid one aside, then the other.

Boxed video tapes were neatly stored on the headboard shelf, labels facing out.

From left to right were WARNER BROS. CARTOONS—#1-#7, with #2 missing. There were three more tapes labeled LITTLE RASCALS—#1-#3.

Brett removed the fourth cartoon tape and put it in the VCR.

After about two minutes of a Daffy Duck cartoon and a few seconds of ant races, Brett saw two young men stroking their penises beside a swimming pool. When one of them gasped, "Okay, *suck* me, *now!*" Brett rewound the tape, ejected it, and replaced it in the headboard.

Mr. Moser was not just curious.

Wondering why they were labeled differently, Brett couldn't resist taking a look at one of the LITTLE RASCALS tapes. He chose #3.

The film—"Our Gang" in *The He-Man Woman-Haters Club*—*was* old with fuzzy black-and-white images and music and voices that seemed to be coming through a wall of gauze.

A fat little boy and a tall skinny one with funny hair were entering a makeshift clubhouse.

The fat one said, "Well, Alfalfa, this is the headquarters of the He-Man Woman-Haters Club."

There were some other boys in the clubhouse and they all waved at Alfalfa, who waved back and said, "Gee, Spanky, I'd sure like to join. What do I have to—"

Ant races.

The ant races were replaced by blackness; Brett slowly realized that the blackness was a room, unlit and unoccupied.

A light came on with a distant *click*, and Brett saw what looked like a doctor's examination table. It was covered with a sheet of heavy plastic. Tied to the table was a naked little boy. Brett squinted at the boy's still face.

It was Jimmy Greenlaw.

A naked man stepped into the picture, his back to the camera. His skin was white and flabby. When he finally spoke—

"Okay," he breathed with anticipation. *"Ooookay."*

—Brett recognized the voice.

It belonged to Mr. Moser.

———————

It was only a matter of minutes before Jason Riley lost his bashfulness and was chatting with Mr. Moser as if they were old buddies.

"Do you like Bible stories, Jason?" Mr. Moser asked.

"Sure do," the boy said with an enthusiastic nod.

"They're my specialty. Tomorrow I'm telling the story of Daniel in the lion's den."

"Oh, that's his *favorite*," Mrs. Riley chimed, putting an arm around her son.

"Good," Mr. Moser grinned. "It's my favorite story to tell."

Mr. Riley politely said it was time to go home and they all stood at once. Pastor Alexander suggested that he and Mr. Moser walk them to their car and they headed down the corridor at a leisurely pace, Jason walking beside Mr. Moser, who rested a hand on the boy's shoulder.

"Looking forward to having you in my class, Jason," Mr. Moser said through a smile.

———————

Brett's fingers dug into the carpet beneath him and he felt something uncoil in his gut as he watched.

His back still turned, Mr. Moser ran his hands over Jimmy's small, still body, his breaths heavy and moist. He turned so Brett could see him in profile, reached under the table, and produced a white, blue-labeled bottle. Brett recognized it as the stuff that Grandma used to remove ring around the collar. As Mr. Moser poured some of the thick liquid soap in his hand and began rubbing it on his rigid penis, Brett sang under his breath, "Ring-around-the-collar, ring-around-the-collar," then closed his eyes for a moment. He opened them again when he heard Mr. Moser sigh, then moan, then pant.

The Sabbath school teacher was holding Jimmy's legs up and apart and lying between them, his dimpled buttocks jutting up and down spastically.

———————

At the Riley's car in the front parking lot, Pastor Alexander suggested Mr. Moser say a prayer and the five people joined hands in a small circle.

"Dear Heavenly Father," he began, "we thank You for bringing these good people to our town and our church. We ask that You watch over them as they settle into their new home…"

———————

Brett sucked in a sharp, sickened breath and diverted his eyes, looking at the room on the screen.

It looked like a garage only smaller, with lots of dusty shelves on the walls. Behind Mr. Moser and Jimmy was a large rusty metal sink; next to that were a washer and dryer. Below the table was a drain centered on the concrete floor surrounded by a large dark stain.

Laundry room… it's a mess in there…

Jimmy screamed and Brett turned back to the television in time to see Mr. Moser lift a hatchet over his head and bring it down with a heavy, wet *crunch.*

———————————

"… We especially ask that you watch over young Jason. Guide him in Your Way, oh Lord, and protect him from the snares and temptations of the Evil One…"

———————————

Blood shot upward in a crimson spray.

Jimmy's scream became a shrill, piercing wail.

———————————

"… Guide them safely home now, Father, and rest them well so that we can all gather tomorrow in Your name. We ask these favors in the Name of Your Son Jesus… amen."

"Amen," they repeated in unison.

Mr. Moser gave Jason a friendly hug and said, "You'll have to come over to my place real soon and well go lizard hunting."

"Okay," Jason said happily. "I'd like that."

Mr. Moser bid them goodnight and walked to his car.

———————————

Another chop.

… a mess…

Brett's fists unclenched and the tight knot in his stomach relaxed as he began to distance himself from what he was seeing.

Just like in church.Driving down the road in his car, Mr. Moser slipped a cassette into his stereo. It was a tape he often played for his children in Sabbath school, an album of Anita Bryant singing some children's gospel favorites. The first song began and he sang along.

"Jesus loves the little chilllllldren ... all the children of the worrrllld..."

He smiled, knowing that in just a few minutes, he would be able to give Brett his surprise.

After Mr. Moser had taken Jimmy apart and milked his penis over the armless, legless, lifeless trunk of the boy's body, the ant races came back on.

Brett watched them for several seconds, his mouth dry. He thought of Mr. Moser teaching Sabbath school, acting out Bible stories, making the kids—Brett included—laugh.

And he thought of what he'd just seen.

I have a surprise for you, Brett...

... a surprise...

Brett stood, left the room, went to the door at the end of the hall, and opened it.

The sink was across the room.

The table was covered with canvas and boxes were stacked on it, making it look like a sort of workbench.

The drain in the floor looked clogged with black soggy lumps.

To the right of the doorway was a tall wooden cupboard. Brett opened it and stared for a while at the tripod and the black and gray camera case beneath it.

He hurried down the hall to the front window and looked out again. He still saw no headlights, but knew he probably didn't have much time to cover his traces.

131

Back in the bedroom, he felt vaguely ill, like he might throw up, but he started to hum a church hymn and the feeling went away; he didn't want to make a mess he couldn't conceal.

He ejected the LITTLE RASCALS tape and returned it to the headboard, then picked up *Ghostbusters* from the floor, wishing he had time to finish watching it; wishing even more that he could see it in a *real* theater on a *real* movie screen...

The idea that came from that thought made his hands tremble.

Hurried by a gnawing feeling of urgency—he *knew* Mr. Moser could not be gone much longer—Brett returned to the living room, rewound *Ghostbusters*, and put it away. He found a brown paper bag in the kitchen, took it to the bedroom, removed LITTLE RASCALS-#3 from the headboard, and stuffed it in the bag. He turned all the lights off on his way out of the house, locked the door, and put the tape in the basket between his handlebars.

Less than a minute after he turned onto Glass Mountain Road, Brett heard a car up ahead. The glow of headlights illuminated the upcoming curve in the road and Brett drove his bike into the ditch, tumbled into the weeds and remained perfectly still, hoping he was out of sight.

The car passed, slowed, turned into the driveway.

It was Mr. Moser.

Brett waited until the crunch of the tires on the gravel road began to fade, then pulled his bike onto the pavement again. Before getting back on, he leaned over and vomited until his eyes burned.

He wiped his mouth on the back of his hand and rode home, already thinking about tomorrow morning.

Mr. Moser came to Sabbath school late the following morning. He rushed in looking rumpled and winded; his hair was mussed and his brow glowed with perspiration. The moment he entered, his eyes locked with Brett's and narrowed briefly to dark bloodless cuts.

He seemed preoccupied as he led the class through song service, kept tugging his tie as he quizzed them on the weekly Sabbath school lesson, and wiped his brow again and again as he stuttered through a retelling of Daniel's stay in the lion's den. He cut the story short and excused himself, asking Mrs. Juarez, the pianist, to take over. Before leaving the room, Mr. Moser looked at Brett and nodded toward the door.

Brett followed him.

In the main corridor, Brett could hear the sanctuary organ playing a hymn; voices sang along glumly, blending and garbling until they seemed to be singing in some ancient long-dead tongue.

Mr. Moser took a handkerchief from his pocket and mopped his face and neck; when he was through, the white cloth looked drenched.

"I don't seem to be feeling too well, Brett," he said nervously. "What do you suppose might be wrong?"

"I don't know. The flu, maybe?"

"I don't think so." He dabbed the underside of his chin with the handkerchief. "Enjoy the movie last night?"

"Uh-huh."

"You, uh... you left before I could give you your surprise. That wasn't very nice. I thought maybe—"

"I took it, Mr. Moser."

He froze, still as a snapshot, his eyes searching Brett's face, his mouth open slightly, tongue darting around inside.

"Don't worry," Brett whispered. "It's in a safe place. And I won't tell anyone. *If...*"

"If?" Mr. Moser breathed. "If *what?*"

"If you do what I ask."

A moment later, Mr. Moser chuckled; his nostrils flared and what might have been a tear glistened in his eye.

"Blackmailed," he muttered, shaking his head in wonderment. "I'm being blackmailed."

"If anything happens to me," Brett said, "someone will find the tape. There's a note attached that explains everything." It was a lie, of course, but Mr. Moser could never know that.

Mr. Moser wiped an eye and scrubbed his shiny face.

"I don't want much," Brett said.

"And what... is that?"

"I want you to take me to the movies. Whenever I want to go."

The music and singing stopped and somewhere in the church a chorus of voices exclaimed, "A-*men!*"

————————

The next day, Brett called Mr. Moser and said he wanted to see the new Clint Eastwood movie. He *really* wanted to see *Bedside Manners* more than anything but it was only playing in San Francisco, which was too far away, and he wanted to see it with Mom; that would make it special. He and Mr. Moser agreed to go to a theater in Santa Rosa so no one they knew would see them.

After hanging up, Brett went to the kitchen and told Grandma he was going for a bike ride and would be back in time for supper.

"You stick close to the house," she ordered. "Don't go riding off someplace where you're all alone. And say your *prayers.*"

On his way through the dark living room, Brett saw Grandpa sitting in the far corner by the phone table. His big gnarled hands were joined on his lap and his head turned slowly, following Brett as he passed.

"See you later," he said, his voice sounding like gravel being crushed. Grandpa did something then that Brett had never seen him do before and he didn't know quite what to make of it at first. The old man's lips pulled back around his scraggly teeth; the corners of his mouth twitched into slight curls. He was *smiling!* "Have a good time," he said.

In the car, Brett and Mr. Moser were silent for the first half of the forty-five minute drive.

Mr. Moser fidgeted at the wheel, drumming his fingers and cracking his knuckles as he drove. He acted as if he was alone in the car.

Brett finally spoke: "Was I going to be next?"

Mr. Moser blinked, wiped his mouth, shifted his buttocks in the seat, but kept his eyes on the road and said nothing.

"That was the surprise, wasn't it?"

No reply.

"Why do you do it?"

Still nothing.

"Because you enjoy it?"

Silence.

"It doesn't bother you that it's wrong?"

Mr. Moser sniffed and ran a hand through his hair; he was crying silently.

It bothers him, Brett thought, deciding not to ask any more questions.

The theater they went to held six screens. Brett stood in the lobby, breathed in the smell of popcorn, and looked at the rows of posters on the walls. He took in each and every detail around him—even the feeling of the carpet beneath his shoes—as if he were in the last hour of his life and wanted to miss nothing.

He looked up at Mr. Moser and said, "I'd like some popcorn."

Without meeting Brett's eyes, Mr. Moser got in line, bought a carton of popcorn, then they went into the auditorium and found seats.

Moments later, the lights dimmed and the screen came alive.

The back of Brett's neck prickled with excitement and he stuffed a fistful of popcorn into his mouth.

The next two hours were everything Brett had hoped they would be.

Two days later, Brett called Mr. Moser again from the upstairs phone and said he wanted to go see the new James Bond movie that evening. Grandma was gone shopping and Brett wanted to hurry out before she returned; the less explaining he had to do, the better. He raced downstairs and through the living room, stumbling to a halt when he heard his name called.

Grandpa was sitting in the corner again by the phone table. He was holding something out to Brett.

"Here," he said.

Brett stepped forward and saw two one-dollar bills held between Grandpa's beefy fingers.

"For Milk Duds," Grandpa whispered conspiratorially with a crooked smile.

Brett chilled for a moment, realizing he'd been found out, but Grandpa's smile was reassuring. He seemed to be saying, *Just between us.*

As Brett took the money, Grandpa said, "Have fun."

Riding his bike to Mr. Moser's house, Brett wondered how often Grandpa listened in on telephone conversations, and how much he'd heard.

Over the following two weeks, Brett had Mr. Moser take him to seven movies; one day they even saw two, back to back.

At first, they said little, but began to talk a bit more each time, until it seemed they were nothing more than two friends going to the movies together.

They did not mention Jimmy Greenlaw or the tape or Mr. Moser's laundry room.

Sometimes Brett spotted Mr. Moser staring at him, like he used to when Brett watched movies on his VCR. But now he stared with tense eyes and chewed his lip nervously; he would look away immediately, but Brett knew—felt, anyway—that he'd been staring at him for a while. Brett tried not to wonder what Mr. Moser thought about while he stared at him because that reminded him of what he'd seen on that video tape, and that conjured thoughts too frightening to entertain.

———————————

During the first week, Brett worried about Grandpa. How much did he know? Most importantly, would he tell Grandma?

By the second week, Brett felt better. Grandma knew nothing yet, and when they passed in the house, Grandpa always gave him a silent secret smile and a wink, something he'd never done before.

For the time being, he seemed to be safe.

It was turning out to be a fun and interesting summer.

Until he came home after his seventh movie—a Steve Martin comedy—and found his mom seated on the sofa talking with Grandpa.

When he walked in, she dashed across the room and greeted him with a laughing, perfumed embrace.

She was beautiful. Her hair fell around her head in a golden mane; tiny stones sparkled in her earlobes and bracelets clicked together on her wrists. She looked like a movie star.

"How *are* you, baby?" she breathed. "*Look* at you, you're such a *big* boy! Oh, give your mom another hug!" She covered his face with kisses and ran her fingers through his hair.

Brett could hear Grandma washing dishes and humming a hymn in the kitchen; naturally she wouldn't be visiting with Mom. Apparently there was no love lost there.

"How about a sundae?" Mom exclaimed. "A big one with *everything!* C'mon, let's go. I've got some surprises for you in the car." She kissed Grandpa's forehead and said, "Be back in a while, Pop."

As Brett followed her out of the house, he heard Grandma's voice behind him.

"*Brett!*" she hissed.

When he turned, she hunkered down in front of him and whispered, "Now, I don't want you eating *any* of that ice cream stuff. Jesus doesn't like you to pour all that bad sugar in your body—it's His temple." She tossed a glance over his shoulder in the direction Mom had gone and her face darkened with intense bitterness. "And I don't care *what* your *mother* says."

Brett went out the front door behind Mom and Grandpa's quiet throaty laughter faded behind them.

On the way to St. Helena, Brett trembled with anticipation, unable to stop smiling; he knew his days in Manning were numbered now and he'd be going to live with his Mom in Los Angeles soon. He'd be able to go to movies anytime he wanted without fear of being caught or punished; there would be no more dreary Sabbaths, no more long church services with long church faces, and—best of *all*—no more Grandma.

"The stuff in the back seat's all yours," Mom said breathlessly. She was bouncing in her seat like a little girl.

Brett put the two boxes in his lap and opened them; one held shirts and pants, another held a blazer and tie.

"Brand new, all designer, expensive stuff," Mom said. "See that blazer? Roll up the sleeves a little and you'll look just like Don Johnson on *Miami Vice*"

Brett had never seen *Miami Vice*. Didn't she know that? Didn't she know what it was like living with Grandma? Sure she did; Grandma was her *mother*.

"You'll be the best dressed guy in church, kiddo!" she laughed.

Church? Brett thought.

"There's more."

He found a bag full of school supplies; paper, pens, and binders with pictures of the Hollywood sign on them, and a drinking mug that read on the side, HOORAY FOR HOLLYWOOD!

"Now you're all set for school in the fall," Mom said.

Something wasn't right.

Brett said, "But I thought I was gonna—"

"Where shall we go for ice cream?" Mom asked quickly.

Brett felt himself sinking into the seat of the rented car as some of his excitement drifted away like a thin mist.

"I thought I was gonna come live with you," Brett said over his hot fudge sundae.

"Well, honey… we'll see."

"But you said—"

"I know, and I *meant* it, sweety. It's just that… well, things are a little different now." She stirred her milkshake thoughtfully, frowning. "I met this man. He's a producer, a very *successful* producer, I should add. Four big hits in two years. He's… I've… well, I moved in with him last week. He's got this *incredible* place, you should see it! A pool, a theater in the back. Clark *Gable* used to live there!"

139

Brett didn't know who Clark Gable was and didn't care.

"Anyway, my producer friend—his name is Jeff—he wants to use me. He thinks I'd be good for a lead. Can you imagine that, baby, a *lead!* A starring role. But… well, for now, there's just no way I could take you back with me. Not now. Maybe later, after I've done a couple of pictures. But not now."

Brett suddenly lost all interest in his sundae. His stomach ached and his head felt bloated with thoughts of staying in Manning, trapped in Grandma's house, listening to those skin-crawling hymns and having to give Grandma more Bengay back rubs.

He had to concentrate hard to steady his voice as he said, "But Mom, you said—"

"I know, honey, but I *can't* Not *now*. But… that's okay, isn't it? I mean, you're doing well here, aren't you? Grandpa says your grades are good, and he says you've made friends with your Sabbath school teacher. That's *great*. I mean, Lord knows, I'm not much of a Bible reader these days, but I suppose it's good for you. C'mon, sweetie-pie. You've waited this long, can't you wait a little longer?"

He put his spoon down and stared at the table.

"Hey, how about a movie tonight?" Mom asked, taking his hand. "I'll go back to my hotel and change and we can go to dinner, then catch a movie. Whatever you want to see. Tonight's your night. Can't be out too late, though. I've got an early plane to catch."

She was leaving *tomorrow?*

Without him?

Panic began to rise in his throat. He wanted to cry, scream, kick something, but he remained silent, thinking of church, trying to shut the feelings off.

They would go to dinner and a movie that night and maybe he could change her mind. At least he got to pick the movie. And he knew exactly which one he wanted to see.

After he showered and changed, Brett went downstairs to wait for his Mom to come back from her hotel and get him. He slumped on the sofa and stared out the window.

Grandpa's chair rumbled into the living room and his gravelly voice said, "You don't look too happy, boy."

Brett didn't reply.

Grandpa stopped in front of him and began drumming his fingers on the wheelchair's armrests.

"Your mom's not gonna take you with her, eh?"

Brett shook his head.

"Well. Guess you'll just have to make the best of things here, eh?"

Brett shrugged.

"Not so bad, is it? You got your friend Mr. Moser to keep you company." He winked and added, "Don't worry, boy, your secret's safe with me. You got Gabby. And, in her own way, I suppose Grandma... well, she thinks the world of you." Then, with a frown, he muttered, "Hell of a lot more'n she thinks of me." His eyes suddenly snapped open wide and he looked around cautiously as if he might have been overheard. In a moment, his face relaxed and he smiled as if he'd just remembered something. "Grocery shopping," he mumbled.

Brett sat up straight, surprised; this was the most Grandpa had ever said to him. In fact, it was the most Brett had ever heard him say, *period.*

"Course, now, if I had a pair of those," Grandpa said, pointing at Brett's legs, "you and me, we would have a good old time."

Brett chuckled. "Grandma wouldn't let us."

Grandpa's head fell back and his wheelchair squeaked beneath the weight of his laughter.

"I suppose not. Fact, I just might be better off *without her* than I would be *with legs*. But..." He waved a hand with resignation. "You going to the movies with your mom tonight?"

Brett nodded. "Have you ever been to the movies, Grandpa?"

"Used to go a lot. Before I met your grandma. I often wish we had a TV in here so I could watch some of them old movies late at night. Don't sleep like I used to. We got enough money saved up to get a good one, you know. Color. Remote control. I look at 'em in the catalogs sometimes. But..." Another wave.

Brett looked at Grandpa for a long moment, seeing a different person in that wheelchair, much different from the silent, empty old man who wheeled around in the dark. He wondered what it would be like to live there with Grandpa, just the two of them. Maybe they'd stay up late at night and watch old movies. Grandpa could tell him about the movies he'd seen when *he* was a boy, about his days in the Army and how it felt to fight in a war. And they could listen to *real* music instead of those depressing hymns, music like he'd heard in the movies.

A car rolled to a stop out front and honked.

"There's your mom," Grandpa said. "You better git. And don't worry. Things won't be so bad."

Brett stood and gave Grandpa a long hug so unexpectedly that it surprised them both, then he rushed out to meet his mom.

Over dinner, his mom asked, "So what movie would you like to see?"

Brett smiled with anticipation and said, "*Bedside Manners*."

Mom's fork stopped half way to her mouth and she slowly lowered it to her plate with a frown.

"Well…" she said, drawing the word out to a troubled sigh. "I don't think so, honey."

Brett's smile disappeared and his spirits dropped even further.

"How come?"

"Well, it's not such a good movie. *Really.* I mean, it's low budget and, and… well, there's one scene where you can see the boom hanging about two feet into the frame, and…"

"What's a boom?"

"Never mind. It's just a bad movie, that's all."

"I don't care, Mom. I just wanna see *you.*"

"Look, sweetie, my part is really small and I'm… well, I get…" She sniffed and straightened her posture. "I just don't think you should see it. It's not a movie for kids."

"But *Mom*, I wanted to see it with *you!*"

"Lower your voice!" she hissed, glanced around to see if anyone had heard. "Now that's *it*, okay? There's a lot of sex and violence in the movie and I don't want you to see it. Maybe when you're older… Hey, how about the new Benji movie, huh? I hear it's pretty good."

Brett clenched his fist around his fork and turned his eyes away from Mom; he knew he could not conceal his anger and disappointment if he looked at her. His appetite was gone.

Mom continued eating, apparently unaware that he was upset.

"Are you really gonna leave me tomorrow?" he whispered.

"I have to, honey. Good grief, you sound like you'll never see me again."

"For how long?"

"I don't know. Until… well, for a while. It's not so bad, babe." She reached for his hand, but he pulled it away. "Don't do this, now. You've got friends here."

No I don't, he thought.

143

"Grandma takes good care of you."

No she doesn't.

"I know she's a little weird. God knows I don't get along with her, but that's different. We've *never* gotten along. Grandma loves you. So does Grandpa. You'll be okay."

No I won't.

"Until you get more movie roles?" he muttered.

"What? Oh, yeah. A couple leads under Jeff and I'll be able to take good care of you."

"A lead? You mean, like a star?"

"Yeah, a starring role. In a good movie, none of this low budget horror crap."

"Is that what you really want? To star in a movie?"

"More than anything, sweetie. More than *anything.* Now eat your dinner."

"I'm not hungry."

"Not hun... well, why didn't you *say* so?" she snapped. "This is an expensive dinner. Now *eat.*"

He stared at the plate silently for a while.

"I have to go to the bathroom," he lied.

"Okay. But when you come back, you'll eat, right?"

He nodded, then left the table and crossed the restaurant. As he rounded the tables and chairs, he thought of a scene from one of the movies he'd watched at Mr. Moser's. *Prime Cut.* Lee Marvin played a gangster who was sent to Kansas City to find and punish Gene Hackman. Not only had Hackman gone back on a few promises made to old friends and business partners and cheated them out of a lot of money, he'd even killed some of them—and had one ground up into hot dogs at his meat packing plant. When Marvin was through with him, Hackman ended up full of bullets and fed to some pigs.

Brett liked that. Hackman had deserved it; it had been a fitting punishment.

Some people simply deserved to be punished.

On the other hand, some deserved to be rewarded, like Luke, the Princess, Han, and Chewbacca at the end of *Star Wars*.

Brett thought about rewards and punishments as he walked toward the RESTROOMS sign in the back and passed by the men's room.

He went on to a bank of payphones, fishing in his pocket for some change.

His Mom tapped her fingernails on the steering wheel as she drove out of St. Helena.

"You're just upset with me, that's all," she said stiffly. "I wanted us to have a nice evening together, but..." She shook her head and sighed.

Brett gazed straight ahead, barely hearing her. His mind was intentionally blank, his body relaxed.

"I'm just tired," he said quietly.

"Then why don't you let me take you home instead of to your friend's?"

"I have to pick up something I left there. Then I'll go home."

She sighed again. "I came a long way to see you, you know. And my friend *paid* for it. What's he going to think when I tell him you didn't even want to be *with* me?"

He pressed his lips together over the sharp reply that came to mind.

Brett watched the road ahead for several minutes, then said, "Turn right here. Then take the first left."

When the car started down the dirt road, Mom said, "Jesus, this is a rented car, you know! *Gawd!*"

Lighted windows at the end of the road drew nearer.

"Is this the house?"

Brett nodded.

She stopped in the drive and Brett said, "Come in. He'd like to meet you."

Mom sighed but turned off the ignition and got out, following him to the door.

"Aren't you going to *knock?*" she asked when Brett walked into the house.

"He doesn't mind." He let her in and closed the door. "He said he was—" He swallowed a dry knot in his throat, "—was going to do some laundry tonight. He's probably in the laundry room."

Brett led her to the end of the hall, opened the door—he wouldn't let his hands tremble—and stepped aside so she could go ahead.

The light beyond the door was so dim the room seemed gray. As soon as Mom stepped down into the room, her heels clicking on the dirty concrete floor, Brett swung the door shut. It hit with a slam like gunfire.

"Brett!" she called. "What the hell are you—"

She stopped, there was a scuffle, then Mom screamed.

Brett stared at the door for a moment, listening to the screaming and the awful, thick hacking noises, the retching and coughing. Then he began to back away, trying to shut the sounds from his ears, realizing that Mom wasn't the only one screaming.

In the living room, he turned and crossed to the front door. Mom stopped screaming, but Mr. Moser continued; his cries of, "I'm sorry, I'm so sorry, my God, I'm sorry!" died in the wet sounds of vomiting.

Brett went outside and stood on the porch, thinking of nothing.

It could have been a minute or an hour later when Mr. Moser came out of the house and into the dim yellow glow of the porch light; Brett wasn't sure.

Mr. Moser held his hands out before him, palms up, fingers clawed, staring at them as if they weren't his own. Blood speckled his twisted face and his sleeveless arms were black with it to his elbows. He was gulping sobs and his eyes sparkled with tears.

"Dear Jesus," he breathed over and over, "dear Jesus…"

"Did you get it?" Brett asked. "On video tape?"

"I… if I'd known earlier, I… I was so upset, so scared… I didn't have time to…"

"You didn't get it?" Brett snapped, anger flaring in his head for a moment.

"I couldn't, I was too… too… Why, Brett? Why did you make me do this, *why?*"

"I thought you enjoyed it," Brett replied flatly, still preoccupied with the fact that his mother's murder had not been videotaped.

"Not this, not an adult, a… a *woman.*"

"Oh. Well. I think it's time you left behind the little kid stuff, Mr. Moser." He turned and stared silently at his mom's rented car.

Mr. Moser paced behind him, muttering, "Oh, God, oh Jesus-God…" He stopped abruptly and snapped in a hoarse, pained voice, "And what am I gonna do about the *car*, huh?"

"It's rented."

"Rented? Oh God, that's just… that's… *rented!*"

Brett stepped off the porch.

"If I get caught, you're in just as much trouble as I am, you know. You helped! You're an *accomplice!*"

Brett turned to him and, genuinely worried for a moment, said, "You think anybody'd believe that? I mean, I'm just a *kid*, and… and you killed all those boys. I've got that tape…" He thought about it a while, then shook his head, feeling better, and muttered, "No. I don't think so, Mr. Moser. I really don't." He started across the drive toward the dirt road. "I think I'm gonna walk home. They don't expect me for a couple hours."

"What will you tell them?"

"I don't know. I'll think of something."

"But... what if they notice she doesn't bring you home?"

"They go to bed real early. Especially Grandma."

Grandma. Brett thought of her stern gaze and the smell of those messy Bengay back rubs.

He turned to Mr. Moser again and said, "Get rid of the car by tomorrow afternoon. I want to go into San Francisco."

"What? *Why?*"

"There's a movie I want to see. *Bedside Manners.*" Then, to himself, Brett muttered, "You saw her die, now I need to."

But Grandma... she was still around to make Brett's life miserable. And Grandpa's.

Mr. Moser bellowed, "Are you out of your—"

"And keep that video camera loaded and ready. Later in the week, I'm gonna bring my grandma over."

Brett watched as Mr. Moser slowly turned his back, then began to kick the side of his house, pulling his hair and screaming like a toddler throwing a tantrum.

Mr. Moser's screams faded as Brett started down the road, looking forward to getting to know Grandpa.

Shock Radio

T he studio was dark but for a soft lamp over the console and, after being cued by the engineer who sat with the producer beyond a long rectangular window, the man leaned toward the microphone suspended before his face, touched his fingertips to the headphones through which he could hear his show's theme music and said, "You're listening to the Arthur Colton, Jr., Show and we're *back!* We have a few more minutes with my guest Melissa Cartwright, who is joining us by phone from Liberal Central, San Francisco, California. Miss Cart— excuse me... *Mizzz* Cartwright—is a writer, a feminist and, in my opinion, another of the whining castrators who has found a way to take out her aggressions *and* make a fast buck by writing a book about the evil that men do. Not people, but *men*, who, according to *Mizzz* Cartwright, are inherently *evil* simply because they have been born *men*" He smirked and winked at Harry, the engineer, who laughed silently beyond the glass.

"No, no, Arthur," Melissa Cartwright said, "that's *not* what I'm saying at all and you *know* it. I simply want to—"

"Let's go back to the phones." Arthur Colton, Jr., whose real name was Andy Craig, looked at the computer screen before

him where the words TAMPA, FLA-FRIEND glowed in amber.
"Tampa, Florida, you're on the air."

"Yeah, uh, Arthur?"

"Yessir, you're on the air."

"Yeah, Arthur, my name's Tom and I'm just calling, uuhhh, to tell you that you're, y'know, uh, right. You're *right*."

"I know I'm right, sir, that's why I'm the host and you're the caller. Do you have a question for our guest?"

"Yeah. I do. I'd like to ask Miss Carter—"

"Cartwright," Andy snapped. "Read my lips: Cart-*wright*."

"Yeah, okay, Miss Cartwright. I'd like to ask her exactly where she thinks women would be *without* men, huh? I mean, like, through *history*, y'know? Where do you think? And, uuhhh, I'll take my answer off the air."

Melissa Cartwright said, "I'm very sorry, Tom, this is not your fault, but I'm afraid there's been a misunderstanding here. It is *not* my opinion that men are inherently evil or dishonest or even ignorantly *wrong*. All I'm saying is that we have to find a way to—"

"It's very clear what you're saying, *Mizzz* Cartwright," Andy interrupted. "Your book, *Women in Crisis, Men in Power*— which, for those of you interested in this kind of whiney propaganda, is published by Putnam—is *clearly* the manifesto of someone who feels that *all* of our problems are the result of men and the *works* of men. Now, I would appreciate it if you'd answer my caller's question, which is quite straightforward. Okay? Oookay. Now, let's hear it."

She was silent for a long time—*too* long—and Andy was about to speak again to fill the dead air, but she spoke first. Slowly and coldly.

"I think that... to speculate on the position of women... without the presence of men... throughout history... would be asinine."

"Well, isn't *that* convenient." The screen read WINSTON-SALEM, NC-FOE. "Winston-Salem, you're on the air."

"Yeah, Arthur, I listen to your show a lot and I just wanna say that I think you're being a little hard on your guest, okay?"

"And why is *that*, sir?"

"Because I've read her book and, as a man, I can say that I think she's—"

"Wait-wait-*wait* a second here. You read her *book*? What, you *enjoy* being castrated? What, you *like* having a woman chew your balls off? And you call yourself a *man*?"

"That's exactly my point, Mr. Colton, you're interviewing her and you probably haven't even read the book."

"Well, of *course* I haven't read the book! I *like* my balls!"

"But you rely on name-calling rather than discussion to make your point, when really you *have* no point to—"

Andy punched a button on the panel, cutting the caller off, and sneered, "You have a good time, sir."

Melissa Cartwright released an explosive breath over the phone and Andy could imagine her rolling her eyes as he flashed a grin at Harry; it was his this-is-good-radio grin.

"Redlands, California, you're on the air."

"Yes, Arthur?" an elderly woman said.

"You're on the air, ma'am, please get to your question."

"Well, I'd just like to say that I'm seventy-nine years old and I don't understand how your guest—what's her name? Cartwright?—can possibly suggest that all men are evil. Speaking from experience, I can say that I've—"

Miss Cartwright interrupted firmly: "I'm sorry, ma'am, but you and the rest of the listeners are being misled by Mr. Colton. I am *not* saying that men are *evil*. I'm simply saying that our culture—along with many other cultures—has given women a back seat in *everything* and it's time to—"

151

"I'm sorry," Andy said as the theme music came up, "but we've run out of time. I'd like to thank my guest, Melissa Cartwright, whose book *Women in Crisis, Men in Power*, is, for some reason, number two on the New York *Times* nonfiction bestseller list. Thank you for joining us, *Mizzz* Cartwright, it's been an education, if nothing else. We're coming up on the news, then well be back with open lines. Stick around."

As Andy leaned back in his chair and removed his headphones, he heard Melissa Cartwright's pinched voice calling from them, "Mr. Colton? Mr. *Colton?*" He glanced at Tanya, the producer, waved toward the phone and picked up the receiver, saying, "Yes?"

She struggled to control her voice. "I'm *very* disappointed, Mr. Colton. I was told you were going to interview me about my book. I didn't know this was going to be the broadcast equivalent of stocks and public humiliation. I didn't know it was going to be an inquisition."

"Oh, please, Ms. Cartwright, don't take it personally. It's just the way I do the show."

She paused. "I'm sorry? Pardon me?"

He shook his head and chuckled. This always puzzled him. Didn't they understand it was just a *show?* That it was just *show business?* "Have you ever heard my show, Ms. Cartwright?"

"No, I haven't. And after tonight, I have no intention of listening.

"Well, if you had," he said gently, "you'd realize that this is just the way the show goes, okay? I mean, *think* about it. My audience is made up of very conservative, aggressive people who want more than just an interview, okay? Otherwise they'd be listening to Larry King. They want *fireworks*, you know? So please, Ms. Cartwright. Don't take this personally. I have nothing against you or your book or your opinion. In fact, you're probably right, I don't know. Anyway, I really appreciate your good sportsmanship. It's just show business, you know?"

Another pause, longer this time. "You appreciate *what?*"

"Your good sportsmanship."

She laughed, but it was an angry laugh. "Are you serious?"

"*Sure* I'm serious. Look, it's just a show, okay? I mean, you want compassion, call *Talk Net;* you want in-depth questions, you go on *Nightline;* and on my show, you get confrontation and a lot of yelling."

"And name-calling and humiliation and some pretty obscene sexist insults."

"Well, that too. But you can't take it personally. It's the nature of the show. You got to make your point and plug your book, right? Myself? I think you're an interesting, intelligent woman. What I say on the show really means nothing."

A cold chuckle. "In other words... you're a whore." She hung up.

Andy rolled his eyes as he replaced the receiver. Why was it so hard for them to understand? Why did so many people get so upset? Not that he minded; they were his best publicity and stirred the controversy that made his show the number one late night radio talk show in the country. He just didn't understand what made them so furious. "About li'l ol' me," he muttered, leaving the studio and heading to the lounge for coffee.

Laurence Olivier had once played a hideous Nazi, but did anyone accuse him of actually *being* one? Of course not. They praised his performance; he was simply a great actor. Nobody accused Stephen King of being a sick bloodthirsty monster, did they? Well, maybe a few... but surely they didn't *really* believe it; he was just a very good writer. But when it came to The Arthur Colton, Jr., Show, otherwise rational people began to foam at the mouth, pound fists into palms and scream for a public hanging. It made no sense.

153

He'd used that argument with Kathrine, a former girlfriend back in Cincinnati who had been irate about the content of his show. It hadn't worked.

"That's different!" she'd exclaimed. "What they do is fiction. Everyone *knows* that what Olivier and King do is *fiction! You*, however, are hosting a *talk show!* You're shaping opinions, *manipulating* them! You aren't writing a novel or acting in a movie. People *listen* to what you say. They respect it, they take it *seriously.* And for you to go on that show and say the barbaric things you say to boost your ratings—things you don't even *mean*—is obscene, Andy!"

It had just been a local show which, for the first four months, was just straight talk with a few guests and a couple hours of open phones; Andy had never expressed an opinion, just kept the conversation going. The ratings were bleak, so he'd listened carefully to his audience, looking for something he could use to breathe life into the show, trying to figure out what they wanted. One night it occurred to him: they were angry and they wanted to scream and shout and kick furniture and if they couldn't do it, they wanted someone to do it for them. His listeners were fed up with everything from crime and poverty to crooked politicians and unfair laws and they wanted someone with a voice—a loud, powerful voice—to represent them.

The following night, Andy opened his show differently than usual: "I've cancelled tonight's scheduled guests," he said, "because I want to talk about something, ladies and gentlemen. I… am mad… as *hell!*"

There wasn't an open line for more than thirty seconds that night. Liberals called to complain about his sudden change of attitude and his unfair generalizations and conservatives called to complain about the tit-sucking liberals. Blacks complained about whites and whites complained about blacks… and Asians and Iranians and American Indians. Men complained about women and women complained about me. AM radios throughout Cincinnati crackled with the wholesale condemnation of Jews and homosexuals and Democrats and Communists and drug dealers and feminists and homeless people and... and anyone who disagreed in any way with the caller. Cincinnati was angry and Andy Craig had given it an opportunity to throw a tantrum. Along with the city's anger, however, came a barrage of racial slurs and profanity which Andy, at first, edited during the seven second delay; but as the show continued that night, getting better by the minute, he left his finger off the button and let the bile flow. He knew he'd get yelled at for it but, in his gut, it felt right.

Two thirds of the way through the show, Dexter Grady, the station manager, burst into the engineer's booth and glared at Andy through the small square window; his face squirmed with anger as he waved his arms and yelled silently at the engineer. Moments later, the show broke, quite abruptly, for a commercial. Grady disappeared from the window and stormed into the studio shouting, demanding to know exactly who the fuck Andy thought he was, allowing all that Goddamned profanity to go out over the fucking radio. He yelled for quite some time, threatening not only to fire Andy, but to see to it that he never worked in Ohio again, not in a radio station, not even in a McDonald's, and then —

—the phone calls started to come in.

Grady had told the engineer to play a few songs, to go to some network programming, *anything*, just as long as he didn't go back to Andy's show.

And people complained. Oh, how they complained.

Andy stayed at the station and continued doing his late-night talk show for almost two years. It didn't last any longer because the sponsors got fed up with the show's controversy; the controversy was the only reason it lasted as long as it did...

In the lounge, Andy poked through a box of stale donuts left in front of the coffee pot and picked out a cruller, which he dipped into the black coffee he'd poured. He was a small, wiry man with short reddish-brown hair and a mustache between his slightly sunken cheeks. His skin was smooth and somewhat pale; he didn't get much sun. He chewed his cruller as he stared out the window at the black, light-smeared city nineteen stories below and listened to the news, which came over the P.A. He'd become addicted to the news; the more current his topics, the more riled his listeners became, and the more riled they became, the better were his ratings.

"You seen this?" Tanya asked, bursting into the lounge.

Andy turned as she tossed a section of the *Times* onto one of the round tables. It was opened to an article accompanied by a photograph of Andy; the headline read, DANGEROUS RADIO, DANGEROUS LISTENERS, OR BOTH?

"No, I haven't," Andy said, glancing over the article.

Tanya smirked. "It's great stuff. The kinda stuff that brings in new listeners, y'know? It was in this morning's edition and my buddy over at the *Times* says they've been getting phone calls all day. I mean, *complaints*. Starting tomorrow, the letters to the Editor section'll probably be full of epistles from your loving fans for a couple weeks." She beamed at him through the smoke from her cigarette.

"Why? What's it say?"

She shrugged. "Oh, the usual bullshit. You're stirring up the masses, using sick jokes and faulty logic that *sounds* intelligent and reasonable to get them so upset that they're willing to *hand over* their freedoms to the first dictator that comes along. The usual bullshit. He says that you're—" She swept the paper up and raised a stiff forefinger, "—listen to this, '... sucking up ratings like a vampire sucks up blood, flashing his fangs all the way to the bank'. Isn't that *great?*" she laughed.

Andy grinned as he finished the cruller and plucked Tanya's cigarette from her fingers, taking a deep drag.

"I thought you quit," she said, slapping the paper down again.

"Just quit smoking my own. It's cheaper that way." He glanced at the clock.

"Don't worry, you got another six minutes." She started for the door as she said, "Got a great call for ya. A pro-choicer raving about the abortion laws."

"Man or woman?"

"Woman. A real bitch. Give her your Jerry Lewis speech." She winked at him as she went out the door.

Finishing Tanya's cigarette, Andy scanned the article. It accused him of stirring up hatred and racism, of helping to destroy the freedoms that made America great—especially the one freedom that provided for radio shows like his own—and suggested that his "careless and irresponsible form of broadcasting" could ultimately bring about "the downfall of American freedoms as we know them."

He chuckled bitterly as he sipped his coffee. He'd gotten the same response from the Cincinnati press since the day he'd changed the format of his show; they'd hated him.

———

But the *women* had loved him. Not just the women callers, but the women who attended his personal appearances... the women who wrote to him... the women he met in bars and restaurants and grocery stores who recognized his name or, better yet, his voice. Building his entire radio show around the political stance that riled his listeners the most—the one that would have sent most feminists into a convulsing, mouth-foaming seizure—Andy had more women hungry for his attention than ever before in his life. The change was so sudden and drastic that Andy had actually been relieved the day he'd come home and found Katherine stripping his apartment of her belongings.

"I can't live with you anymore," she said, throwing her toiletries into a satchel.

"But you don't live with me. We agreed you'd keep your apartment, I thought that was—"

"*Listen* to yourself!" she snapped, stabbing a forefinger at his chest. "You're such a *stickler* for details, like my fucking apartment. What difference does my *apartment* make? It's just a little section of a building in which I get my phone calls and keep my *cat!* When I say I can't live with you anymore, I mean that I can't live with the fact that you're such a stickler for details and yet, when someone tries to point out the details of what you're doing, you blow up, or just *laugh.* I can't live with the fact that I'm wrapping my life around a person who can, so very *casually*, do such vicious damage to things that so many people have died to protect, things that have taken so many decades to finally realize and are already being dismantled fast enough as it is without any help from *you!* I can't live with *you*, Andy. And how *you* possibly *can* will be one of the greatest mysteries of my life." She was gone in ten minutes.

Half an hour later, he had a dinner date, and only a few hours after that, he had her in bed. Suddenly, life was good, *really* good. Suddenly, everything was going his way, and that included his breakup with Katherine.

Then, a few months later, someone threw a brick through the windshield of his car at a red light. Not long after, the first death threat was phoned into the station, followed by a few more over the following months. At first it had, like everything else, worked in his favor and stirred up some publicity-grabbing controversy. But during the week of the second bomb threat received by the station, the sponsors began to drop like computer generated aliens in a video game and the manager and owners became so afraid for their lives that they saw no alternative but to let Andy go.

At first, he'd been very depressed. In fact, for a couple of days, he hadn't left his apartment or answered the phone. But only two days after his firing had been announced, he was offered a job by TBN—Talk Broadcasting Network—the biggest talk radio network in the country. He'd responded with appropriate nonchalance, asking for a few days to give it some thought and talk it over with his agent; he needed the extra time to *get* an agent.

The network's offer was impressive: a nation-wide weeknight call-in talk show with timely guests covering controversial topics. Andy would have to move away from Cincinnati, of course, but that was okay. The only problem was Andy's certainty that the show would be watered down by the network to satisfy their sponsors, eliminating, at the very least, the profanity allowed on his show and, at the most, restricting his broadcasting style. But TBN surprised him. Countless polls had shown that, due to the overwhelming popularity of television, very few people listened to the radio unless they felt they were missing something unique or unusually popular, so the sponsors *wanted* Andy to be profane and aggressive and controversial and they didn't give a damn about his politics. Controversy usually attracted publicity, which *always* drew listeners. And listeners listened to advertisements.

After his recent experiences with bricks through windows and telephoned bomb threats, Andy was reluctant to use his real name on national radio, so, after acquiring the job and moving to the big city, he decided to come up with a pseudonym.

The Arthur Colton, Jr., Show began without fanfare, a strategic move by the network; they were confident that it would generate its own publicity and saw no reason to pay for any. They were right. The show created a wave of controversy and, within the first two weeks, inspired newspaper columnists across the country to write a column in response; some were positive, but most were vicious protests, some calling him a broadcasting whore who was willing to say anything, no matter how damaging or dangerous, that might garner a few more ratings points.

Once again, Andy was puzzled by his critics. He could understand if they just didn't *like* the show, but they made it sound *dangerous.* Didn't they understand that he wasn't really that person on the radio? He didn't even use his real voice anymore, let alone his real name; his radio voice was deeper, more authoritative than his regular speaking voice. And of *course* he didn't share the opinions of his radio alter ego; nobody *really* thought that way about everything, it was *ridiculous*, a caricature. In fact, Andy had very few opinions of his own. He watched the news and read papers only for the benefit of his show. He wasn't that concerned with world events; they were out of his hands. Didn't they realize that it was—

—"Just show business," he muttered, leaving the lounge with the paper and his coffee. He ducked into the control room where Tanya was occupied with a caller and didn't notice when he snatched up her cigarettes. In the studio, he tried to read the rest of the article, but the dim shadowy lighting only made his eyes water, so he leaned back in his chair with a sigh and pinched the bridge of his nose.

The night before, he'd gotten less than an hour of light dozing scattered between bouts of rolling and rutting in bed with a voluptuous, squealing co-ed named Debi, and that morning he'd had a brunch date with Jaretta, his hairdresser, who had agreed to grab a hotel room halfway through brunch so they wouldn't have to waste time deciding on his place or hers. Andy had seen them both before and would see them again, along with the several other women he saw regularly— Sherrie and Dina and Kaylee and Lynda and Melonie and Shawn—and the many others whom he had not yet met. His social life was better than it had been in Cincinnati despite the fact that he protected his identity and no longer used his celebrity status to impress women; it made no difference because, back in Cincinnati, he'd gained a lot of confidence with women, learned a lot about being funny and charming and tap dancing around commitment and exclusivity like Fred Astaire. And he was making a *lot* of money now, which didn't hurt a bit.

But tonight, he was taking a rest. After work he was going to call Sol's All-Nite Deli and order a pastrami and Swiss on an onion roll and one of Sol's fat dill pickles, take them home and eat them with a cup of hot tea in front of *Shane*, which was on the Late Late Movie, then he was going to sleep until noon. Maybe later. He lit a cigarette and sighed the smoke from his lungs, looking forward to his evening with relish.

"This is the Arthur Colton, Jr., Show and we are now entering the final hour of the show with open phones for those of you who have something to say. Anything you want. You got a gripe? You want to bitch about something? Give me a ring. Any questions? I'm almost *always* right, you know. Give me a call. And if you have a personal problem and would like to benefit from my experience, strength and wisdom, as the sniveling drunks say at AA meetings, don't hesitate to pick up the phone. Janice is calling from Wichita, Kansas. Janice, my dear, you're on the air."

"Yes, Arthur, I'm calling about your previous guest, Melissa Cartwright. I'm not a regular listener, but I heard Ms. Cartwright was going to be on tonight and I'm a big fan of hers, so—"

"Why am I not surprised?"

"—I listened and I was very disappointed that you never allowed her to make her point. I mean, she is a very wise and warm person who has an open mind and she is *not* a man-hater. I think it's sad that you deprived your listeners of what she has to say, but I think it's indicative of a frightening trend in this country today toward *woman*-hating, a trend to which you seem to be a powerful contributor."

Andy smiled. This was the pro-choice woman Tanya had warned him about earlier. Andy didn't give a damn about abortion one way or the other—it meant *nothing* to him—but the great majority of his listeners were against it, and that was what mattered. It had been a hot topic ever since abortion laws had been reintroduced back in the eighties and he got a lot of calls for it, so he'd prepared a stock response—a funny, sarcastic, *angry* response—specifically for callers like Janice from Wichita.

"Janice, my dear, I may be a lot of things, but I am *not* a woman-hater. Women are my favorite living beings. Anyone who knows me will tell you that Arthur *loves* women. But I do not love *castrating* women. This is a free country, so you're entitled to your opinion just as I am, and my opinion is that *Mizzz* Cartwright *is* one of those castrating women. Believe me, I think there are plenty of men who *deserve* to have their balls chopped off, but not *all* of them, for crying out loud, and the women who think so are, in my opinion, no better than the psychotic *men who beat women.* Now. Why did you call? What's your question?"

"I don't really have a question, I just wanted to point out that this kind of attitude—the attitude you've exhibited on your show tonight—is greatly responsible for one of the most frightening changes to take place in this country in my lifetime."

"And what is that, pray tell?"

"Within the last several years, laws have been passed in every state in the country, stripping women of the right to do as they please with their bodies. Abortion has become a *crime.* It's like our bodies are now the property of the *state!* I don't see any laws prohibiting *men* from doing what they want with *their* bodies! How would you feel if a law was passed that *required* you to have a vasectomy? How would you like to be arrested if you weren't *circumcised?* And if you feel abortion is a moral crime, why can't you at least give women that choice? Why can't you allow them the *right* to commit that sin if they feel it's necessary?"

"Are you finished?" he asked calmly. "Is that your question? Because if it is, I have an answer."

"Yes. That's my question."

"First of all, that business about vasectomies and circumcision is just bullshit and I won't dignify it with a response. Okay, now. You and the women who agree with you claim that it is your right—your inalienable *right*—to do with your bodies as you wish. But I disagree, and I'll tell you why. Have you ever heard of Jerry Lewis?"

"Of course."

"Have you seen his Muscular Dystrophy Telethon?"

"Well... I'm familiar with it."

"Okay. Here's a man who has performed financial miracles for the battle against muscular dystrophy, and yet children continue to have their bodies withered by this disease. Do they have that *right?* Do they have the right to be crippled by this disease?"

"That's the most—"

"Do I have the *right* to get cancer?"

"That's the most—"

"Does my father have the *right* to have a stroke? Does my mother have the *right* to have a heart attack? Which they both *had*, and they are now *dead*."

"That is without a doubt the most—"

"What I'm saying is that our bodies are really not our *own*. When it comes right down to it, we don't *own* them. If we don't have the right to choose whether or not we get these horrible diseases or are stricken with these deadly ailments, what gives *you* the *right* to *kill* the life that is *growing* inside *your* body?"

"That is the most *ludicrous* thing I've *ever* heard in my *entire*—"

"Thank you for calling, Janice. We go to Tucson, Arizona, where David is waiting to speak with the *host*. David?"

"Hey, Arthur, it's great to talk with you, man, really."

"Thank you."

"I love your show and I think this country needs more people like you who's willing to tell it like, well, like, y'know, it *is*. I mean, I get so fed *up* with, like, all these liberal talk show hosts who... well, who think this whole fucking country should be run by a bunch of communist faggots who... who, um... well, and women! They think the country can be run by, y'know, *women!* I mean, women like the one you had on tonight... *what's* her name? The one who hates men?"

"Melissa Cartwright."

"Yeah, like women like her can *run* the damned country, I mean... give me a *break*, okay?"

Andy smirked. Ignorant as he sounded, David was a typical listener—friend, not foe—and required a green light. "You're right on the money, David. You've got your fingers on the pulse of America and I appreciate your call. Paul in Anderson, California, what's on your mind?"

"I hear you get death threats."

"Pardon me?"

"I understand that you get threats against your life."

It was true; he still got some pretty scary threats. But his pseudonym and the anonymous nature of the network protected him. "Yes, that's true. There are people out there who don't like what I do and would like to kill me for it. Why, are you one of them?"

"Does it worry you?"

"Of *course* it worries me. Anti-American lunatics who want to kill me because of what I do? *Sure* that worries me."

"Well, I don't think you should be worried about that."

"And why's that, sir?"

"Because I don't think you'll be killed for what you do. I think you'll be killed for what you are."

The back of Andy's neck shriveled like a raisin and his hand trembled as he hit the button. "Rest well, sir, and be sure to take your medication regularly." He sighed heavily into the microphone. "Is the moon full, Tanya?"

She laughed beyond the glass.

"Tanya, of course, is my immensely talented producer, a lovely woman and a fine human being. You *see?* You see how *nice* I am to women? In fact, our next call is from a woman and her name is Mary. How are you tonight, Mary?"

"Oh… not so good, Arthur." Her voice was soft, breathy and tremulous.

One of his devoted female listeners with a personal problem. Arthur shifted in his chair, got comfortable. "First of all, I need you to speak up, dear. Okay?"

"O... kay."

"Now, tell me... what's wrong?"

"Well, it's about my boyfriend. He's... he's really hurt me, Arthur, and I just don't know—"

"Physically? Has he *hit* you?"

"Oh, no, no."

"Well, thank God for that. What's his problem, honey?"

"I don't know. I thought you could help. I listen to your show all the time and you seem so smart, so... worldly and wise."

"That I am. So how can I help you."

"All I want, see, is for him to let me into his life. And to let me let him into *my* life, see?"

Andy glanced over at Tanya, and rolled his eyes. "Oookay, if you say so."

"I mean, we don't really share anything, you know?"

"Do you sleep together?"

"Yeah."

"That's sharing in my book."

"Yeah, but... but... well, it's little things. *Important* things. I don't know anything about him, about his life, his past. Y'know, those little things that make people close. And he doesn't *wanna* know anything about me. Like, what I want to do with my life and, well, what I've been *through*, I mean, just a year and half ago I was in a... in the hospital."

"Oh? Anything serious?"

"Well, I had some, um, a few nervous problems. It wasn't a... *regular* hospital. Um, it was a... a..."

"You were in the cracker factory, Mary? Is that it? C'mon, spit it out."

166

She giggled. "Yeah. Guess so."

"Okay, so you blew a fuse for a while. How are you now?"

"I'm... well, I'm—" She sniffed a couple times, "—better. I'm doing better. Anyway, he just doesn't seem to... *feel* anything. You know. It's like he doesn't have any real *emotions*. And I also think he's sleeping around."

"Oh-ho, now, whoa, hold the phone. You mean, this guy is *your* boyfriend and he's sleeping with *other* women?"

"Uh-huh."

"Okay, now, honey, were you listening a few minutes ago when I said there are some guys who deserve to have their balls cut off?"

"Uh-huh."

"Well, this clown sounds like a prime candidate to me. So why don't you just chop the lousy bastard's gonads off and stuff 'em down his lying throat. And tell him Arthur Colton, Jr., said he deserved it."

Tanya grinned through the glass and made a scissor-like cutting motion with two fingers.

"Martha's been on hold for a while. Go ahead, Martha, you're on."

"Hello, Arthur, dear." And old woman. "Oh, my, I've listened to you for so long I feel like I know you." She said that every time. "I just called to tell you my son got that position I told you about a few weeks ago."

Oh, God, Andy thought. "Oh, really?" he asked.

"Yes. He and his wife are moving to New Jersey now, which is where the company's main plant is. Only problem is, they can't take their dogs with them and the children are *so* disappointed."

"Oh, too bad." He drummed his fingers on the console.

"And speaking of dogs, my Pookie is getting bigger every day. You remember the dachshund I got last month?"

167

"Mm-hm."

"Well, he's just as cute as a button and—"

"Take care, Martha, talk to you in a week or so. Keith in Provo, Utah."

"What gives you the right, man, what gives you the *right* to just dismiss people the way you do. You talk about freedom of speech, but you just cut people off like they're *nothing*. Who do you think you *are*? What gives you the *right*?"

"Well, I may not have the right, but I've got the button, which I'm gonna use... right... *now*. Lancaster, Pennsylvania, you're on."

"Yeah, Arthur, I hope you'll let me make my point and not cut me off."

"We'll see."

"I think maybe that last caller was onto something when he mentioned freedom of speech. You talk about it a lot, and yet your show is anything *but* an example of free speech because you hang up on anybody who disagrees with you before they've even made their point or asked their question. *That's* not freedom of speech. If you're so convinced you're right, why don't you let them speak? What are you afraid of? Why can't you *discuss* it with them?"

"Okay, okay, I get this question a lot. Listen, sir, when I talk about freedom of speech, I'm talking about freedom of speech *within the country*. This country was built on freedom of speech and continues to uphold that freedom, and it's one of the reasons I love my country so much."

"Continues to uphold—whatta you mea—what about *flag-burning*?"

"Just hold onto your dick a second, sir, I'm getting to that. If you think I'm so anti-free speech, why do you *listen*? It's a *free country*, sir, you don't *have* to listen. If it weren't a free country, there might be a law requiring you to listen to me, but there's not, so why *do* you? I think it's because, deep down inside, even the people who hate me know, in their heart of hearts, that I'm right. As for flag burning, don't start with that bullshit argument the faggot liberals used back in the eighties when this whole thing came up. Freedom of speech doesn't mean freedom of *vandalism.* Men *died* for that flag and to burn it—"

"They died for what it *stands* for, there's a big—"

"And that flag *stands* for the thing for which they *died*, so to burn it has been made a crime, as it should be, and people are now in prison for it, where I hope they rot. It's barbaric, it's treasonous, and nothing less than criminal.

"Now *this* is what I'm sick of, sir, people like you who— look, I'll *tell* you why I run my show the way I do. Because I... love... my... *country!* And I'll explain that. Like I said, one of the things I love most about America is it's freedom of speech. It's in the constitution, it was granted us by our forefathers. It is available to all who live here. I support it. But sometimes, ladies and gentlemen and Lancaster, Pennsylvania, *sometimes* it frustrates the hell out of me. Because this freedom is often abused by those who represent everything that is *un*-American. And I'm talking, now, about these people who think it's just fine and dandy to burn our flag, who think that it's just a piece of cloth and that burning it is a *statement*, when you and I, dear listener, *we* know that it's no different than *pissing* on our country, no different than *shitting* on the graves of those men who have given their lives so that ours might be free. Those who think *that* shouldn't be a crime—which it is—abuse the freedom of speech.

And I'm talking about these women, these, these... okay, I'll say it, I'm not afraid ... these *sluts* who think they have the right to fuck everything that moves when they know full well they might get pregnant, then, and *then*... when they *do*... they feel they have the right to kill—to *scrape out* and *dispose of*—the very life they've created. These women who think abortion—which is *also* a crime—is a fine and dandy method of birth control because the life they've created just isn't con-*veeeenient* for them are abusing America's freedoms. And the list goes on.

The faggots who continue spreading AIDS among innocent people. What, you think AIDS just *appears* in bags of plasma in some blood bank? You think it comes out of *nowhere?* Those queers who can't keep their dicks in their pants are abusing America's freedoms.

The people who vote into office the liberal scum who pass laws requiring a white boss to hire a black employee when a white man is more qualified just because the black employee is *black!* Do *you* like that? *I* don't. I have nothing against blacks, some of my best friends are black, but some of my best friends are *white*, too! Those people—not the liberal scum, but the people who vote them into office—*those* people are abusing America's freedoms.

And the Jews who have gained control of America's film and television industries so they can degrade the Christian values and beliefs that we all hold dear—*they* abuse America's freedoms. Those people make me sick. But I realize that they have just as much access to those freedoms as I do.

"However, folks, my show is not a country. It's my *show.* I'm in control here. Those people, those scumbags, those shitheels, they have all the rights they need, and they abuse them to hell and back. On *this* show, they do *not* have that right. And neither do the people who support them. My critics say I'm a danger to American freedoms but I say they're full of shit. My show is for the throbbing heart of America: the people who love and value their freedoms and use them as our forefathers *meant* them to be used. My show, sir, is *not* for people like you, and I would appreciate it if you didn't call again. Ever. In fact, I would appreciate it even more if you didn't - *listen* anymore.

And I would *especially* appreciate it if you would kindly take your fly-eaten, shit-soaked, un-American opinion and blow it out your ass. Have a *wonderful* evening." He hit the button. "And if this wasn't America—God *bless* her—I couldn't say that." He sighed heavily. "We've got a couple minutes of commercials, then we'll be back for more open phones. Stick around."

Andy looked up to see Harold and Tanya standing and applauding in the control room. It was one of the best—maybe *the* best—speech he'd ever given and he was exhilarated. He laughed, knowing that many of his listeners throughout the country were probably standing in front of their radios doing the same thing as Harold and Tanya. It tickled him pink.

———————

... I don't think you'll be killed for what you do. I think you'll be killed for what you are...

... for what you are...

... what you are...

Andy shuddered. He'd never had any trouble leaving his work behind him when he went home, but as his cab drove through the warm, dark city, he couldn't shake that one call... one of the shortest calls of the night...

It haunted him.

He even remembered the caller: Paul from Anderson, California.

... I don't think you'll be killed for what you do. I think you'll be killed for what you are.

Andy leaned forward and said to the cab driver, "Right here, on this corner." The cab stopped and he walked into Sol's All Nite Deli where he heard Sex Talk with Dr. Tracy Connor, the show that followed him on TBN. It was playing on the radio beside Sol's cash register.

"Andy!" Sol shouted with a grin and a wave. He was in his late sixties, short, fat, balding and loud.

"Hey, Solly, how you doing?"

"Shitty. I'm *shitty!* I been listening to this Arthur Colton shmuck. You hear him tonight?"

"Never listen, Sol."

"Aaah." He swiped his meaty hand through the air, grimacing. "Dreck. That's what it is. Talkin' about how the Jews control movies and TV so we can destroy Christianity. What, like we haven't been through *enough?* Like we don't have enough troubles as it *is?* He's gotta stir the goyim sommore? Aaah, *meshuganuh*"

"Why do you listen, Solly?"

He shrugged, stuck out his lower lip and cocked his head.

Andy grinned. "Well, if it's any help, Solly, I'm not Jewish and I think you're the bee's knees."

Sol laughed. "You want the usual?"

Andy nodded.

As he left the deli with his sandwich and pickle, Andy shook his head, puzzled. Why didn't they understand? And if they didn't understand, why did they listen?

As he walked into his dark apartment, his mouth watering for the sandwich, Andy was startled by the smell of a familiar perfume. He stood in the entryway a moment, staring into the dark, before he switched on the light.

"Andy?" The voice—a woman's—came from down the hall.

"Who's there?"

"It's me."

It was Sherrie. First, Andy rolled his eyes, knowing his plans for the night were shattered, then, heading down the hall, he shouted, "How the hell did you get in here?"

Andy froze in his bedroom doorway. The room was bathed in candlelight, and so was Sherrie, who lay on his brass bed wearing a sheer negligee that left little to the imagination. One knee was cocked up, one hand rested between her legs and her blond hair fell around her shoulders.

"Holy shit," Andy muttered with a smirk.

"I convinced the super to let me in," she whispered. "After all, he knows me, right? He's seen me before. It's all right, isn't it?"

"Wuh-well, I did sort of have other plans..."

She slid her hand up between her breasts and spread her legs. "Were your plans *this* good?"

"Ummm... no." As he entered the room, she stood and lifted a satchel from the floor, holding it between them, her eyes twinkling.

"I thought we'd try something different tonight."

"Different?" He tingled.

She nodded, dropped the satchel and embraced him, giving him a long, deep kiss as she began to remove his clothes. When he was naked, they moved to the bed, kissing again, and, removing something from the satchel, she told him to lie on his back.

Sherrie held up four lengths of velvet. "Have you ever been tied up?"

He laughed. "No. But I'll try anything once!" Smiling, Andy decided that *Shane* could go fuck himself.

Sherrie tied his wrists and ankles to the brass, put the satchel on the edge of the bed, then straddled him and began covering him with kisses. His cock was erect long before she took it in her mouth and began moving her head up and down on it as she ran her fingertips over his body like feathers.

Andy felt as if his brain were melting and he moaned deeply, moving his head back and forth, eyes closed.

She stopped.

He lifted his head as she fished through the satchel.

"You up for something *really* kinky?" she asked.

He gasped, "You kidding? *Sure!*"

She removed something long from the satchel.

A *vibrator?* he thought. *Oh, my God!*

There was a click and the object she held began to hum.

"Oh, my God," Andy moaned, dropping his head back on the pillow and closing his eyes.

She cupped his balls in her hand.

The electric hum continued.

Sherrie giggled.

Andy lifted his head, smiling, and saw it.

Its quivering blade caught the light as she lifted it.

An electric carving knife.

"What the—"

Sherrie grinned. "Arthur Colton, Jr., said you deserve this."

As her arm moved downward—so slowly, unbelievably slowly—Andy understood with terrifying clarity, remembered the call, remembered his response, and screamed, "No no wait you don't know you don't underst—"

He heard the sound.

He felt the pain.

Before he could react, something was stuffed into his mouth...

Dr. Krusadian's Method

1.

They were screaming in the Campbell house again.

The bitter, garbled shouting was something to which the other residents of Galaxy Heights had grown accustomed over the years. The Campbells weren't the only ones; the Graftons two blocks north had their share of window-rattling shouting matches and the Tillys one street over seemed to destroy all the glassware in the house each time they had a disagreement. But none fought with the tireless regularity of the Campbells. And none were as private about their disputes.

When the Graftons fought, Suzie Grafton covered her street like a missionary handing out religious tracts; she went from house to house to have coffee and talk about her husband's latest affair.

The Tillys went one better. For a month or so after one of their domestic battles, they tried to get everyone on their street to take sides. They became politicians canvassing the street for votes until they finally made up again; then they laughed about

175

their differences as if the whole thing had been a joke staged for the amusement of their neighbors.

The Campbells weren't like that. They said nothing of their quarrels, their domestic uprisings. In fact, they said little to their neighbors at all, with the exception of the Royers, who lived four houses down. Dani Campbell and April Royer were best friends; they often spent mornings together ironing clothes and sometimes took turns sitting one another's sons. Other than that, however, the Campbells kept to themselves and probably would have gone unnoticed entirely if it weren't for the screaming. Even that went largely ignored; it had become as commonplace as the barking of dogs and the chirping of crickets.

So no one knew exactly what went on within the walls of the two story gray house with white trim at 3575 Milky Way in Galaxy Heights when the screaming started, only that things were not as right as they might be.

But then, when were they ever?

The Campbells kept a neat and tidy yard. The grass was mowed each week; the shrubbery that grew along the front wall of the house was always evenly trimmed. Dani kept a flower garden along the front of the lawn that was visible through the redwood post fence running along the sidewalk the length of their yard. It was an immaculate garden in which a single weed was never allowed to see the light of day.

Their nine-year-old son Jason always put his outdoor toys in the garage when he was through playing with them, unlike so many of the other neighborhood children, who often left their front yards littered with skateboards and Big Wheels and wagons. The neighbors took this to mean that Jason was an orderly, well-behaved boy and, for the most part, he was. But the real reason Jason put his toys away was that he was afraid of what would happen if he didn't.

Dani Campbell did not care much for housework and when she did it, she did it haphazardly and without conviction. Before Jason was born, she'd kept the house spotless, but in the last six years or so, she'd lost interest in dusting and sweeping and scrubbing. It seemed pointless when she knew that her work would be virtually unnoticeable within twenty-four hours. She still did it, but not with the regularity she once had and she supposed not as well.

In fact, there were a number of things Dani did not do as well as she used to. During the first few years of her marriage, she'd exercised regularly and watched her diet and weight as intensely as a broker watches the rise and fall of the stock market. Back then, her body was picture perfect and she was proud of it; she shopped for clothes that best displayed the results of her devotion to fitness and went to the beach regularly to bask in the sun as well as the admiring stares of both men and women.

Not anymore.

Somewhere along the way, she'd slowed down. Her activity had decreased by minute intervals over the years until the only exercise she got was walking from one end of the shopping mall to the other and climbing the stairs in her house. She began to pay scant attention to what—as well as how *much*—she ate and it wasn't long before she was ignoring the more revealing outfits on the racks at Macy's and Weinstock's and searching, instead, for baggy, more concealing clothing, hoping to hide the porridge-like lumps on her thighs and hips and the roll of flesh that now oozed over her belts. Even her hair, the color of rich honey, had lost its shine and taken on a dull, unwashed look that no amount of shampoo seemed able to erase.

Some days—not often, but once in a while—it would suddenly occur to her, just hit her like a slap in the face, that her lack of enthusiasm toward those things that had once been so important to her had something to do with the fact that she and Richard ended each day by polishing off a couple bottles of wine. Maybe three. Or so. Sometimes she didn't wait for Richard to get home to open a bottle, and on those evenings, she usually just slipped frozen dinners into the microwave or got some take-out from the Colonel or Wong's Cantonese Palace. She didn't care much for cooking anymore, either.

On the evening of what would be the last chorus of hoarse screaming to come from the Campbell house before Dr. Krusadian arrived, they had eaten Kentucky Fried Chicken and coleslaw on paper plates in front of the television set. The Colonel himself smiled from the side of the red and white striped bucket that sat in the center of the coffee table. Two empty wine bottles stood at attention at the end of the table closest to Richard's recliner where he sat eating, a Coors glass filled with Sutter Home white zinfandel on the lamp table beside him. On the floor next to the chair was a third bottle, half full.

Dani sat on the sofa staring blankly at the television. A pile of unlaundered clothes clogged the other end of the sofa and four days' worth of newspapers were scattered over the floor beneath the coffee table.

Jason knelt on some of the papers, hunched over his untouched dinner on the coffee table. His Daffy Duck glass was filled with grape Kool-Aid, watered down by melting ice cubes. Beside it stood Dani's Tasmanian Devil glass; a few drops of wine were growing stale in the bottom.

They ate in silence, as always.

A rerun of *Family Ties* was just getting over on the television.

Richard browsed through the paper during the commercials.

Jason toyed with his food noncommittally.

Dani ate the last of her chicken breast and muttered, "Jase, pour Mom another glass of wine, will you?"

He took the bottle by the recliner and emptied it into her glass.

Dani chased her meal with a couple gulps of wine. She'd finished off a bottle of Blue Nun by herself earlier that afternoon, so by the time she sat down for dinner, her thoughts were covered with peach fuzz and her vision was only slightly, but pleasantly, unfocused. Now things were beginning to clear up and she planned to nip *that* in the bud.

She looked at the pile of laundry beside her as she drank, deciding she would have to get it done tomorrow. And she could probably stack the papers beside the fireplace, get them out of the way.

They seldom used the fireplace anymore. There was plenty of wood stacked in the back yard, but no one ever brought it in. The nights were getting crisp as October neared November and they'd been using the gas heater to keep warm. Dani decided to bring some wood in tomorrow, too. Might as well if she was going to do laundry. Wouldn't hurt to pick up around the house a little, too.

Staring at the black, lonely fireplace, Dani noticed that two of the pictures on the mantle had fallen forward. Although she couldn't see them, she knew exactly which ones they were: One was a picture of her, Richard, and Jason at Disneyland with Mickey standing behind them, arms raised happily. The other was of the three of them at Richard's parents' farm in Colorado. The two other pictures on the mantle—Richard and Jason at the County Fair and herself and Jason on a horse at a friend's ranch—were laced with cobwebs. She would have to dust tomorrow, too.

Funny, she thought, squinting at the pictures through a Zinfandel haze, *Jason never smiled.*

179

Dani had noticed that Jason was smiling in none of the pictures several times before, but, as always, she noticed it again as if for the first time. Wondering if the two pictures lying face down were any different, she set her plate aside and rose unsteadily, went to the mantle, and righted the fallen pictures.

Jason stared at her from within the chrome frame, standing between her and Richard and in front of Mickey; his chin was tucked in slightly, the corners of his mouth turned downward just a bit, eyes shadowed and deep. He was a Dickensian urchin, a lost little elf far from home.

Does he always look like that? she wondered.

He did in the four pictures on the mantle.

Dani returned to the sofa, splashed some more wine into her glass and took a couple healthy swallows.

The telephone rang.

On the third ring, Richard said slowly, "I suppose I should get that?"

"Mm-hm," Dani nodded, suddenly interested in the newsbreak on television, because *she* didn't want to answer the phone.

Richard set his plate aside, stood, and stretched. He was just under six feet, wiry but muscular, hard, with impossibly wavey brown hair that refused to be combed or styled; it just did as it pleased, curling here and sticking out there, defiant. He went to the telephone in the hallway with a put-upon sigh. His voice was muffled by the opening theme of *The Cosby Show*.

They used to have a telephone in the living room, but Richard had broken it a few weeks ago and neither of them had gotten around to switching the hall phone into the living room jack.

Dani watched Jason do everything with his dinner but eat it as he watched television. He was a small boy with his mother's blond hair and light freckles and his father's strong features and deep brown eyes. He prodded his chicken leg with his fork.

Richard laughed in the hall, but it sounded forced.

"C'mon and eat your chicken, Jase," Dani said, reaching over to pat his shoulder.

"Not very hungry." His voice was hoarse, his words garbled by the fork as he slipped it between his lips and bit it.

"Well, you've gotta eat, hon. Wanna grow up, don't you?"

He shrugged, using the fork to stir his coleslaw.

"Do you feel okay?"

He nodded.

"Well, why don't you at least—"

Richard slammed the receiver down so hard, Dani heard the sharp ring of the phone in the living room.

Jason's fork slipped from his small hand and clattered to the plate.

Dani silently braced herself.

"That was George Winter," Richard said as he came back down the hall. His voice was different. The lazy dinnertime drawl was gone; his words were succinct now, crisp.

Dani looked over her shoulder, knowing what she would see; she was correct.

He stood at the hallway entrance the way he always stood when he got started: hands in his back pockets, elbows out at his sides.

"You know George Winter, Jason," he said. "Randy's dad? Any idea why he might call this evening?"

Jason stiffened and his lower lip trembled.

Randy Winter was Jason's best friend. Dani had met the boy's parents at a school picnic; Richard had stayed home.

"Seems there was a little program at the school tonight," Richard went on. "A student art show. All the parents were invited." He crossed the room as he spoke until he reached the

Ray Garton

coffee table, where he leaned forward, his face tensing, eyes narrowing. "All the parents but *us*."

Jason slumped forward a little, pulling his shoulders up to his ears.

"How come, Jason?" Dani asked softly, puzzled.

"Forgot," he whispered.

Richard repeated the word, spat it from his mouth with contempt as he spun around and got his drink from the floor by the recliner. He finished it off and quickly reached for the bottle, but it was empty.

There was a brittle silence as Richard walked a slow circle around the recliner.

Dani knew what was coming, what always came when Richard paced and circled and, as always, she gave it no thought. Instead, she wondered why Jason hadn't told them about the art show. They always attended his school programs; *she* did, anyway, even if Richard sometimes didn't. Why would Jason deliberately keep this one from them?

"Do you know how this looks?" Richard asked. "Do you know how this makes *us* look? Like we don't care about our son's progress in school, like we don't—" He stopped abruptly and wiped a palm over his mouth once, twice, a third time. Another sign of what was coming. "Get out of here!" he barked, sweeping a hand through the air in Jason's direction.

Jason was up and running for the stairs before Richard had finished the sentence.

Richard paced again, still holding his empty glass, muttering to himself every few steps. "... have everyone thinking we don't give a damn about him... don't even show up at his goddamned art show... and he won a prize, for Christ's sake." He spun around to face Dani and shouted, "Can you believe he won a goddamned prize and didn't even *tell* us?"

182

Before she could respond, he went to the kitchen to open another bottle.

Dani listened to him slamming cupboards and throwing things. Glass shattered, he bellowed, *"Shit!"* and broke something else. "Why don't you clean this goddamned place up once in a while? *Huh?* Just once in a while?"

She knew he would come out with a new bottle, sit in his chair, and change television channels rapidly with the remote control as he mumbled and cursed. Half way through the new bottle, he would decide enough had not been said and would go upstairs to shout at Jason some more.

Why would Jason do that? she wondered. It was such a small thing, but so unlike him. Jason loved arts and crafts, was very creative; it seemed he would be proud of his art project, would want them to see it.

The only explanation Dani could come up with was one she didn't want to think about... one that made her want some more wine.

Richard returned to his recliner and strangled the freshly opened bottle of wine between his thighs as she shot at the television with the remote control. "... goddamned kid... what'm I supposed to say when someone asks why we weren't there at the... Jesus..." He curled his lip back, shaking his head back and forth as if he were running his teeth over a file.

The room moved just a little when Dani got up, drank the last of her wine, and went to the kitchen for her own bottle.

Two coffee cups were shattered in the sink.

She opened their last bottle of Sutter Home, making a mental note to buy more tomorrow, and poured until the wine rose above the Tasmanian Devil's head. As she drank, she heard Richard slam the bottle onto the coffee table and get out of the recliner.

Dani lowered her glass, closed her eyes a moment, then drained it and poured another, starting on it immediately. She felt calm, a little numb, relaxed. Prepared.

"Unlock this door, goddammit!" Richard screamed in the hall upstairs.

Dani went back to the living room, sat in the recliner, found a movie on television that looked interesting and turned up the sound until Richard's words were indecipherable. She could never shut out his voice completely, not once he got started.

Something crashed against the wall upstairs.

Dani wondered vaguely if it was Jason and turned the sound up a bit more.

Cosby's over, she thought, realizing it was later than it seemed. She looked out the window and saw that it was indeed dark outside. Had been for some time, she knew.

Dani relaxed a bit more. She found it comforting, seeing blackness outside the windows; it meant the day was over.

She changed the channel to an old rerun of *The Brady Brunch;* she'd always liked that show.

Jason's voice rose above the television's volume in a shrill scream: "No, Daddy, I'm sorry, *don't*—"

Glass shattered.

Dani finished her wine, released a sweet, quiet belch, and filled her glass again.

"—cause you're ashamed of us? Huh?"

"—please don't—"

"*I'll* give you something to be ashamed of, goddamned little—"

"—*noooo!*"

Dani's knuckles burned; she looked down at her right hand and saw that she was clutching the glass so tightly that her knuckles were the color of skim milk. She gulped the rest of the wine like cold water and put the glass on the coffee table beside the bottle.

There was a clamor at the top of the stairs and Dani turned as Jason tumbled from the hall onto the landing. He shielded his face with his arms as Richard stood over him, fists clenched, teeth bared like an angry dog.

"Don't you *ever* do that again," he growled, towering over the boy, "you understand? *Huh?* Or by God, I'll... I'll..." Richard paced three steps forward, spun, stalked back, his face a mottled red and, pulling a foot back abruptly, he kicked Jason in the ribs.

The boy rolled once and stopped a foot from the stairs, eyes clenched, head pulled back with his mouth yawning open as he made a long miserable retching sound.

Richard paced again, cursing under his breath.

Dani saw it coming, saw it clearer than she'd been seeing the television all evening, and she surprised herself by shooting to her feet and calling her husband's name in a voice ripe with warning. Her shin hit the coffee table and the bottle fell over and rolled a few inches. Wine made gulping noises as it spilled to the carpet.

Richard ignored her.

He kicked Jason again.

The floor tilted beneath Dani's feet and her vision blurred as another wine flavored gas bubble burst in her chest and she watched, rooted to the floor, as her son went down the stairs in a blur of small arms and legs.

It happened so fast, and yet it seemed to take forever for Jason to reach the bottom of the stairs. Dani heard a sound rise above the thump and tumble of Jason's body hitting the carpeted steps; it was an instantaneous sound, there and gone so quickly that she realized she might not have heard that brief wet crunch at all.

When he finally hit the floor, landing flat on his back, Jason released a burst of breath, as if he'd been holding it all the way down. Then he lay still, staring up at the ceiling with those big fudge brown eyes that blinked so rapidly, as if he'd just awakened and was thinking, *Boy, that was some dream!*

Dani couldn't move or speak at first, couldn't even breathe, could only listen to the thick liquid rushing sound in her ears—as if she were moving underwater—and stare at her son.

Jason lifted his head, gave it a little puppy-like shake, and sat up. His left arm lay between his legs and he dragged it over a thigh, started to lift it, then let it drop to the floor as if it were just too heavy for him.

"Mommy?" he croaked, sounding puzzled, confused, as he stared at his arm, his round little face clouding with worry, "Mommy?"

"Yes, Jason, yes, yes, Mommy's here," she slurred, hurrying to him unsteadily, nearly falling when she dodged the lamp table by the recliner. She saw the bone when she was half way there, dropped to the floor, and scuttled the rest of the way on her knees as he began to scream.

"Mom-*meee!* Mom-*meee!* Mom-*meee!*"

His left arm had broken half way between the elbow and wrist and a jagged shard of bloodied gray bone jutted from his broken skin like a steak knife trying to slice off a bite of meat.

Dani felt the blood drain slowly from her face until her cheeks felt ice cold and her mouth worked numbly for several seconds before words actually came out; even as she spoke, she knew it was the wrong thing to say.

"Oh, we'll have to put some ice on that, Jase. That's gonna swell."

In fact, it swelled right before her eyes, like a flesh-colored banana shaped party balloon with a pretty red and gray design in the middle. It seemed a long time before she realized it wasn't the swelling that really mattered; no, it was that bone...

Richard was groaning at the top of the stairs, groaning in black, sticky waves...

As Jason continued to scream, distorted thoughts limped, wounded, through Dani's mind: *Listen to Richard groan... look at Jason's bone...*

The horror of what Richard had done finally sank in and, before it could become the horror of what she'd *allowed* him to do, Dani took in a long deep breath as she slowly lifted her head to scream at him and—

—he was still standing at the top of the stairs groaning, such a deep, sickening groan, and—

—when her eyes finally found him, her voice lodged in her throat like a thorn because—

—Richard was doing something, a horrible thing that made Dani think for a moment that, somehow, her whole life had been a tragic mistake, and—

—it was that thing, that horrible thing that her husband was doing, not the sight of her son's exposed and splintered bone, that made her sick on the carpet.

2.

Jason felt better after the shot.

The nurse who'd given it to him was nice. Tiny, like him almost, with bright red hair and freckles, *lots* more than he had. Her voice was very high, like an elf's, and her name was Tina.

Tina had been so afraid of hurting him, acting like maybe he was going to start crying when she brought the syringe to his bedside.

"Okay, Jason," she'd chirped, "you're gonna be a big boy for me now, aren't you? 'Cause this'll only hurt for a second, and it'll make you feel a whole lot better."

He'd been in too much pain to protest, even if the needle *had* scared him. It hadn't, though. A needle wasn't so much.

Tina stood by his bed after the shot, rubbing the stinging needle prick gently with a rubber-gloved little hand. As the minutes passed, ticked away by the unholy throbbing in his broken arm, Jason began to relax, stopped crying and breathed easier until he began to feel like... like... yeah, like cotton candy, the kind you get at the fair, real light, fluffy and sticky.

"Feelin' a little better?" Tina asked, lightly patting his behind.

"Mm-hm."

"So how'd this happen, big fella?" she asked, tossing the needle and syringe into a plastic-lined silver trash bucket. "Were you fightin' off the girls?"

"I tripped on a rollerskate and fell down the stairs," he replied without a second for thought.

"Mmm." She walked around the bed to face him. "Well, that ice'll make the swelling go down, then Dr. Saunders'll fit you up with a brand new shiny white cast for all your friends to sign. How's that?"

He tried hard to smile as he nodded, but his lips felt a little numb.

Tina left him alone behind the mint green curtain.

If everyone in the hospital was as nice as Tina and as funny as the chubby man who had taken X-ray pictures of his arm earlier, Jason hoped he'd get to stay for a while.

Otherwise, of course, he would have to go home.

At least he'd done nothing more to upset his dad. When he left the hospital, he could honestly tell his dad he'd answered the doctor's and nurse's questions just as he'd been told to do in the car on the way there.

The curtain squeaked in its plastic track on the ceiling when Dr. Saunders pulled it aside and stepped through, smiling.

"Jason," he said, "how's that swelling coming? You got it down for us yet?"

Jason just smiled a little; his tongue was much too heavy to speak.

Dr. Saunders had snow white hair that was very short, cut high above his big ears. He wore black rimmed glasses on his craggy face; the lenses made the little twinkles in his eyes look much bigger. He was tall and skinny and his long arms seemed rubbery within the sleeves of his white coat. His voice was rough but soft, and his breath smelled of sweet smoke, like burning cherries.

"That shot's a whopper, huh?"

Jason nodded.

"Makes you feel sorta like your head's a balloon and the string's coming loose, huh?" He perched himself on a stool and wheeled it over to the bed, adjusting his glasses on his sharp nose and looking down at Jason through the bifocals.

"That falling down stairs, Jason," he said solemnly, "that's no good. That'll have to stop." He took a good look at the ice bag wrapped around Jason's arm, then looked at his face for a long time. "Tell me, Jason. How did you get this little scar here?" He touched a fingertip to Jason's upper lip.

"Fell on the sidewalk."

"Well, what're we gonna have to do with you, son? Put you in a wheelchair?"

Jason laughed wearily. He wasn't used to adults joking with him; it was a pleasant, refreshing surprise.

"You're all alone in here, Jason. Most kids want their mom or dad in here with them. Keeps them from crying. But not you. You're a brave boy."

Jason closed his eyes for a moment; Dr. Saunders' voice was soothing.

"Don't you want your mom or dad in here? Don't you wonder where they are?"

After a few seconds of warming up his rubbery lips, Jason said, "S'okay if they had to go."

"No, no. They haven't gone anywhere. They're right outside. You don't really think your mom and dad would go off and leave you. Do you, Jason?"

He licked his lips slowly; his mouth had gone dry. "Maybe to clean the carpet. 'Fore it stains. S'okay."

Dr. Saunders frowned and took Jason's right hand from the bed, holding it in his big palm as he looked at the pink, slightly raised scar on the pad of flesh between thumb and forefinger.

"And where did *this* come from?"

"I was... playing with... matches." Jason was beginning to feel very sleepy and didn't really feel like talking, but the responses came automatically, cutting through his foggy head, just as rehearsed.

"And this one on your finger? A cut?"

A heavy, slight nod. "Mom's... sewing... scissors."

"Aaahh. Jason, where was your dad when you fell down the stairs?"

"Be... side me."

"I see. Too bad he couldn't have stopped you."

"S'o... s'okay."

Jason's leaden eyes closed very slowly as Dr. Saunders said, "You just relax, Jason. I'm gonna give you another once-over."

"I want a cigarette," Dani whispered. Her voice sounded harsh in the empty waiting room.

"I thought you quit."

"You *know* I quit. But I want one."

Richard stood and the sofa's green vinyl upholstery crackled its relief. "I'll get you a pack."

"Where are you going?"

"Cafeteria. For coffee. You want some?"

"Yeah. A cup."

Dani realized they were both speaking in flat monotone voices, barely above a whisper, like alien invaders in a bad movie.

Richard left and Dani stared up at the black and white television mounted on the wall. *Cheers* was on, but the sound was too low to hear. It was an old episode, way before Diane Chambers ran off with her ex-fiancé to write a book instead of marrying Sam. That meant it was one of the syndicated episodes, so it had to be somewhere between eleven and twelve o'clock. She tried to remember when they'd arrived, couldn't, and gave up trying.

Her gray shirt was splotched with blood from holding Jason in her arms in the car. The blood was drying to a stiff crust.

The ride to the hospital had been a nightmare. Jason screaming in her arms, quaking in pain... Richard trying to keep an eye on the road as he said over and over, "Now, what are you going to tell the doctor, Jason? Remember? About the roller skate? What are you going to tell the doctor?"

Dani was glad Richard was gone, glad she was alone. She didn't want to be near him. She leaned forward, folded her arms over her knees, and rested her vaguely aching head.

"Where's Mr. Campbell?"

She snapped upright. Dr. Saunders stood over her, hands in his coat pockets.

"He... went for coffee." She stood clumsily and hugged her purse to her stomach. "How is Jason?"

"Heavily sedated and in a tremendous amount of pain. Will you come with me, please?" He didn't smile or look her in the eye, didn't even wait to see if she was coming, just turned and started out of the room. He stopped at the reception window and said to the graying woman at the desk, "Jessie, when Mr. Campbell comes back, would you send him straight to my office, please?" Then he was gone, out the door and down the corridor.

Dani tried to keep up with him on weak legs, thinking, *It's serious, bad, maybe they'll have to operate or... Christ, what if he loses it, what if Jason loses his arm?*

She followed Dr. Saunders into a small cluttered office that smelled of pipe tobacco. He closed the door, cleared some books from a folding chair, and gestured for her to sit. When she did, he leaned his hips on the corner of his desk, folded his long arms over his chest and said, "Which one of you beats Jason, you or your husband?"

Dani's jaw dropped, she released a gush of breath and stammered, "Wh-what—what're you—I don't under—"

"Or whatever it is you do, beat him, burn him, cut him. You or your husband? Or do you take turns?" His creased face was colder than death and his eyes were steel bearings glistening in their sockets.

"W-w-we *told* you, he slipped—"

" —on a roller skate, yes, you told me. But, unfortunately for your son, I'm neither blind nor stupid, and *I'm* telling *you* that I don't buy it. You have a lot to drink tonight, Mrs. Campbell?"

"I-I-I..." She stopped, knowing that any further attempts at speech—let alone an explanation—would be futile.

"Your husband, too, hm? Smells like wine, am I right? And it *does* smell, Mrs. Campbell, don't kid yourself. It's a wonder you weren't all killed on the road."

Dani felt lightheaded, trembly, like she might pass out. She let her purse slide down between her feet and clutched the edges of her chair, as if to keep from floating away.

"We... just had... some wine... with dinner."

"Some wine," he said doubtfully. "How many bottles?"

Before she could attempt a reply, there was a knock at the door.

"Come in," the doctor said.

Richard peered in uncertainly, stepped inside and closed the door. His face was expressionless at first, but when he looked at Dani, he frowned, sensing her discomfort.

She took in a deep breath to tell him... what? She didn't know and didn't try to speak.

"I'd offer you a chair, but I'm short," Dr. Saunders said. "Which is too bad, because I think you'll need one. I was just explaining to your wife here that it's pretty obvious to me you're unfit parents. Both of you."

Richard stared at him blankly for a moment and when the words registered, his eyes became stormy. "What... what the hell're you—"

"Shut up, Mr. Campbell. Give me any trouble and I'll have you canned for DUI. You'd probably set a blood alcohol *record* in the lab." Saunders spun, stepped around his desk, and took a seat.

Dani felt sick.

"By law," Dr. Saunders said, "I'm required to turn you in, no questions asked. But I've been that route before and I'm not too keen on the way the system handles this kind of problem. They seem to think that—"

Richard's face was the color of strawberries when he barked, "Wait just a minute, here, just who the hell do you think you are, goddammit, telling us—"

"I think I'm what you've been dreading, Mr. Campbell, and if you don't shut your mouth and listen to what I have to say, I'll make things much worse for you than you've imagined, I promise."

"B-but... he *slipped*," Richard said, his voice suddenly drained of anger.

Dr. Saunders gracefully locked his boney fingers together beneath his sharp chin and he spoke softly. "Mr. Campbell, that boy has more nicks and scars than my favorite pair of black leather motorcycle boots, which I've had since seventy-*four*. No one... no one... is that clumsy. Now, if I turned you in, Jason would be taken from you. But that usually does more harm than good. So I'm not going to do that. I know of something better."

Dani looked at Richard; his face had become slack, cheeks sagging, jaw loose. Even his shoulders drooped in a physical display of guilt and defeat. He leaned back heavily against the door looking sick.

Dr. Saunders went on. "I know a doctor. Dr. Krusadian. He works wonders. I don't know what his methods are, but I've seen the results. So here's what we'll do. No trouble, no hassle, we're just going to handle your problem in the quickest, most efficient way I know. If it doesn't work, we'll go from there. I'll call Dr. Krusadian and tomorrow—"

Richard stepped forward suddenly, face white, mouth working. "Listen to me," he breathed, lips trembling. "Listen to me, please, I... I don't want any trouble. If we can just... just forget about this, maybe I could... well—" A desperate, pathetic little chuckle wiggled from his throat and Dani, for a moment, almost pitied him. Almost, "—maybe I could add a little something to... to your bill? You know? May... maybe?"

Dani suddenly wanted to throw up.

Dr. Saunders stared at Richard for a long time. Smiling. When he finally spoke, he did so softly at first, slowly building to a growl as he rose to his feet and dug his knuckles into his desktop.

"Have you ever seen a ruptured anus, Mr. Campbell? I don't mean one that's just torn a little and bleeding. I mean an asshole you can stick your arm into up to the elbow. I've seen that, Mr. Campbell. I used to be a prison doctor. Ugly. *Ugly.* That's the kind of thing they do to child abusers in prison because they hate them. All those murderers and rapists? They *abhor* people like you, and to tell you the truth, I wouldn't mind running an industrial power drill up your ass my*self*, but because I'm not in a position to do that, I'm trying to help you straighten up and keep your family together, and if you don't shut the fuck up and cooperate, I promise you, I'll recommend they throw you into prison for the rest of your miserable life and you'll be shitting into a colostomy bag within your first *week.* Do I make myself *clear*, Mr. Campbell?"

He stared at Richard with hateful, deadly eyes, and when he got no response other than a look of impossible horror and dread, he returned to his chair and cleared his throat softly.

"I'm going to have Dr. Krusadian drop by and see you tomorrow evening. He will then proceed with his treatment and, whatever it is, you will cooperate. You will cooperate happily. Otherwise, I will, quite simply, ruin your life." Another smile, big and flashy and filled with satisfaction. "I'm keeping Jason here for the night. You can pick him up tomorrow afternoon. I will see him once a week for the next six months. If he shows up with so much as a mosquito bite that I don't like, I'll crucify you. Clear?"

They both stared at him silently. Dani knew she would vomit soon.

"I said... *clear?*"

Richard nodded silently.

"Now," Dr. Saunders said, "if you don't mind, I'd rather not look at you anymore. Call a cab. If you drive home in your condition, I'll have the cops on you so fast you'll think you died and went to hell. Good night."

Dani couldn't stand up.

Richard didn't move.

Dr. Saunders raised his snowy brows. "Alcohol effect your hearing? I said, good *night.*"

As soon as they were in the corridor, Dani looked for a restroom but didn't find one in time and vomited into a drinking fountain.

Dr. Saunders leaned out of his office and said quietly, "Get some paper towels and clean that up before you go."

3.

The weather was changing.

"Clouds were curling across the night sky, blocking the stars and, finally, the platinum moon.

Dani stood on the sidewalk in front of their house and watched the night lights disappear from the sky as Richard paid the cab driver, her back to the idling car. She looked at the house; they'd left quickly and the lights were still on, making the windows glow.

So that's how it looks, she thought. *From the outside.*

Richard walked by her as if she weren't there, went through the gate, and up the front path.

She followed him into the house and asked, "What about the car?"

"What about it?"

Well, if you take the Samurai to work, how will I pick up Jas—"

"Call April. Have her drive you." He crossed the living room, turning off the lights as he went, and slowed to step over the caked patch of vomit on the carpet. Climbing the stairs wearily, he said, "Clean that up."

Dani watched him, her gut seizing up. An unbearable weariness washed over her and she began to cry quietly although she fought the tears; she knew Richard would be annoyed if she cried, aggravated, maybe even angered, but she had to speak.

"Richard? Don't you think we should talk?"

"About what?"

"About… about what we're going to do."

"Do?" He turned at the top of the stairs and laughed at her coldly. "We're going to do exactly what the doctor ordered." He shuffled toward the bedroom.

"But… but—" She couldn't just drop it; they hadn't spoken a word in the cab and she felt empty, gutted, " —shouldn't we… talk? Richard? I'll pour us a drink." There was a long silence as Richard stood in the hall staring at the floor, then Dani whispered, "Please?"

"Come to bed. You've had enough to drink."

When she heard the bedroom door close, Dani muttered, "No, I haven't."

She had a tall glass of wine over ice before she cleaned up her sickness on the living room floor.

Shortly before dawn, Dani sat up in bed and choked back a scream.

It had happened again in a dream, the accident. But seeing Jason fall again was not what had shot her from her sleep.

It had been Richard.

He'd stood at the top of the stairs again, butt naked and in murky shadows, groaning and shining with sweat as he did that thing…

That horrible thing.

4.

The next morning, April drove Dani to the hospital to pick up the car. The cloudy sky was the color of dirty steel and the breeze was armed with a cutting chill.

Over coffee, Dani had explained about the roller skate and told April how terribly worried she and Richard were about their son. That was all she'd told her, all she'd needed to tell her. For now. If it was necessary later, she would come up with some explanation for this Dr. Kru… Dr. Krusa… whatever his name was.

"He'll be fine," April assured her. "Kids bounce back fast, you know. You just watch. But you… you seem a little, you know, upset about something else."

Dani shrugged, heaving nonchalance from the gesture with constipated effort.

"Richard and I had a fight. You know, just before… the accident." *Careful*, she thought. *Don't tell one you can't cover later.* "I think it upset Jason. You know, made things worse."

"I'm telling you, don't worry about Jason. He'll be fine. Kids're tough. Like Timex watches. Remember last year when my little Kenny fell off the monkey bars and broke his ankle? He hardly noticed it. Even enjoyed it, I think. All the attention, you know? They're like TV evangelists, kids," she giggled. "They keep coming back for more. Wish I had a little of what they've got in 'em."

April pulled into the hospital parking lot and stopped in front of Dani's car.

"How about I park and go up with you?" April suggested.

"Oh, no, hon, that's okay. I know you're busy."

"Busy? Hell, I'm bathing the dogs today, f'Christ's sake. I'll park the—"

"No, no. I can't stay anyway. I've gotta go pick up his school-work."

"Oh. All right," she conceded. "See you later today? Got some wine coolers in the 'fridge."

"This afternoon. Thanks for the ride."

Dani smiled until April's station wagon was out of the parking lot, then she leaned against her car and sighed, looking up at the gray hospital building.

She couldn't go up and see Jason. Not yet. She wasn't ready.

Dani could not get out of the parking lot fast enough.

5.

Jason was groggy, but not too groggy to laugh. He was propped up in bed, the new cast on his arm resting in his lap as he watched a Donald Duck cartoon on the Disney Channel. He'd never seen the Disney Channel before and was nearly happy enough to jump out of bed when he learned the television in his room had cable.

Dr. Saunders had said his arm wasn't as bad as they'd thought and would probably heal nicely. He'd told Jason to rest in bed until his mom came to get him.

Jason didn't want to think about that. He hoped she was late.

Ramona, his nurse, a squat woman with big smiling eyes and a musical voice, bustled into the room; she held a Styrofoam cup with a straw sticking through the lid.

"Here you go, sweetie pie," she said, handing it to him. "Chocolate, just like you asked."

"Thank you, Ramona."

"Not supposed to have milkshakes this soon after breakfast, but I smuggled it outta the kitchen for you."

Jason was laughing at the cartoons again.

"You gotta roommate coming in a coupla hours. But your momma'll probably be here by then, I'm sure. Bet you can't wait to get outta here, huh?"

Jason's laughter crumbled as she fluffed his pillows. He sipped his shake, frowning, and whispered, "I can wait."

6.

The fourth-grade class at Millhouse Elementary School was at recess when Dani arrived and the teacher, Miss Carmody, greeted her on the playground.

Miss Carmody was a tall, svelte woman with a pleasant face but a timid, breathy voice. She clicked her tongue sympathetically as Dani told her of Jason's accident.

"We'll have to work on that boy's coordination," she said good naturedly, walking to the classroom. "He seems to fall a lot."

Inside, Miss Carmody gathered up the week's remaining assignments, put them in a folder, and gave them to Dani.

"You can take this, too," she said, going to a long table in the rear of the classroom. On the table were several stacks of large rectangular sheets of heavy-duty paper; they were rumpled from dried watercolors. Miss Carmody lifted a sheet with a red ribbon taped to the cover and held it before her. "Too bad you missed last night's art show," she said. "Jason won second prize."

Dani clung to her smile as if for life as she stared at her son's painting. Acid began to sizzle in her stomach.

She knew, suddenly, why Jason had kept the art show a secret.

Miss Carmody said hesitantly, "He's very... imaginative. Don't you think?"

"Oh... yes. He is. Imaginative."

"You know, some of the other faculty members found this very interesting."

"Yes. Interesting." Dani stepped forward and took the painting, clumsily rolling it up on the table.

Miss Carmody joined her hands before her, fingers fluttering like moths. "We thought there might be... well, some... significance to Jason's painting. We thought maybe you'd—"

"I have to go to the hospital now, Miss Carmody. Thanks for your help." She started for the door, dropped the folder, and papers hissed over the floor.

Miss Carmody hunkered down beside her to help gather them up and said quietly, nervously, "If you ever need to, Mrs. Campbell, you can come talk to me. Or the school counselor. He's—"

"Thanks again."

In the car, Dani wrung her fists around the steering wheel until she caught her breath, then she unrolled the painting again.

It *was* very good, bright with colors, even dark with shadows in most of the right places.

A pretty green long-necked bottle stood in the center of the picture with fire and smoke bursting from the top. Peering from the flames were two hideous, monstrous faces. On the left, a scaled reptilian face glared with fiery eyes, a gaping mouth lined with needle-like fangs, and, on the top, a tuft of wavey curly brown hair. The fangs dripped with red-black blood. The other face seemed softer, somewhat feminine, more human, with gold worms coming from the head instead of hair. A big black padlock pierced the thin lips, locking the mouth shut and, worst of all, the creature had no eyes.

Written at the bottom in red pencil was: THE MONSTERS FROM THE BOTTLE.

Dani almost tore it up into small pieces. She knew she'd have to sometime because if Richard ever saw it, he would... he would...

She didn't want to think about it.

She wanted a drink.

Dani rolled the picture back up, started the car, and drove away.

7.

Dani stopped a few feet away from the open door of Jason's hospital room when she heard an unfamiliar sound. She stood in the busy corridor and listened, took a cautious step forward and craned her neck to peer into the room.

At first, she thought he was in pain, then thought perhaps he was crying because he'd been left alone in a hospital.

She was wrong.

Jason was laughing.

Dani started into the room but spun around when someone touched her shoulder. She looked into the stern face of Dr. Saunders.

"Dr. Krusadian will call you at two this afternoon," he whispered. "Don't let me hear you weren't there. Understood?"

He went into the room ahead of her.

"Well, Jason," he said, smiling, "ready to go home?"

Jason turned his smiling eyes from the television.

"Your mom's here."

When he looked at Dani, Jason's smile disappeared as if it had never been. His eyelids dropped half way and his brow creased slightly.

"Yeah," he said in a low monotone. "I'm ready."

Once again, he was the Jason Dani knew.

8.

They drove home in complete silence.

Jason usually spoke little anyway, but his silence in the car was a nervous one, cautious. He kept eyeing the rolled-up painting on the seat between them.

When they got home, Dani said, "Your teacher gave me this," handing him the painting as she sat down on the sofa. "Jason, is there anything... well, would you like to talk about this picture?"

He stared at his cast silently, reading some of the nurses' inscriptions. Finally, without lifting his eyes, Jason shook his head.

"It's... well, you know, it's *good*, but—"

"Thank you."

"Um, look, Jason, there'll be a man coming here tonight. A doctor. He's coming here to... to talk with us."

"Is he gonna talk about my arm?"

"Well, sort of. See, this doctor might be able to fix it so... so your dad... doesn't get so mad... you know, like he does? He's... I don't know, he's just gonna talk to us, that's all. To your dad and me. I think he might want to talk to you, too, okay?"

He nodded.

She looked at him for a while, waiting for him to look at her, just lift his head, anything. But he didn't. Dani touched his chin with a forefinger and he raised his head first, then, a moment later, his eyes, and looked at her.

"You're… you're so pale," she whispered. "You wanna go to bed, sweetheart?"

He nodded again.

"I'll bring you a bunch of pillows. And how about a popsicle?"

Another nod as he started up the stairs, holding the rolled-up painting.

"Um, Jason? Um, your painting… well, just for now, could you, um, you know…"

"I'll put it away," he said without looking back.

Before getting the pillows and popsicle for Jason, Dani went to the car for the groceries she'd bought earlier. She took them to the kitchen and opened the day's first bottle of wine.

It was one of her last.

9.

The phone rang at exactly two o'clock that afternoon. Dani's hand trembled as she reached for the receiver; her other hand was wrapped around a glass of wine.

"Hello?"

"Mrs. Campbell? Dr. Krusadian calling."

His voice was deep as an arthritic ache and curled by an accent of some kind. Jamaican, perhaps, but she wasn't sure. He was definitely black.

"Um, yes, this is Dani Campbell."

"Good. I'm calling about this evening. I will be there at seven. I wanted you to know so I wouldn't interrupt your supper. I'm very prompt."

"Well, Doctor, I appreciate that, but… well, it would be much easier if we could come to your office."

"I don't have an office."

In the dead silence that followed, Dani wondered about Dr. Krusadian.

"I see," she said. "Well, if you don't mind my asking… if you don't have an office, what kind of doctor are you? Exactly?"

"A very good one, Mrs. Campbell. I'm calling to verify your address."

After he recited their address succinctly, Dani said, "That's right. Do you know where that is?"

"Exactly. Seven o'clock. Good afternoon."

He hung up.

10.

Richard didn't say a word when he came in from work that evening. By that time, rain had begun to fall outside and, occasionally, thunder rolled in the distance. Dani had gotten to the bottom of a large cheap bottle of chenin blanc and was relaxed on the sofa watching M*A*S*H when he arrived. She'd managed to stack the newspapers by the fireplace and do the laundry, but she hadn't quite made it into the back yard for firewood.

After changing his clothes, Richard opened a bottle of wine, got a glass, and sat in front of the television to drink and read the paper during the commercials. He did just that for a long time without saying a thing or even acknowledging Dani's presence.

When she could take the silence no longer, Dani said, "Dr. Krusadian's going to be here at seven.

Mm-hm."

"Do you think he'll want to talk to Jason, too?"

Richard made a little humming sound, like saying *I don't know* without bothering to open his mouth.

"Richard?"

"Hm?"

"You… you're making noises. Why won't you talk to me? What have I done?"

"Nothing. Just don't feel like talking. Been talking all day. We'll do plenty of talking later, probably. When he comes. He say how much this is gonna cost me?"

"No," she sighed. "He didn't say."

"Probably plenty. What's for dinner?" He didn't look up from the paper.

"Soup and sandwiches. Is that all you can think about? How much it's gonna *cost?* I mean… Richard, I'm *scared.*"

"So'm I. I just don't want to talk about it."

They didn't.

11.

The ringing of the doorbell mingled with a growl of thunder.

Richard seemed not to notice; he was still reading the paper.

Dani leaned forward and ran a hand over her hair, patting. She took one more drink of wine and her hand froze with the glass half way back to the coffee table.

My God, she thought, *we're drinking. He's here and… how much wine have we had?*

There were two bottles on the floor beside Richard's chair. Empty.

"Richard, put those bottles away. Please?"

"Why? I'm not drunk. I have nothing to hide. S'only wine, for Christ's sake. Answer the door."

Dani walked through ankle-deep mud to get to the door. It sucked at her feet, making each step an ordeal as the doorbell rang again. She looked down, actually expecting to see the mud, but there was only carpet. She stood with her hand on the doorknob for a moment, took a deep breath, and pulled the door open.

Dr. Krusadian filled the doorway. Only a small amount of light from the porchlight squeezed past him over his shoulders. Below that, there was only Dr. Krusadian in the doorway from side to side, all the way down to the threshold.

He wore a black raincoat, open in front. Beneath that, a black suit, narrow black tie, white shirt, and, on his head, a black fedora tilted forward slightly.

His face was as black as his clothing, coal black, so black it was like looking into a night sky that held only two glittering stars: his eyes.

Dr. Krusadian smiled; his lips pulled back to reveal a bit of their chocolate brown and pink undersides and two rows of enormous pure white teeth.

"Hello, Mrs. Campbell. I am Dr. Krusadian."

Dani realized she was nibbling on a knuckle nervously and dropped her hand suddenly.

The thick meaty fingers of his left hand were wrapped around the handle of a black bag, a doctor's bag, just like in the movies. His right hand held what looked like an overnight bag.

Dani covered her mouth to hold in a nervous giggle; it surprised her, bubbling up from her chest like an unexpected belch.

"My goodness," she said, "it looks like you're moving in."

He was still smiling as he said, "Only for the night."

Dr. Krusadian moved forward, turning his bulk slightly and easing through the doorway shoulder first.

Horrified by the thought of being in his way, Dani stumbled backward, gasping so suddenly she choked and coughed.

Dr. Krusadian put his bags down, took off his coat and hat and handed them to her, then closed the door behind him.

And locked it.

Without taking her eyes from him, Dani draped his coat over a chair and put down his hat.

"And where is Mr. Campbell this evening?"

Dani stammered before she finally got her reply out of her mouth; she was suddenly very, *very* uncomfortable.

"He's in the living room."

"Well, why don't we join him." He gave a little half-bow as he picked up his bags and said, "After you."

She was reluctant to turn her back on him but walked quickly and didn't stop until she was standing beside Richard's recliner.

Richard folded up the paper and started to stand but froze with hands on the armrests, elbows jutting and shoulders hunched, frowning at the doctor's suitcase. He muttered, "What… what're you…"

"Mr. Campbell? I am Dr. Krusadian." He put his bags down again, filling the room with his smile. "I've come to help."

12.

Dr. Krusadian lifted his cup of cafe mocha from the kitchen table to his lips, which were waiting, stuck out and puckered, as if he were about to whistle. He sipped carefully, loudly, eyes closed and sausage pinky delicately cocked.

Richard stood by the refrigerator, hands in the back pockets of his jeans, gawking at Krusadian as if the man had just come up through the floor.

When Richard realized earlier that Krusadian was planning to stay the night, he'd begun to show signs of smoldering anger that had set off alarms in Dani's head. She'd quickly suggested they go to the kitchen for coffee, hoping to hold Richard's anger back a while longer.

Now Richard was setting off her alarms again by the way he looked at Krusadian. He stepped forward and leaned against the table.

"Look," he said, "if you don't mind my asking, I'd like to know—"

"Many things, I'm sure, Mr. Campbell. But first, why don't you sit down and let me explain what we'll be doing together and perhaps that would answer some of your questions."

Dr. Krusadian's voice was creamy, rich, and his accent covered his words like a dark chocolate coating.

Dani stood by the counter watching both men. Richard didn't move and Dr. Krusadian rolled his eyes slowly upward to him.

"Sit down," he said, his big lips moving slowly around the two words and coming to rest in an expression that was almost, but not quite, congenial.

Dani and Richard each took a seat at the table.

Dr. Krusadian's cup disappeared between his mitt-like hands as he began, his words accompanied by distant thunder and rain on the windows.

"You have a problem. Both of you. *All* of you. Three people with one single problem. I am here to help you deal with it. I am here to help all three of you, but my foremost reason for coming is Jason. I will focus on your son. Through working with him, a solution will most likely… reveal itself. That has been my experience."

He sipped his drink and savored it a moment before taking it down. "You may think this presumptuous of me because we've never met, but I'm quite confident that I know exactly what you've done to your boy, Mr. and Mrs. Campbell. Oh, I'm not sure what you've done to him physically, but here—" He tapped his forehead. "—I know what you've done to him up here.

209

"They are such amazing people, children. So… *sturdy*. They have to be. They must endure so much, don't you think? Or—" He grinned, "—do you give any thought of that sort of thing? Probably not. Like so many people, you are probably too wrapped up in your own many problems to concern yourself with such a little, insignificant person. We *all* have problems. Demons, they are. Build up inside you like a sickness until you must, *some*how, expel them. But too often, they are expelled onto… *into*… the children."

Lightning flashed in the window, shining like inspiration on Krusadian's broad face.

"But they have demons, too, you know, the children," he went on. "Demons we know nothing about. We had them, too, back then, but adulthood has a way of sweeping them up and putting them away. Or dressing them up and calling them nostalgia. We remember the school bully and we smile. We forget that, back *then*, that bully was the stuff of nightmares, a dreadful monster waiting around the next corner with his fists clenched. We forget that, and the children, then, must endure it alone. And they *do* endure.

"But they must also, too often, deal with *our* demons because we *can't* endure them, we've forgotten how. So we pour them into the children, beat them in, as if we sense their strength and wish to exploit it. But, strong as they are, the children, they are not *that* strong. No one is.

"And yet, they endure somehow. For a while. Until they can no longer. And they… they change. It becomes too late. They grow up with their demons—so *many* demons—from their childhood, from their parents. And *those* demons must be expelled. So those children turn to *their* children. And it goes on and on."

He smiled at Richard warmly, sympathetically. "Perhaps you're like that, Mr. Campbell. Perhaps you've had too many demons pounded into you for too long, and now you are continuing the chain." He turned to Dani. "You, too, perhaps. I don't know yet. If that is the case, you have my sympathies. I grieve for your pain. But." His smile evaporated and his face became stern, hard. "That is irrelevant. You are *adults* now. You're all grown *up*. You should know better. My concern now is with Jason. Which is why I am here. The chain breaks with *me*. Here and now."

Dr. Krusadian sipped his cafe mocha, put down the cup, and sat very straight and stiff.

Dani chilled.

Suddenly, Dr. Krusadian meant business; the small talk was over and he seemed to be rolling up his sleeves in his mind.

"My job," he said, "is to remove from Jason all of the demons you have inflicted upon him. They are ugly, I promise you. Hideous. Once I have removed them—if I *can*, that is, but I have confidence—once I have done that, do you know what I'm going to do next?" He smiled, tapping a thick finger on the table and turning looking back and forth between the two of them. "After I have removed your son's demons, I am going to *show* them to you. And I promise you this: you will learn from them." He took another loud sip. "It usually takes only one night, but each case is different and I will work at whatever pace I deem necessary. During that time—by the way, Mr. Campbell, what is your occupation?"

"I'm… uh, I'm a contractor. My company, we, uh, built this neighborhood. Galaxy Heights."

"How nice for you. And you?" He turned to Dani and hiked one thick brown high over his right eye.

"Nothing. I mean, um, I'm a housewife."

"Fine. Tomorrow is Saturday. If it will be necessary for you to go to work tomorrow, Mr. Campbell, you will have to make arrangements to be away from the office. Until we are finished

211

here, neither of you will go anywhere or see anyone. Is that understood?"

"Hold it," Richard said, raising his palms. "Just… *hold* it." He stood and began to pace.

From the way he was chewing on his lips, Dani could tell he was trying very hard to temper his words, and she was somewhat relieved.

He said, "I was willing to cooperate with whatever, uh, counsel Dr. Saunders saw fit. Whatever problems we may have, I don't think they're as serious as Dr. Saunders makes them out, but I figured it couldn't hurt to, you know, talk to someone. Besides that, Saunders didn't give me much choice. But… Jesus, this is just… you can't just barge into my house, just move *in* like this, and tell me I can't even go to work—I mean, that's our *living.* How do you think I'm gonna *pay* you? I'm… well, I'm sorry, Dr. Krusadian, but I don't like the way you work. I'm very uncomfortable with you. I'd like to cooperate, I really would, but… I can't. Not like this. I'm gonna have to ask you to leave."

Dani was moved. She knew how difficult it was for Richard to remain so calm and speak so eloquently. She found herself actually feeling proud of him and thinking that maybe things weren't so bad after all, maybe they *could* change.

Dr. Krusadian had listened carefully to Richard, sitting straight in his chair, one hand over his cup. A few seconds after Richard stopped talking, the doctor said, "Are you finished?"

"Yes. As far as I'm concerned, this *conversation* is finished."

Dr. Krusadian nodded. "First of all, unlike Dr. Saunders, I take no payment for my services. None. This is not my business. It is my calling." He looked beyond Richard and eyed an open bottle of wine on the counter. "Also unlike Dr. Saunders—" He scraped his chair backward and stood and the room seemed to darken. "—I am giving you no choice whatsoever. You will cooperate with me fully."

The doctor moved forward and Richard, wide eyed, scooted quickly out of his way.

"If you do not," Krusadian continued, lifting the bottle and sniffing with disapproval, "I will notify the proper authorities. I will not waste my time with the police or the county or the state, nothing like that." He turned the bottle over and wine gurgled into the sink. "I will notify… the *proper*… authorities." Holding the bottle, he turned to Richard. "I will, in fact, Mr. Campbell, come down upon this household like the iron fist of God and you will regret the day your mother opened her legs for your father."

Richard clenched his fists, eyes darting between the empty bottle and Krusadian's face, as if trying to decide which outraged him more.

"Dani," he growled, "call the police."

"If you call the police, Mrs. Campbell, they will come. But when they leave, it will not be I who leaves with them. They will take away your husband, I assure you, accompanied by flashing red and blue lights that will attract the attention of everyone in the neighborhood." He turned to Richard. "Within hours, everyone you know as well as God knows *how* many total strangers will be aware of your dirty little secret. That does not, of course, include all of the newspaper articles and court appearances. All very public. And, if your luck is especially sour, perhaps Geraldo Rivera will decide to do a live prime time special on child abuse and one night after you're out on bail, he will burst into your bedroom with cameras and—"

"All *right*, Jesus *Christ*, all *right!*" Richard screamed, hitting empty air with down swinging fists. He went on quietly, taking shallow staccato breaths between his words. "All right, all… right, all… right…"

"That *is* what concerns you most, isn't it, Mr. Campbell? That others might find out? What you do? In your home at night?"

Dani was shocked to see Richard's shoulders hitching with sobs. He turned his back to her and leaned his forehead against the refrigerator door and cried quietly.

Dr. Krusadian put his hand on Richard's back; the hand engulfed an entire shoulder blade. The gesture was sympathetic; his voice was not.

"Do it my way," he said, "and no one knows. No one but us."

Richard did not respond, but Dr. Krusadian nodded as if he had.

"First," the doctor said, "under no circumstances are either of you to question anything I do at any time. Ever. Now, we will empty all of these." He handed the bottle to Dani. "Every swallow of alcohol you have in the house goes into the sink. We don't need it."

Numbed and walking through a stranger's dream, Dani took the bottle, went to the wine cupboard, and removed all the others.

Dr. Krusadian asked Richard, "Do you have a basement?"

Richard moved away from the refrigerator rubbing his eyes. "What... what has that got to do with—"

"I believe you are about to ask a question, Mr. Campbell. Don't. It is against the rules, remember? Now. A basement?"

Richard led him to the back of the kitchen to the basement door.

Opening the door, the doctor reached in, flicked on the light, and peered down the stairs. "Mm-hm. Fine." He closed the door and smiled at them. "Just fine. Now, why don't you introduce me to Jason?"

Dani stepped away from the sink, suddenly on guard. It struck her all at once; they weren't going to get rid of him, this strange and frightening man was going to *stay*, and worst of all, he was going to be alone with Jason. She was about to protest when Richard spoke.

"Is there... anything else you want to tell us? Doctor?"

Krusadian grinned. "One more thing. If either of you raise a hand to the boy while I'm here I'll kill you. Both of you if necessary. Now." He gestured gallantly toward the kitchen door and took one step backward. "After you."

13.

He'll terrify Jason, Dani thought as she followed the boy downstairs.

Jason wore his ALF pajama bottoms and a T-shirt Dani had cut to fit over his cast.

Dr. Krusadian was standing at the fireplace, hands joined behind his back as he looked down his broad nose at the pictures on the mantle.

The gurgling of bottles being emptied into the sink came from the kitchen.

In the living room, Dani said, with the slightest tremble in her voice, "Jason, this is Dr. Krusadian."

The doctor turned quickly, spread his arms, and grinned enormously.

"Jason!" he said as if greeting an old friend. "How nice to meet you. I see you've been to the Land of Disney." He waved toward the picture. "You must tell me all about it. I've never been." He quickly moved to Jason's side and leaned forward, putting his arm around the boy, leading him to the sofa.

Dr. Krusadian seemed a different person suddenly, sparkling and animated, almost... childlike. As far as Dani could tell, there was no fat beneath his black suit. Nothing shifted or jiggled when he moved; his body was concrete.

"Wait right here for me, Jason," he said. "I'll be with you in a moment. I have something for you. We'll have a grand time together." Krusadian lifted his head, dropped his smile, and bellowed, "Mr. Campbell? Time to go upstairs."

Richard came from the kitchen. "What?"

"Come." Krusadian went to his black bag and removed two things: a golden box the size of an average alarm clock and a small metallic object that chittered when he dropped it into his suitcoat pocket. He went up the stairs and, after exchanging a quick, unsettled glance, Dani and Richard followed.

"You listen to the doctor, honey," Dani said over her shoulder as she climbed, not really meaning it. Tears were burning in her throat and she wanted to tell Jason he didn't have to listen to a goddamned thing that black monster said, but—

—*I'll kill you. Both of you if necessary*—

—she knew she couldn't do that.

"You listen to him," she repeated, stopping on the stairs to look at her son, so small on the big sofa below, "but… if you want me, honey, you… you just holler. 'Kay?"

He nodded and looked away.

Dr. Krusadian stopped outside their bedroom and faced them, gestured to the door and said, "After you." He didn't look inside to see if it was a bedroom; he just… knew.

He followed them in.

Richard leaned on the dresser with both hands, watching Krusadian in the mirror.

Dani sat on the bed, craving a drink. But they were all gone, every drop. She remembered some Valium in an unmarked bottle in their bathroom medicine cabinet and turned her eyes to the door, to the rectangular mirror over the bathroom sink, deciding to take one of the pills when Krusadian left them alone, even if she had to chew it dry.

The doctor stood before her, swallowing her field of vision, and said, "Mrs. Campbell, will you please give to me all of the pills and any other consciousness altering drugs you have in this room." It was not really a request.

Dani said, "But I don't... well, we don't keep any—"

"Don't make me look for them." He looked around the messy room distastefully. The bed was unmade and clothes and underwear were strewn over the floor. "I wouldn't particularly care to do that."

She went to the bathroom shaking, still fighting tears, and got the pills. She considered keeping a couple—just a couple— even dropped them into her quivering hand, but—

—*I'll kill you*—

—she knew she couldn't do that, either.

Dr. Krusadian dropped the little bottle into his pocket and held out his hand again, saying curtly, "The cannabis. I can smell it."

"The-the-the—"

"Mari-juanaaaa."

Vision blurring, she went to the dresser, nudged Richard aside, opened the top drawer and got the little plastic bag of grass, muttering, "My God, Jesus, Jesus Christ..." It was just a little bit, not even an eighth, and they only smoked on the weekends, not even *every* weekend, and it was so *old*, hardly had any aroma at *all*, how could he *possibly*—

"Thank you." Into the pocket. He put the gold box on the corner of the dresser. "A music box, in case you would like some music. I am going to work with Jason for a while." He went to the door. "You two... work with each other."

They stared at him blankly.

217

"In other words, Mr. and Mrs. Campbell... talk." He grinned. "Just... *talk* for a while." After he pulled the door closed, there was a brief insect-like chittering sound on the other side, metallic, as if he were tapping two spoons to the door.

Then he was gone.

Richard looked at her as if to say, *What the hell was that?* then crossed the room and tried the door. The knob turned, but the door wouldn't budge.

"Jesus Christ!" he barked, pounding the door with a fist. "He locked the—" He spun on her, glaring, "—can you believe this? He locked the goddamned door!"

"Richard..."

He began to pace. "We're locked in our own goddamned bedroom!"

"Richard..."

"How did he *do* it? He must've put a—"

"Richard, maybe we should—"

"Shut up. Just shut up, okay? I don't want to talk. I just... I just want... I want a *drink*, is what I want." He turned on the nine-inch color television on his nightstand and first sat on the bed, then laid back, hands locked behind his head. "I just... don't want to talk," he sighed.

Dani went to the bathroom to find the Maalox; her stomach was rebelling, shooting great bursts of flames up into her throat. She heard the roar of a crowd coming from the television; Richard was watching some sports event. She wished she could lose herself in something so easily.

When she found the Maalox, the bedroom door burst open and she quickly left the bathroom to find Dr. Krusadian in the room again, staring with burning disapproval at the television.

"This will never do," he said, crossing the room. He picked up the set, jerked the cord from the wall, and started back out.

"Son of a bitch!" Richard shouted, shooting to his feet. "That's it, I mean, that is really *it!* You can't—"

The television flew across the room. Dani did not see Dr. Krusadian throw it, just saw it miss Richard's head by spare inches and hit the wall with a thick pop. Glass shards sang together in chaotic harmony as they scattered and fell. The back of the set came off when it hit the floor.

Richard stood swaying in the middle of the room, then lowered himself to the bed.

Dani blinked again and again, hoping she'd imagined it. She hadn't.

"Do you have a question, Mr. Campbell?" Dr. Krusadian's voice made Dani's teeth vibrate and ache as if they were being drilled.

Richard stared, swallowing frantically again, as if something had caught in his throat.

"There is much to be done," the doctor said. "You have no time for television."

He pulled the door closed.

Locked it from the other side.

Dani heard the soft thumps of his footsteps on the carpet fade down the hall.

From downstairs, she heard him laugh, "Jason, my boy, alone at last!"

In the bathroom again, Dani didn't bother with the small measuring cup she usually used; she took three generous swigs of the thick chalky liquid straight from the bottle and waited for it to dowse the fire in her gut.

Before it had the chance, she threw it back up.

14.

Jason heard the television implode.

He remembered a man who spoke on career day at school last month, a television repairman named Buddy. He talked about all the things a television repairman is required to know and do in his work and Jason remembered Alicia Brandstetter—a mean, sour-faced girl—asking what would happen if you kicked the television screen really hard, like she wanted to do last week when a newscaster came on to show pictures of the president going on some stupid trip to Russia right in the middle of *Thundercats*. Buddy said it wouldn't just crack or break open, it would implode. That, he explained, was the opposite of exploding; the picture tube would blow inward on itself instead of out because it had a vacuum inside.

At first, Jason was confused, wondering how anyone could possibly get a clunky old vacuum into a television screen, but Buddy explained that a vacuum wasn't something Mom used to clean the carpet.

A vacuum was nothing.

Absolutely nothing.

A television's picture tube, according to Buddy, is so empty that the emptiness is *hungry*, so desperate to be filled that, if its shell were cracked, it would collapse on itself, violently sucking in as much air as it could take.

Jason often imagined himself inside a giant picture tube. He imagined that he actually *was* a vacuum, not just inside one, because that would be impossible. No one—nothing—could be inside a vacuum.

A vacuum was nothing.

Absolutely nothing.

He sometimes wondered what an implosion would sound like. Somehow he knew—he wasn't sure how or why, he just *knew*—that the sound from upstairs was exactly that.

Someone had thrown his dad's little television set.

Probably his dad.

But in front of company? That was odd.

He didn't think about it, though. Instead, he thought about picture tubes and vacuums and implosions as thunder purred like a jungle cat and lightning peeked in the windows.

"Jason, my boy! Alone at last. Forgive my tardiness," Dr. Krusadian said as he came slowly down the stairs shaking his head. "You must never listen to people who criticize you too harshly for occasionally breaking or forgetting the rules. Even parents sometimes, I'm terribly sorry to report, forget them. Break them. Ignore them. No one is perfect."

Never in his life had Jason seen a human being so big. Or so black. His cheeks shined like black apples.

He effortlessly pulled the recliner around so it faced Jason and sat down, leaning forward.

"Jason, do you know why I've come?"

Jason didn't know exactly, but he knew it was big and important. He'd heard shouting when he was upstairs in his bedroom. When he finally realized that it was a stranger shouting—well, not shouting, exactly, but speaking in a very loud, threatening voice—at his dad, and his dad wasn't breaking things up in the living room, he knew something was up. But he didn't let on that he knew; he was afraid his dad would get angry about it later if he did.

"To talk about my arm?" Jason replied.

"Yes, to talk. With you. I've come to talk about lots of things. Like that picture." He turned to the Disneyland picture on the mantle. "I'd like to talk about that. Yes... yes, I would." Dr. Krusadian looked at the picture as if he were looking out a window at something beautiful and a smile spread over his face like warmth over a cold windowpane. "Must be a wonderful place, Disneyland."

"I had fun," Jason lied.

"Is it big?"

Jason nodded.

"A place where everyone can be a child. Mmm. Must be absolutely delightful."

Jason nodded again, only slightly this time, lowering his gaze to his broken arm. He could feel Dr. Krusadian looking at him.

"But there's one thing I don't understand, Jason. About that picture. How is it that a boy like you could go to such a place—a gigantic land made up of fairytales and pirate ships and trips to outer space—and spend one tiny little second without a joyous smile on his face? You're not smiling, Jason."

There was another cavernous silence.

"You don't look like you were having fun."

The silence of a vacuum.

"Were you? Having fun?"

No reply.

"I don't think so. But if you don't want to talk about it yet, that's perfectly all right. Do you like music?"

"Uh-huh."

"Good. I have something for you." Dr. Krusadian went to his black bag and removed a white cardboard box shaped like a big cube. He sat down again and put the box on the coffee table. "Powerful thing, music. *Magic.* It can make you happy, make you cry. Some makes you angry, some relaxed and soothed. I don't know what I would do without music. How about you?"

"I like music."

"Of course you do. All children do. They have to. Because sometimes it isn't easy to be children, is it?"

Jason didn't speak, but he looked up at Dr. Krusadian finally. He could tell by the darkness in the man's eyes that he already knew the answer to that question.

He *knew.*

"Music has always been my refuge," the doctor said. "I turn to music for comfort, for protection. I put music into my life the way one puts a bandage on a wound so the wound can heal. Like that cast on your arm. It's there to protect your arm while it gets better. Sometimes," he whispered, "I wrap my whoooole life in music. Like a broken arm in a great big cast." He spread his arms before him as if embracing a huge cast. "Have you ever done that, Jason?"

Jason gave that careful thought and realized he'd never done anything of the kind. It made him feel bad, that realization, because he'd *felt* that way before, lots of times: like a great big wound that needed bandaging.

"No," Jason said, "but... I know what you mean."

"I thought you might. What is *your* refuge, Jason?"

He chewed his lip while he thought about it.

At first, he was going to say his bedroom, but that wasn't true. When his door was closed, his dad just came in anyway, sometimes even kicked the door open without bothering to turn the knob. He'd broken two locks that way.

Jason had a lot of books in his room and sometimes turned to them for comfort and diversion. He didn't have as many as he used to, though, not enough to call them his refuge. If his dad ever caught him reading when he wanted Jason to pay attention to his shouting and hitting, he usually swiped the book from Jason's hands and ripped it into three or four pieces.

Feeling lost, Jason looked up at Dr. Krusadian and, sounding surprised, whispered, "I don't have one."

The doctor's face fell. "I am truly sorry to hear that, Jason. But—" He held a finger, "—that is why I am here."

Dr. Krusadian reached into the box and removed what looked, at first, like a gold-colored ball with fascinating intricate designs carved into its smooth surface.

But it wasn't a ball because it had a little stand attached to the bottom with tiny legs to stand on.

When he spoke again, Dr. Krusadian's voice was quiet, secretive.

"Different music does different things, Jason. Some music is meant to make you dance, while other music will put you to sleep." As he spoke, the doctor opened his other bag and removed a heavy black tarpaulin folded into a square. Standing, he pulled the coffee table back a few feet and began spreading the tarpaulin over the carpet in front of the sofa. "Music like that—dance music, lullabies—fills you up. It puts something inside you. Do you understand, Jason?"

"I think so," Jason said as Dr. Krusadian took a long sturdy rope from his bag and began threading it through brass rings in the corners of the tarpaulin.

"Some music, however, does the exact opposite." He sat in the recliner again, still speaking softly, his twinkling eyes holding Jason's attention. "Instead of filling you up, some music lets *you*... fill *it* up... with anything you wish. Does that make any sense to you, Jason?"

It didn't, really, and Jason frowned at Dr. Krusadian.

"Perhaps it would be best to simply show you." The doctor touched the globe gently with a fingertip. "This is a music box. Of sorts. A very *special* music box. This music does not give you anything. Doesn't make you want to dance or sing. This music... *takes*. It takes whatever you need to get rid of, Jason, whatever you need to let go of. But before I play it for you—and this is important—I must tell you that it is to remain our secret. Ours alone. You must never tell a soul. Not even your parents. Promise?"

His eyes wide with fascination, Jason nodded.

"Now," Dr. Krusadian whispered, placing a big hand on the globe, "listen."

When he lifted his hand, the globe began to turn very slowly and Jason noticed something startling.

There was another globe inside, turning in the opposite direction.

And inside *that* globe was *another*, turning in the direction of the first.

Each had minute designs carved into them, as the outer globe did: wiggly openings, round ones, triangular ones, all passing one another with each revolution, giving the illusion of movement.

The openings seemed to blink like eyes...

The globe appeared to breathe with life...

And its music began to play...

For a moment, it sounded nothing like music at all. It sounded instead like the cracking of wood, the slow falling of a great tree in the distance. Then other sounds joined in: a high, wistful pinging, a gut-deep thrum, a hollow, mournful whistle...

They blended, the eerie sounds, locking together like cogs until they were one single, unified sound. Achingly beautiful music bled from the rotating globes and embraced Jason, held him like a guardian angel...

Stroking him...

Rocking him...

"Isn't it beautiful?" Dr. Krusadian asked.

His deep resonant voice reached Jason's ears as if from a long distance. The boy's gaze was held firmly by the spinning globes but, peripherally, he could see Dr. Krusadian rise to his feet and walk to one of the room's four shining lamps.

"The music is forever changing," he whispered as he clicked the lamp off.

The room dimmed slightly.

"And the globes never remain the same... do they?"

225

Click.

Dimmer still.

Lightning fluttered in the windows like playful ghosts.

"The music is waiting, Jason. Waiting for you to decide what to give it. If you listen carefully... if you'll watch closely..."

Click.

"... sometimes you'll... *see* things..."

Another click and the murky darkness fell unnoticed around Jason.

"... pictures... some pretty... some not. Lie down, Jason."

He did, still watching the globes. He wasn't sure, but... Jason *thought*... he saw something inside... something glowing, pulsing, blinking a bluish white inside Dr. Krusadian's music box.

Sitting down again, the doctor whispered, "Watch closely. Look inside, Jason... *deeeep* inside... and perhaps you'll see them, too..."

As Jason stared intensely, he began to feel sleepy, groggy, like he had just before having his tonsils removed.

Then the pictures began...

15.

After the volcano in her stomach began to subside, Dani drank some more Maalox and fought to keep it down.

Richard was sprawled on the bed staring at the ceiling. His eyes appeared glazed, dead.

Dani listened for noise from downstairs, but heard nothing.

"He's gonna pay for that fucking set," Richard croaked. "He doesn't *know* it yet, but he's going to."

When Richard wasn't talking and the thunder was still, the room was so silent Dani could hear her blood flowing.

"We won't say anything right now," Richard went on. "Well just go on with him while he's here. Cooperate quietly."

Dani stood in the bathroom doorway looking around the room for something. A book, a magazine. Anything to take her mind off of... *everything*.

The music box caught her eye.

"But as soon as that son of a bitch is gone, I'm gonna sue his fat nigger ass from here to the goddamned Second Coming, you just *wait*."

She ignored him. He wasn't talking to her, anyway; he was talking to himself, the way he so often did.

Dani sat in her chair at the dresser and studied the box, frowning.

There were holes in the gold-colored cube, finely carved holes of all different shapes and sizes.

The more she looked at it, the more beauty she saw in its patterns and the more she realized that—

—there was something *inside*.

"We'll call that other doctor—what's his name?—Saunders. Find out a little more about this asshole. Not gonna throw *my* - fuckin' television at me and get away with it." He was beginning to sound sleepy. "Honey, turn the light off, will you?"

Dani didn't hear him. She was trying to figure out the shape of the object inside the cube. It looked like... maybe... a pyramid carved with more intriguing curlicues and squiggles...

"Dani? Dammit, Danielle, will you turn the god—" He got off the bed. "Okay, I'll get the goddamned light."

The sudden darkness startled Dani from her concentration. A small yellowed nightlight in the shape of a daisy was plugged into the outlet above the dresser, always there, glowing day and night. It came alive in the darkness, shedding a pool of dull yellow light onto the dresser.

Onto the cube.

It shined a hazy gold, like sunlight filtering through heavy, dirty clouds.

"I'm gonna take a nap" Richard said. "Wake me up when that bastard comes back." He rolled onto his side and mumbled into his pillow. "Locking us in our bedroom… moving into our fucking house… Jeee-zus."

Dani's stomach began to burn again. It had eaten the Maalox, sucked it up, and now was chewing on itself again like a mad animal caught in a trap. She leaned forward, hugging her stomach, and belched Sulphur as she looked at the box.

Thinking…

That was her problem; she couldn't stop thinking…

About Jason: one year old and giggling in his highchair, pink round face splotched with applesauce.

That image came often, always turning up the fire in her gut, fueling it with… what? Sorrow? A feeling of loss? Both of those, she knew, and something else, the worst of all.

Guilt.

Because that was the last time she could remember Jason laughing, really laughing through a genuine grin. She'd tried to remember others, but couldn't. That was the last.

It was easy to think Jason's laughter stopped when their drinking—their *nightly* drinking—started, but maybe not. Maybe the drinking came after, in an attempt to silence the constant shouting.

That, she decided, *is when Jason's laughter went away. When the shouting started.*

The shouting was one thing, but the *hitting*… It was the hitting that had done so much damage.

No, a voice said, a guttural fiery breath voice in her stomach, the damage came when the hitting didn't stop. And why didn't the hitting stop?

She scrubbed her face with her hands, trying to reroute her thoughts.

Why, Dani? Why didn't it stop?

"I tried," she breathed into a curled fist.

Coward.

"No."

Coward.

"I tried... once..."

Once wasn't enough, was it?

"But... I did... *try*...

Her head dropped heavily and she put both hands on the cube and—

—it came alive.

Dani gasped and jerked her hands away.

But it was too late...

16.

"Do you see the pictures, Jason?"

"Mmm... hmmm..." His eyelids were stones and his body was turning to warm smooth milk and soaking into the sofa. But he never took his eyes from the globes within globes... from the tiny pictures that flashed from the holes and were magnified for an instant in his head.

"Can you see the pictures, Jason?"

"Uh... huh..."

"Good. I... I would like you to do a favor for me, Jason."

"Wha... ?"

"I'd like you to look for particular pictures for me. Will you do that for me, Jason?"

"'kay."

"Find for me the last time you remember being happy. Truly... *truly* happy. Can you do that?"

He looked. Searched. The pictures flashed through his mind like a slideshow being projected on the side of a moving roller-coaster until—

—there.

Jason willed the picture to stay in his mind, in focus.

The globes stopped turning, just held, and the picture grew bright, vivid, *real*, and—

—Jason slipped his right thumb in his mouth.

"How old are you, Jason?"

He started to reply, but speech was now a distant memory that took a moment to recapture.

"Don't... know..."

"Can you hold up fingers for me?"

Jason's fingers wagged slowly, stopped, then disappeared, tucked beneath his chin, giving up.

"Where are you?"

"Kitchen."

"What are you doing?"

"Eating. Nummies. Ap... applesau... ap..."

"Applesauce?"

He nodded. "Mommy's... laughing. Feeding me."

"Mommy's happy?"

Another nod.

"Where's Daddy?"

"Work. Home soon."

"Find Daddy in the picture, Jason."

Jason frowned, listened.

He heard the front door open, heard Daddy's footsteps.

"Daaa-*eee!*" he cooed.

"Is he home?"

"Just came in."

Jason's smile disappeared; he pulled his thumb from his mouth. This, he knew somehow, was the bad part, like the monster finally coming into the light in a scary movie. He didn't want to look, but the picture remained inside his head, held by the globe, vividly superimposed over the dark living room.

"He's... he's gonna..."

Goddamned son of a bitch Steevers... at work... fucking idiot doesn't know what the hell he's doing... we got any wine?

"He's mad," Jason said.

Mommy said, but it's only five—

I don't give a damn what time it is, goddammit.

A fist slammed the table.

Jason started, bumping the little jar with the baby's face on it.

The jar shattered on the floor, sending small gobs of applesauce through the kitchen.

Daddy's foot crunched some glass.

Son of a bitch, *that little*—

Daddy's fist flew—

—hit Jason's chair—

—and the world tilted.

"Falling! Daddy h-hit... the ch-*chair! Falling!*" Jason screamed.

"Not really. It's okay, Jason, it's—"

His body jolted on the sofa when he—

—hit the floor, bumped his head, and screamed—

—*Jason! Oh,* God, *Richard, what did you*—

—*Well, look at this, it went right through my goddamned shoe, the little*—

"Daddy's... hurt. Glass with... blood. He's showing me... screaming because ... I hurt Daddy. I cut him." Jason's arm flew up in front of his face. "No, Daddy, no, *nooo!*"

The entire sofa jerked with each invisible blow as Jason screamed...

... then cried...

… then whimpered as thunder growled.

Jason tried to focus on his faint, dark surroundings, tried to look through the images projected over them, but something else directed his attention away from them. He felt something leave him, felt a pull, then a silent, internal fear, like a tooth being pulled slowly from its socket and—

—something moved beside the sofa between Jason and the doctor with a thick, liquidy slushing sound, making the tarpaulin on the floor crackle softly.

"It's all right, Jason," Dr. Krusadian whispered as lightning X-rayed the room. "It's gone. You've let go of it. Gotten rid of it. It's gone. Just close your eyes for a while and relax."

He did, and for a few honey-thick moments, Jason slept…

The pyramid inside the cube began to turn and something inside glowed softly and Dani shook her head whispering, "No… I tried… I *did* try…" The dark bedroom became a ghost and she was suddenly on the stairs hurrying down to the living room where Richard sat in his recliner, bottle between his thighs, the newspaper crumpled on his knees.

You hurt him, she hissed, *goddamn you*, Richard, *you* hurt *him*. He ignored her.

Dani rounded the chair and faced him, her eyes tearing with fury.

Did you hear me, Richard? You hurt his head! He's just a baby, for Christ's sake, you could've killed him!

Did I?

But you could've—

I didn't, did I?

I can't believe you're—

Just drop it. I had a shitty day and—

If you ever do that again, so help me God, I'll—

Richard's face caught fire and he exploded from the chair and swung the bottle. Wine rained over them and the bottle struck her neck. Dani went down and he began to kick her.

She clutched the edge of the dresser, feeling herself slipping from her chair. Dani *knew* she was still in her bedroom, could still *see* it, but—

—she was reliving the beating that had made her pray for death, that gave her such a clear vision of her family's future. It was the first time Richard raised a hand to her and she decided as she bled that it would be the last, if she could help it.

Richard screamed at her as he kicked and slugged and jerked on her hair, but she heard none of it. There was a strange calm inside her as she smelled her own blood, a calm brought on, perhaps, by the inevitability of it. So many times, she'd caught a glimpse of Richard's potential for violence—temper tantrums, broken dishes, a crack in the bedroom wall where he'd struck out with a fist one angry night—but she'd always turned away from it, ignored it.

She couldn't ignore it that first horrible evening he'd beaten her until death seemed a good idea.

She couldn't now, either.

Dani fell from the chair to her knees, still holding the dresser, eyes still gripped by the cube, now only faintly visible through the pictures it was showing her. She vaguely felt the floor come up and hit her in the back when she fell and her breath exploded from her lungs, but that wasn't as important as the fact that—

—Richard's fist was plummeting toward her face, a knuckled flesh-colored meteor that filled her vision and finally struck, bringing blackness and pain.

His knuckles chipped a bottom tooth and cut both her lips badly. He broke two of her ribs, the middle finger on her left hand, and cut the back of her head with his shoe, sending blood dribbling down her back.

But he wasn't finished.

Don't you ever... ever... talk to me like that again! he screamed. His face was the color of blood and his entire body quaked as he began kicking her some more. *Ever! Ever! Ever!* Dani vomited onto the living room carpet. You *don't know anything, hear me?* he screamed, circling her with clenched fists. *You don't know what's going on with me, at work, in my head. You don't know shit!*

The beating went on for an eternity; Dani passed in and out of consciousness, sometimes forgetting who was beating her. But even when confusion washed over her like fevered chills, a part of her brain remained detached from her situation and processed a series of orderly thoughts. They were thoughts about what she would do when Richard was finished and she was able to walk. She would go into Jason's room, gather him up in some warm clothes, maybe get a few things of her own, and go—

—where? She had no idea, but she couldn't stay with him. *Could* she? It would only happen again, maybe in a few days or weeks, maybe next year or the year after that, but it *would* happen again, she had no doubt. She might go to April's. Or maybe her mother's. Anywhere. And she would file for divorce immediately. And then she would—

—what? Get a job? Doing what, waitressing? Working in a 7-11? A Burger King? She had no skills. She hadn't gone to college; in fact, she'd barely gotten through high school. She and Jason would have to live on mere scrapings. Richard had always supported her well. His business was not always good—in fact, it frequently became quite rocky, and that was usually the reason for his tantrums and shouting fits—but he was a very good provider and kept her comfortably surrounded by both necessities and luxuries.

So. Maybe they could see a counselor. Weren't there shelters for battered women and children? Maybe they could go to some group therapy, or whatever people did when they had problems like this. Maybe. Maybe not.

Maybe not.

As Dani writhed on the bedroom floor and Richard slept a few feet away, she felt something move inside her, twist and turn, as if trying to... come out. It was not unlike the sensation of giving birth, but without the pain. She couldn't tell if it was something she was actually feeling, or if it was a part of the vivid, frightening vision she was having.

The sensation stopped.

The beating stopped.

She sensed Richard standing over her, heard him... *groaning.* It was the same wretched groan that had come from him after he'd kicked Jason down the stairs... the same groan that had come from him as he stood on the landing doing that horrible *thing...*

She remained on the living room floor, pain dancing over her body like some vile fanged elf, as Richard went downstairs, his miserable groan fading down the hall, finally silenced by the slam of the bedroom door.

Except she wasn't *in* the living room.

She was on the bedroom floor hugging her knees.

Dani lifted her head and looked for the blood she'd been shedding, but it wasn't there.

The room was dark and Richard was snoring.

Dani hugged herself and lay still on the floor, awaiting the return of the numbness she'd worked so long and hard to perfect, the numbness that enabled her to go on. But without alcohol, it had abandoned her.

In the stillness of the dark bedroom, Dani listened to her nerves scream.

───────────────

The foggy half-sleep that fell over Jason reminded him, vaguely, of the lead blanket the chubby man in the hospital had spread over him before taking X-ray pictures of his arm. It was heavy and cool but felt protective and safe. He managed to lift his eyelids a fraction of an inch during his odd rest; along with the room's darkness, his vision was smeared with a murky film that made the room seem filled with smoke. Even the lighting, which was actually becoming brighter and more frequent as the weather grew fierce, was dimmed to a mere flickering of pale light from outside.

Through cotton-stuffed ears, Jason heard sounds: a wet, snotty sucking, like Jell-O being scooped from a bucket; heavy plastic crackling with movement; Dr. Krusadian's puffs of exertion; the hush of something being dragged over the carpet. With a great heaving effort, Jason opened his eyes and lifted his head an inch from the sofa. Through the clouds in his eyes, he saw Dr. Krusadian pulling on the rope he'd threaded through the tarpaulin's brass rings. The dark plastic was gathered around something squat and bulbous and heavy that slid with each pull of the doctor's big arms.

And within the plastic, something moved.

"Rest, Jason," Dr. Krusadian whispered. "Just close your eyes and rest."

Jason was far too weary to ask the question that wriggled just behind his lips. He let his head fall back on the cushion and felt himself disappear into the air like a rising cloud of vapor.

17.

When Jason opened his eyes again, he was aware that some time had passed, but had no idea how much.

The room was still dark. Dr. Krusadian was at his side once again, hands joined between his knees, elbows resting on his thighs. His teeth gleamed within the broad frame of his smile and he asked, "How do you feel, Jason?"

"Fine. I guess." He wasn't sure. Of *anything*. He scanned his memory for something—he wasn't sure *what*—but came up with only fleeting blurred images and the vaguest of sounds. When he saw the globe, though, something fell into place, dowsing his apprehension.

Dr. Krusadian put his hand on the globe and whispered, "Ready?"

He nodded, even though he couldn't quite remember what he was ready for.

The music began.

Haziness overcame him.

And the pictures returned.

Dani moved her arm first, sliding it over the carpet to push herself up, and her hand slipped through a thin coating of cool slimy wetness.

Did I throw up? she wondered, rising to her knees and brushing her palm over the carpet again. The glow from the daisy nightlight above the dresser wasn't enough for her to see what was on the floor, so she reached up and flipped a switch on the wall. The light in the walk-in closet before her came on; the louvered door was open a crack and light striped the carpet.

Dani squinted down at the glistening strip of moisture and reached for it again to touch it, smell it, but something moved within the closet and she jerked her hand back and slapped it to her chest, staring open-mouthed through the two inch opening.

The doorjamb was wet; a drop of clear gelatinous fluid dribbled down to the carpet.

Dani leaned closer to the closet and peered inside, her eyes wandering below the hanging clothes to the dark places where tennis racquets and shoe boxes and rolls of decorous wrapping paper leaned in the shadows.

And something else.

Something wet and puffy, the color of drying semen.

It moved with the sound of phlegm being sucked through a straw, sloshing out of the shadows toward her and Dani threw herself forward, slamming the door and holding it shut with her weight as she screamed.

"Where are you now, Jason?"

"My bedroom."

"What are you doing?"

"Hiding. Daddy's screaming again."

"Why is he screaming?"

"I don't know."

"Where is he?"

"Downstairs. He's... no, wait, he's..." Jason's voice became a trembling whisper as he listened to his father's bitter, drunken shouting growing louder. Closer. "... he's coming up *stairs!* Up *here!*"

The bedroom door slammed open and Jason saw his father standing in the doorway holding a G.I. Joe action figure in one hand and a toy Jeep in the other.

You know where I found these? he bellowed. *On the living room floor, that's where. You know how I found them? I nearly broke my goddamned ankle, that's how!*

He stormed across the room toward Jason, dropping the toys, and Mom appeared in the doorway behind him. She leaned heavily against the doorjamb, her head falling to one side like a rag doll's.

Jason was relieved to see her, certain she would intercede, hoping she would be able to somehow dampen his father's anger. But the sadness and utter helplessness in her face told him otherwise. She looked at Jason with a pain in her eyes he'd never seen before but would see many times after that, a pain that made him ache; then she turned her gaze to her husband and Jason saw surrender.

She disappeared down the hall and his father's fists began their work.

Jason began to scream pleas for mercy as his body jolted on the bed, bouncing as if receiving electrical shocks. He felt no actual pain, but seeing his father's fists falling on him again and again filled him with such terror that he screamed and writhed as if in agony.

Through his father's roared epithets and battering fists, through his own ragged cries, Jason heard two things: the messy slurping sound he'd heard earlier and his mother screaming from far away, "Let me out! Let me out of here, please! Plee-heeeze!"

They were screaming in the Campbell house again...

When the music stopped and the brutal vision faded, Jason opened his sleepy eyes to see Dr. Krusadian once again dragging the bulky tarpaulin out of the living room.

"You just relax, Jason," the doctor said as the thing in the tarpaulin squirmed wetly. "You relax and... back in... few minutes... we'll..."

His voice faded as Jason slept. But even in his sleep, he could hear his mother screaming.

18.

"Jesus *Christ*, Dani, what're you screaming about?" Richard rose clumsily from the bed as Dani slammed a chair against the closet door. "What the hell is—"

"There's something in the closet."

"What?"

"Something's in the *closet*, I *saw* it, it *moved!*"

"Oh, Christ, Dani, you're drunk." He started for the closet, reaching for the chair.

"No! Please, Richard, don't open it!" She stepped in front of him and put her hands on his chest, closing them over his shirt desperately. "Please."

He rolled his eyes and pushed her aside.

Dani gripped his arm and pulled hard, snapping, *"No!"*

With the speed of the lightning that brightened the windows, Richard spun and slapped her face hard, knocking her onto the bed as—

—something clattered in the closet, rattling the door against the chair and—

—with a brief metallic clicking, the bedroom door opened and Dr. Krusadian glared at them in an electric flash of lightning and the thunder that followed could have been his voice.

"What is it?" Dani screamed at him. "What have you done? *What the hell is it?*"

"Leave the room," he said, his voice level but deadly. "Now. No questions."

Dani ignored his words and shouted again, "What is it? What have you—"

Dr. Krusadian's lips pulled back over his teeth and his voice hit the walls of the room like a wrecking ball.

"Leave! This! *Roooom!*"

The thing in the closet threw itself against the door and the wooden chair crackled weakly, preparing to give way.

Dani stopped breathing and wrung her hands at her chest as she looked at Richard. His face was blank.

Dr. Krusadian gave them room to pass and Richard left the room first with Dani behind him, not wanting to be separated. A tightly rolled length of barbed wire was unrolling itself in her stomach slicing her insides to shreds.

In the hall, she could still hear the closet door being rammed from the inside and she wanted to run screaming from the house.

Krusadian stopped outside the bathroom between Jason's room and theirs. He opened the door and gestured for them to enter.

They did so without question.

Krusadian closed the door and locked them in without comment.

Richard sat on the edge of the bathtub, loudly grinding his teeth; anger was alive in his face now, like maggots beneath the decaying skin of a corpse's face.

"What the fuck did you do?" he growled.

"I-I-I didn't d-do *anything*, Richard! I... didn't do... anything."

He looked into her eyes and for a moment she thought he was going to hit her. Then he turned away, stood, and began to pace in the small space.

"Richard?" she whispered.

He said nothing.

"Richard?"

Impatiently: "*What?*"

Dani leaned over the toilet and threw up.

The bathroom seemed to grow much smaller as Dani and Richard waited for Dr. Krusadian to return.

Richard said nothing and, although she wanted to speak, just to break the funereal silence and cover the endless steady dripping of the sink's faucet, she said nothing either.

With no clock in the bathroom, their stay was timeless and Dani feared, after a while, that Krusadian might leave them there for the night.

Maybe he's left the house, she thought, realizing there were no sounds in the hall or from downstairs. Then the worst thought of all: *Maybe he's taken Jason with him.*

Richard sat on the tub's edge with his face in his hands, occasionally murmuring into his palms, but only to himself.

Sitting on the toilet, Dani watched him, willing him to look at her. She needed to be touched, held, reassured, but knew better than to expect those things from Richard in a time of crisis, or any *other* time. She could not remember what the touch of Richard's hands felt like; she was now only familiar with the pain of their blows.

There was a sound from their bedroom, muffled through the wall, and Dani lifted her head to listen. She recognized the rattle of the closet's louvered door being opened. Objects clattered, something thumped the wall.

"What's he doing?" she breathed, knowing she would be ignored. She stood, listened.

He left the bedroom and moved into the hall. Slowly.

Dani went to the door and cocked her head.

Dr. Krusadian was dragging something past the bathroom.

Unable to resist, she asked, "What are you doing?"

"With you in a moment," he replied, dragging... dragging...

Until he was gone.

A few moments later, she returned to the toilet and waited, only to stand again when she heard the door being unlocked from the other side. It opened and Dr. Krusadian grinned at them.

He said, "Let's take a break."

19.

In the kitchen, Dani put a mug of water in the microwave for tea as Richard drank a Coke silently at the table.

Hushed voices drifted from the living room where Dr. Krusadian was talking with Jason; he refused to let Dani or Richard see him until Krusadian had a word with Jason.

The rain sounded like battle outside.

The microwave beeped, Dani removed the mug and began dipping a tea bag in the steaming water.

"What the hell is *that?*" Richard asked, firmly but quietly, glaring across the kitchen.

Dani turned in the direction of his stare and the tea bag plopped into the mug.

There was a lock on the basement door. *Two* locks, she realized as she looked below the doorknob. They were padlocks, *enormous* brass padlocks twice the size of a man's fist, locked through hasps that had not been there earlier that evening.

Richard went to the door, jerked on the upper lock, and whispered, "Son of a bitch."

At his side, Dani touched the lock's perfectly smooth, cool surface. There was no brand name written on the lock, nothing to suggest it had been purchased in a hardware store. It was perfect and spotless, the biggest padlock she'd ever seen.

"Son of a *bitch!*" Richard repeated, louder, pounding the lock with a fist. "What the hell are these for? The *basement*, for Christ's sake."

"Remember, Richard, what he said about questions. No questions. Let's just leave it alone for now and get this over with."

"Yeah, for now. But I'm gonna sue him. Sue his black ass." He returned to the table and his Coke.

Dani looked down at the bottom lock and a glistening wetness on the floor caught her eye. It was just a thin strip on the tile, flush with the door and disappearing through the crack beneath it. She hunkered down and gingerly touched it with two fingers.

Cold and slimy. Thick.

Just like the clear sheen of gelatinous fluid on the closet doorjamb in the bedroom.

Dani wiped her fingers on the cold floor, grimacing with disgust at the feel of the substance, about to point it out to Richard, when—

—something moved deep within the basement.

Something heavy and slow.

Something that made a sound like that of a person climbing out of a bathtub full of lard.

Dani felt her insides roll over and she stood, whimpering, "Richard? Rich—"

Dr. Krusadian entered the kitchen as Dani turned and her mouth shut so suddenly that her teeth clacked together.

"Jason will be here in a moment," he said. "He may seem lethargic, quiet, a little... *different*. Don't be alarmed. My method is swift and covers a lot of ground in a short time. It can be exhausting. One negative word from either of you will force me to have him removed from this home. Do you understand?" he asked, grinning.

Richard nodded.

Dani moved her head loosely, as if she had forgotten exactly how to nod.

"Good, then. You both look very tired. Not used to being held powerless and against your will in your own home, are you? Well. Think of what Jason has endured these past nine years. Perhaps you should put on some coffee, Mrs. Campbell." Over his shoulder, Dr. Krusadian called, "Come on in, Jason."

Jason shuffled into the kitchen in the middle of a jaw cracking yawn. He smacked his lips and said, "Mom, can I have some chocolate milk?"

Dani knelt before him and touched his pale face, whispering. "Sure, sweetheart. How are you?"

His eyes darted to Dr. Krusadian and back. "Fine."

Looking up at the doctor, Dani ached to ask what he'd been doing with her son, but his narrowed eyes and cold razorblade smile told her not to.

"Chocolate milk coming up," she said, going to the refrigerator.

Dr. Krusadian cleared his throat. "Excuse me while I use the facilities. Ehhh, the sooner that coffee is ready, Mrs. Campbell, the better. We're all going to need it."

When he was gone, Dani knelt before Jason again and whispered, "Jason, listen to Mom. Does Dr. Krusadian scare you?"

He shook his head.

"Is he… well, what has he said to you? What has he done?"

"Talked. Just talked, is all. And played his music box."

"Mu… mu…" Her tongue froze. She thought of the golden cube on her dresser, the music it had played, the things she'd seen as she listened to it and, worst of all, the thing in the closet.

Dani spun her head toward the basement door so quickly, her neck popped.

Light from the overhead fluorescents glittered reflectively in the strip of slime beneath the door. She noticed more of it streaked on the doorjamb just below the knob.

Demons...

The word passed through her mind like a ghost and Dani closed her eyes a moment, searching for it again. It was something Dr. Krusadian had said earlier that evening—although it now seemed days ago—one of his annoying melodramatic proclamations.

My job is to remove from Jason all of the demons which you have inflicted upon him.

Demons...

She opened her eyes again and looked at the substance on the floor.

Demons...

Something roiled up inside her; it was not quite guilt and not just fear, but a thick acidic mixture of both that bloated her stomach and gushed through her entire body until she could smell it clogging her nostrils.

"Richard," she hissed, rushing to the table, trying to ignore her sudden dizziness. "Richard, we have to get out of here!"

His heavy-lidded eyes rolled to her slowly and he mumbled, "Shut up, Danielle."

"But Richard, he's—"

"I *told* you, I'm gonna sue his goddamned—"

"No, we have to get out of here *now*. Before it's too late."

"Too late for what?" His voice was heavy with contempt and annoyance.

"I... I don't know, Richard." Dani fought back a sob; her trembling hands fluttered up and down his arm pleadingly. "I don't know yet, but I'm telling you he's doing something horrible, I'm telling you whatever was in the closet is—"

"How is that coffee coming, Mrs. Campbell?"

Dr. Krusadian put his black bag on the table, reached in and removed a small notebook and seated himself across from Richard, opening the book with a slight flourish of his arm.

Taking a pen from his breast pocket, he began making notes, reading over the pages, and acting as if he were alone in the room.

Dani rose and got Jason's chocolate milk, unable to hold the carton or glass steady in her quaking hands.

Standing in the middle of it all, Jason turned round eyes from Krusadian to his dad to Dani and back to the doctor again, the seat of his pajama bottoms sagging, the nails of his right hand scratching nervously over the scribbled inscriptions on his cast.

When Dani gave him the chocolate milk, he whispered, "Thank you, Mom," in a voice so soft and hollow that tears stung Dani's eyes and she reached out to embrace him, but he was drinking, eyes closed, head tilted back, and a part of her heart shriveled.

She hurriedly put some coffee on, then waited for Jason to finish his chocolate milk. When he went to the sink to rinse his glass, she glanced at Dr. Krusadian, saw that he was still involved with his notes, and leaned toward Jason's ear. "Come upstairs with Mommy, sweetheart," she whispered, slipping an arm around his shoulders and leading him out of the kitchen.

She'd made a decision; she would call Dr. Saunders and, if she reached him, would tell him she thought her family was in danger at Dr. Krusadian's hand and if any harm came to them, she would see that the blame would fall on Dr. Saunders for forcing them to take the strange doctor into their home. She wanted Jason with her when she made the call; she'd also decided that she would not let him out of her sight until Dr. Krusadian was gone.

Before either Dani or Jason could step out of the kitchen, Dr. Krusadian said casually, "Jason stays with me at all times."

Dani turned to find that he hadn't even looked up from his notes. She said, "I... I was j-just going to—"

"At all times, Mrs. Campbell. You may go if you wish, but Jason does not leave my sight." He sounded distant, preoccupied with the notebook, then he looked at her and smiled. "Go on, Mrs. Campbell, it's all right. I'll let you know when it's time to go back to your room."

Dani couldn't let go of Jason; she looked down at him through her tears and saw, to her horror, that he was smiling at her.

"S'okay, Mom. I like Dr. Krusadian."

She pulled her hand away from him slowly, turned to Richard, who was staring blankly out the window at the stormy night, then Dani hurried from the kitchen and up the stairs.

In her bedroom, she looked up Dr. Saunders' number in the telephone directory, placed the call, and reached his answering service. After a few minutes of trying to impress the woman at the other end of the line that her call was urgent, Dani said, "Listen to me, please, this is not a medical emergency, it's *personal*, do you understand? If Dr. Saunders doesn't call me back immediately, he could be in a *lot* of trouble." She left her number, hung up, and sat on her bed, waiting.

The phone rang nearly ten minutes later and Dani picked up before the ring died.

"Hello?"

"Mrs. Campbell? Dr. Saunders."

"Oh, thank God. Dr. Saunders, please, you've got to help me, you've *got* to."

"What's wrong? Is it Jason?"

"No. Well, *yes*, in a way. It's actually, it's that man you sent over here, that horrible man, Dr. Krusadian. Dr. Saunders, he locked us in our *bedroom!* My husband and me, he locked us in our bedroom and just *left* us there for, Jesus, I don't know *how* long, but he was alone with Jason all that time, down in the living room, and he left this music box with us and, and —"

"Mrs. Campbell, please, hold on, just calm down, now. Okay? Just calm down."

Tears flowed freely and she sobbed loudly before she covered her mouth and took several long deep breaths. When she regained some composure, she said, "Yes. Okay. Yes."

"Now, Mrs. Campbell. What are you talking about?"

"Dr. *Krusadian.* He got here about... well, I don't know what time it is now, but he came at seven, so I guess he's been here for about—"

"Dr. who?"

Dani pressed the receiver to her ear so hard it made her head ache. "Kru... *sadian.* The doctor you sent, the doctor you *made* us see."

"Well, Mrs. Campbell, you're certainly free to see another doctor regarding your son, but if you've done so, it hasn't been at *my* recommendation."

She couldn't find her voice for a moment. "What? *What?*"

"I don't know who you're referring to, Mrs. Campbell. I've never heard of the man."

"But... but you... you-you-you—"

"Sounds like maybe you need some rest, Mrs. Campbell. If you'd like, I could prescribe some—"

"Why are you doing this?" she sobbed.

"Um, Mrs. Campbell, I'm sorry, but... look, I don't really have time for—"

"You son of a bitch, why are you *doing* this? He's here now, in my *house!* With my *son!*"

Silence.

Then: "Goodbye, Mrs. Campbell."

Dr. Saunders hung up.

Screaming behind tightly clenched lips, Dani slammed the receiver into its cradle and lay on the bed sobbing for long minutes before she picked up the telephone again. She clumsily punched 9-1-1—

—but the dial tone would not go away.

Dr. Krusadian's voice bled through the endless hum: "No phone calls, Mrs. Campbell." He was speaking on the kitchen phone. "I'm leaving the telephone off the hook."

The dial tone went on and on and on...

Dani threw the receiver down and bolted from the room, descending the stairs in a staggering run, stumbling to a halt at the front door, no longer trying to hide her sobs. They echoed through the house with the thunder as she turned the doorknob.

Only after a moment of blindly throwing herself against the sturdy door did she see it.

A padlock.

An enormous shiny brass padlock...

20.

Later—Jason had no idea how long—after his parents had been sent back to their room, Jason lost count of the times Dr. Krusadian started the globe spinning and played the music that never sounded the same twice. He lay on the sofa, the plaster cast heavy on his chest, and passed in and out of a heavy sleep each time the music stopped. Under Dr. Krusadian's gentle guidance, Jason relived incidents he'd tried so hard and so long to forget that when he experienced them again, it was like returning to an old forgotten nightmare that had disturbed his sleep long ago...

The time his dad made him sweep up a dish he'd dropped and broken in the kitchen, then beat him with the broom...

The Christmas Jason accidently broke an ornament on the tree and his dad stripped all the ornaments from the branches, cornered Jason in the living room and pelted him with the brightly colored bulbs, shattering them on his head and face and hands, inflicting small cuts that opened like new eyes and cried tears of blood...

The weekend his dad got *really* drunk, even drunker than usual, and decided Jason was being too pampered by his mother—"pussified", he called it—and spent all of Saturday and most of Sunday teaching Jason what it meant to be a man, getting drunker and drunker as he tried to make Jason cry; he pinched him and poked him and stuck him with pins, burnt him with cigarettes, plucked his eyelashes with tweezers, stomped on his feet and pulled his hair, and the moment Jason so much as allowed his lip to quiver, his dad beat him mercilessly, screaming, "This's what my pop did to *me* when I cried, and I'll be goddamned if I'm gonna do any different with you! Pussified, your mother's *pussified* you, and by Christ, I won't *have* it!" Jason was never able to stop crying that weekend and the tears lasted through the first part of the following week. The beatings stopped only because his dad finally got too drunk to stand up and make a fist...

There were others, *countless* others, and Dr. Krusadian gently led Jason through each one, touring his young past like a museum of pain and fear with exhibits that screamed, bled. And through it all, one image returned again and again: the sight of his mother cringing in the shadows or peering around a corner, looking, at first, as if she might step forward and scream for her husband to stop, might pull him off Jason and bring an end to the violence. But that look lasted only a moment and, each time, she retreated, backed away, disappeared silently to find a bottle and turn up the volume on the television set until the laughter and applause of a studio audience blanketed Jason's screams.

Always she was there, silent and watchful, looking numbed, then she was gone.

Always.

Except once…

"Can you hear me, Jason?"

"Mm-hm."

"Are you relaxed? Comfortable?"

"Mm-hm."

"Good. Now. I've noticed, Jason, that your mother is always *watching* when your father becomes violent. Is that right?"

"Al…ways."

"She never does anything else?"

He did not respond.

"Never?"

Still no reply.

"Tell me, Jason. Has your mother ever hurt you?"

Nothing.

"Ever?"

"Yes," he finally whispered, and the music began…

21.

Dani no longer felt she was in her own home. It was a replica, a decoy meant to fool her, holding in its deceptively familiar shadows and corners the things of childhood nightmares.

When they returned to their room, Dani cautiously approached the closed closet and found that the slimy substance on the doorjamb was gone.

"It was here," she muttered.

Richard sounded impatient and annoyed when he snapped, "What?"

"I swear to God, Richard, *something* was in this closet."

"You're still drunk."

"I'm *not*. Look, the carpet is still damp."

"Okay, so you threw up again. Jesus, Dani, will you give it a rest." The bed squeaked under his sudden weight and he groaned as he squeezed his head between his hands. "You said you called Saunders. What'd he say?"

"He denied it. Said he didn't *know* a Dr. Krusadian."

"What?"

She turned from the closet and faced him, hands fluttering. Her voice was a quiet midnight breeze, her sentences punctuated with quick breaths. "He's done this to us, Richard."

"Done what, Dani?" he sighed.

"Sent this man. This Krusadian. He's not a doctor, not really, I'm *sure* of it. I don't know *what* he is, but he's *not* a therapist, not like we thought. He's... wrong, Richard, there's something *wrong* with him, something *not right*, and he's come here to... to, yes, to punish us. Yes. That's it. He's come here to *punish* us, Richard."

"Punish us for *what*, for Christ's sake?"

"For what we've done all these years. For all the horrible things we've done... things I *haven't* done."

"Will you take a couple Valiums and shut—"

"There *are* no Valiums, Richard. There's no wine and no pot. Don't you see, there's *always* a Valium or a drink or a joint, but they're gone now. They've always been our answers to every problem and now they've been taken away from us. We're being *punished*."

Richard got to his feet, fists clenched, and growled through his teeth, "Goddammit, will you shut the fuck up. We're not being punished because we haven't done anything wrong. We're just like everybody else in this neighborhood, this town, this whole goddamned *country*. We've got problems, we have bad days, we fight, just like everybody else, you hear me? There's nothing *wrong* with us, we just had an accident that looked suspicious to one doctor, one miserable fucking doctor, and if he denies siccing this black bastard on us, I'll sue *his* ass, too, by Christ. So shut up. We're *not* being punished. There's nothing *wrong* with us." He paced as he spoke and, when he was finished, he sat heavily on the bed, breathing as if from a run, and spoke quietly to the floor. "I'll go into the city and get a really good lawyer. Top drawer. A Jew. Somebody who'll—"

"We're not going to sue anyone, Richard. Can't you see that we're *trapped* in this. Because we're guilty. We're dirty. Filthy." Tears rippled calmly and quietly down her face. She went to the dresser and leaned on it, staring down at the music box, afraid to touch it.

"Christ, Danielle, you talk about us like we're pornographers, or something! This... this is just insane! *You're* insane if you think we deserve to be—"

"You know it as well as I do, Richard. You most of all."

He clutched her shoulder and spun her around, spitting, "And what the fuck does *that* mean?"

"I let it go on. I watched. I said nothing, did nothing. Because I was afraid of what you would do to me. After you beat me that first time—"

His face twisted. "You lying bitch, I've never laid a hand on you and you know it, I've never so much as—"

"*Stop!*" she cried. "Please stop, Richard, it's making me sick, physically *ill*, this... this selective memory we've developed."

"I may have a temper, but—"

"No, Richard. You have more than a temper. I let it go on because I was afraid of you, so that makes me dirty, too. But you *did* it. You were the one who always *did* it, kicking him, hitting him, throwing him—" She stopped for an instant as a sob hit her in the midsection, "—throwing him around like a beanbag doll. The way you always—"

He was on her in an instant, fingers digging hard into her shoulders as he shook her back and forth, his face darkening with blood, eyes pushing from their sockets like a toad's, his mouth spraying her face with spittle as he roared, "That's bullshit, that is such *bullshit*, goddamn you, I was *not* always the one, was I, Dani, *was* I?" He slammed her back against the dresser, then quickly moved away from her, pacing. "*Was* I?"

She knew the answer, but she could not say the word…

22.

"How old are you now, Jason?"

"Seven."

"And where are you?"

"My… room."

"Where are your parents?"

"Dad's in… his room… dressing, I think. Mom's in the… hall bathroom. They're… going out, I guess."

"Who will stay with you?"

"Probably Tracy. From down the street. Or Mrs. Royer."

Jason was silent a while, lying on the sofa, eyes half open, but not seeing the living room ceiling, not really. He was, in his eyes, leaving his bedroom and going down the hall to the bathroom, where his mother was curling her hair. He stood in the doorway and watched her, unnoticed.

The phone rang and Jason heard his dad answer in the bedroom. Moments later, the curses began.

"Goddammit. Son of a *bitch!*"

Jason turned to hurry back to his room, but it was too late; his dad was coming down the hall, shirtless, a blue and red tie held in his fist.

"Forget it," he said angrily. "Just forget it. She can't come. Tracy can't come. Dammit." He pushed Jason aside and stepped into the bathroom. "She just called. No sitter. I'll call and cancel the reservations."

Jason ached when he saw the shattered disappointment on his mom's face.

"Can't we get someone else?" she asked hopefully.

"This late? *Who*, for Christ's sake?"

"But… but I've been looking forward to… you *promised* we'd—"

"Well, what the hell am I supposed to do? We're sure not gonna take him *with* us!" He spun and returned to the bedroom.

Jason stepped toward the doorway again but collided with his mom, who shoved him into the doorjamb and snapped, "Dammit, Jason, *get-out-of-the-way!*" Hurrying down the hall, she called, "April's gone tonight, but maybe Ken would watch him for us."

"Christ, Dani, he's not gonna want to—"

"Well, just let me call and ask."

Jason regained his balance, went into the bathroom, and stared at himself in the mirror as his parents shouted at one another.

"No," his mom said, "we *never go* out, we haven't been out in over a *year*, and now that we've actually made plans—"

"Well don't bitch at *me* about it, *you're* the one who wanted to have kids so bad, what the hell'd you think, they come *equipped* with babysitters?"

"Just let me call and ask Ken—"

"You're not calling to ask him anything."

When Jason heard his mom begin to cry, he decided to go back to his room and read a book, stay out of the way, but as he turned around, his arm caught on something—a cord—and when he pulled his arm back, his mom's curling iron slid away from the sink and fell to the floor.

Jason stared at it.

He knew he should pick it up, but Mom had always told him never *ever* to touch her curling iron and he was scared he'd make her angry.

So he stared, thinking about it, trying to decide what to do—

—as smoke began to curl upward from the blackening carpet.

The smell was awful and, terrified, certain of the punishment that would come, Jason bent down and picked up the curling iron, but—

—the smoke alarm in the hall began to scream and the noise so startled him that he dropped it again.

He was trembling now, quaking uncontrollably with fear, but he tried to pick it up again before too much damage was done and, as he bent down, he felt the presence of someone behind him as the smoke alarm wailed on.

When fists began to fall on his neck and back, Jason knew that it was his dad, knew that his mother would be standing in the hall, watching, her eyes dead, until she could take it no longer.

But he was wrong.

"Goddamn you! Goddamn you!" his mom screamed again and again, her fists pounding in turn with each syllable. "How many times? How many times have I told you not to touch it? How many times? Don't you know it's hot? It's *hot!*" She slammed him against the sink, clutched his wrist and pressed something into his hand, screaming, "Here! *Here!* Feel this? Feel it? Didn't I say it was hot?"

257

When Jason felt his skin melting, he began to scream, "No, Mommy, no, don't, *noooo—*"

"Why don't you do what you're told? All you do is make trouble! *Trouble!* All the screaming and crying—"

"—doooon't Mommyyy—"

"—because of *you!* Now we can't even go *out!* Because of *you!* Everything's turned to *shit—*"

"—*noooo!*"

"—because of *you!*"

The alarm stopped.

His mom fell away from him, staring with disbelief at the now messy curling iron held in her fist, her knuckles as white as her face.

Jason could not get enough breath to cry out loud; he simply shook with muffled sobs as his mom began touching him, caressing his face as she cried, "What have I done? What have I done?"

And from the hall, there came a groaning, long and deep and tremulous.

"Oh, dear Jesus, what have I done? What have I done?" his mom sobbed as his dad stood moving oddly in the hall, blurred by Jason's tears.

Groaning... groaning...

Jason clutched the sofa cushions beneath him, grinding his teeth.

"Relax, Jason," Dr. Krusadian whispered as the thing that now hunkered beside him shifted its gelatinous bulk. "Just relax. Take deep breaths."

Jason did, took them in deep and let them out slowly, gradually relaxing, feeling his body sink into the cushions.

Dr. Krusadian stood and gathered the tarpaulin together. As he began to drag it, full and heavy and shifting, from the room, Jason spoke.

"What's that?"

Dr. Krusadian stopped, smiled, and replied, "Something for your parents."

23.

As Jason lay on the sofa reliving the relentless punishments of his seventh and eighth years, working his way to the previous night's fall down the stairs, the shouting upstairs continued without pause. They had been shouting in long uninterrupted circles and by the time Jason had forgotten all about his mom's curling iron and was into the next torment, they had come around to the beginning again.

"It only happened once," Dani gasped, "and I hated myself for it, I *still* hate myself. I've never done it again and you know it, but I've let *you* do it and that's just as bad. You do it constantly. Every day, sometimes. You don't have a *temper*, Richard." She spat the word "temper" through a burst of bitter, hateful laughter. "You have a *prob*-lem, Richard."

Veins stood out on Richard's neck and his hands opened and closed over the pockets of his tan chinos; his lips tore back over his teeth, then bunched into a rectum-like hole through which he puffed bursts of air as he slowly advanced toward her a step at a time.

"You're *sick*, Richard," Dani went on, not caring that his anger was stretched over his face like thin transparent plastic, transparent but disfiguring and suffocating. "You're sick and you *know* it, and that just makes you worse, doesn't it? Knowing that you're so *sick*, that you're such a *monster*."

He was closer, actually tearing his pockets from his pants now with fingers hooked into claws.

"Know that you *enjoy* beating up on children and women. That you actually *get off* on—"

He struck. His arm whipped through the air and his palm connected with her face with the sound of cracking ice.

"That's bullshit!" he hissed, cheeks quivering as they deepened in color. He repeated "bullshit" again and again, striking her each time, driving her backward until she fell against the dresser. The back of her head cracked the mirror and shards of reflective glass rained over her, dancing together musically like blood-speckled wind chimes. He dragged her away from the dresser by her hair and threw her to the floor, then swept his arm through the perfume bottles and powder puffs and lipsticks and jewelry, sending it all to the floor with her in a clatter of plastic and glass. A dozen different perfumes mingled and rose in an eye-watering cloud, filling the room with flowers and spices and sexual promise. Richard stood over her and dropped to his knees, straddling her chest. He began to beat her shoulders and face and head, spitting "*Bull*shit! *Bull*shit! *Bull*shit! Nothing's wrong! There's *nothing* wrong, goddammit, nothing's *wrong!*"

Dani tried to scream for help, certain that Dr. Krusadian, however sinister he might be, would not allow this to go on while he was in the house, but the fists were coming too fast and hitting too hard and she was afraid she would lose consciousness soon and—

—then she felt it. Against her. Pressing between her breasts.

Through the thunder in her skull, Dani heard the music box begin to play. It had fallen from the dresser to the floor with all the other things and lay beside her head, so close that she could hear its insides moving again, coming to life, turning slowly with soft clicks and whispers and—

—Richard struck her cheek and her head snapped to one side and her eyes, swelling and blurred, locked onto the box and held and she saw it, Dani saw—

—that horrible *thing*.

She'd seen it so many times before and each time she dragged it from the center of her attention like some bloated incriminating corpse and she'd buried it, hidden it away in one of the many secret compartments of her memory, compartments she kept locked and covered so no one— including Dani herself—would notice them.

She'd seen it and ignored it.

That horrible thing.

And she saw it for the first time once again. And the second and the third, countless times, on and on through the nine years they'd had Jason. She saw it pressing and throbbing against the wall of its small prison, trying to expose its one glistening eye so it could watch, firsthand, the pain and violence that inflamed and excited it so. The images rushed through her mind with painful dizzying velocity, sickening her, inflating her with such hatred for herself that she felt she would burst and then—

—they were gone.

And she was left with only one.

Richard had stopped shouting, had even stopped beating her, but he was still on her.

Groaning.

Moving against her.

Pressing his sickness between her breasts.

He pulled one bloodied hand away from her face and placed it over the bulge between his legs, smearing his crotch with her blood and squeezing his erection, letting his head flop back, mouth gaping to make way for the dreadful groan that slithered up from deep in his chest and rose to become a trembling cry as his hips began to convulse on her and a dark wet spot appeared over the bulge and spread slowly like a soggy cancer as his back stiffened and he gulped air and sputtered, "Nuh-nothing's wruh-wrong! Nuh-nuh-nothing's *wrong!*"

Richard's body quaked for several seconds, then calmed to a brief shiver, and finally became still as he stared forever at the ceiling without even taking a breath. Then he lowered his head and blinked his wide confused eyes, looking at Dani, then his hands, then his soiled pants. His hands trembled as he dragged himself off Dani and crawled on all fours over broken glass to the bed against which he leaned as he sat and stared at his hands. They were imbedded now with tiny shards and slivers, but he didn't seem to notice; he dropped them in his lap, gasping suddenly for breath as he whispered, "There's... nothing wrong... is there? *Is* there? Please. There's nothing... wrong..."

"Yes, there is," she said, spitting blood. "And I'm going to fix it."

A clatter at the door signaled Dr. Krusadian's entrance.

He stepped into the bedroom and, silently and without expression, surveyed the mess. He went to Dani's side, bent down and retrieved the music box, then studied the two of them closely before saying, "My work with Jason is finished. It is your turn now. Please clean yourselves up and come downstairs."

24.

Jason sat up slowly on the sofa, feeling as if he'd taken a long nap filled with muddled dreams. He looked around the darkened living room and recognized Dr. Krusadian's bags beside the recliner. But there should be something else... the music box and tarpaulin; they were gone. He was alone and the only sound was the rain falling outside. When he tried to stand, Jason felt very dizzy and wondered why; he'd been doing nothing more than lying on the sofa talking with Dr. Krusadian and listening to the music box.

Hadn't he?

Jason tried to think back over the past few hours but could come up with nothing clear or solid. Just music. Beautiful, restful music. He couldn't even remember where his parents had gone.

There were voices upstairs, so he wasn't alone in the house, but that didn't quell the fear growing inside him, brought on by his confusion and disorientation.

"Mom?" he called, quietly the first time, then again, louder and with urgency.

"What, Sweetie?" she cried, her footsteps thumping down the hall. "What's wrong, honey? I'm coming! It's all right!" She hobbled down the stairs, clinging to the banister with both hands, and knelt before him.

In the shadows, she was an obscene clown; one blackened eye was swollen into a ghastly lingering wink and blood smeared her pale face like dark red greasepaint.

"What is it, honey?" she whispered, clutching his small knees.

He was inclined, at first, to ask about her face, but didn't because he knew she would lie and he already knew the truth, anyway.

"I was... scared, is all."

"There's nothing to be scared of, baby. Not now. Not anymore. I promise." She leaned forward and embraced him, pressing her bloody face to his chest and crying softly. "Your mom's not gonna let anything happen to you anymore."

Voices shouted upstairs; Jason recognized Dr. Krusadian's rising like flames to the very top of the house. He sounded much the way Jason had always imagined God to sound.

"Is Dr. Krusadian angry?" Jason whispered. "Did… did I do something wrong?"

"No, honey, nobody's angry at you. You haven't done a thing."

The shouting stopped. Dr. Krusadian came down the stairs, turned on the lights and put something in his black bag.

Jason watched his dad descend to the living room one heavy step at a time, shoulders wilted, head sagging forward. He was wearing different pants.

Jason squinted at the sudden light and rubbed his eyes.

Dr. Krusadian said, "Mr. and Mrs. Campbell, if you would come with me to the kitchen, please."

Jason opened his eyes when his mom pulled away from him and said, "I'd like to talk to you, Dr. Krusadian."

"We will talk."

"Alone," she whispered, glancing at her husband. "Please."

"In the kitchen, Mrs. Campbell." He took a step backward and gestured with his arm. "After you."

Jason watched his parents go, his dad first, his mom following reluctantly. She stopped in front of the doctor and whispered, "Look, whatever you've done—"

"The kitchen, Mrs. Campbell."

"—I've decided this has got to stop and I'm going to take Jason out of here. Tonight. Now. He… my husband… is sick. I can't let it go on anymore. I'm getting out."

"That's very noble of you, but out of the question for two reasons. It won't solve the problem, first of all. And secondly—" He grinned. "—I'm not through with you yet. Now, Mrs. Campbell. After you."

Dr. Krusadian turned to Jason, gave him a wink, and followed them into the kitchen.

When they were out of sight, Jason stood, crept to the kitchen entrance, leaned his back against the wall, and listened.

25.

"Please sit down," Dr. Krusadian said, seating himself at the table.

Reluctantly, Dani pulled up a chair but she did not want to sit down; she wanted to take the doctor aside and explain that she had finally, after so many years, come to her senses and wanted to take Jason away from the house immediately. She had no idea where she would go or how she would support herself and her son, but she'd decided upstairs, only a few minutes before, that poverty—even *homelessness*—would be preferable to living on in the nightmare her family had become.

Along with that, she was afraid—*terrified*—of what Dr. Krusadian was going to do.

"It is time, Mr. and Mrs. Campbell, to face what you have done to your boy."

"Dr. Krusadian," Dani said, "if you'll just listen to me for a—"

"There will be plenty of time for listening afterward."

Dani flinched. "After... ward? After what?"

He simply looked at her with a gentle smile.

Richard sat at the table with his face in his hands, looking at neither of them. He jerked to attention when Dr. Krusadian spoke to him.

"I'm curious, Mr. Campbell. Can you explain this? Your wife's face? The cuts and bruises?"

No reply.

"Teaching her a lesson, were you?"

"We… had… an argument. That's all." His hands trembled noisily against the tabletop.

"Ah, an argument. You enjoy them, don't you? These arguments."

"It was just an argument. *Everybody* has arguments."

"Then you don't think this is a problem?"

Richard steeled himself, stopped the trembling and leveled an icy glare at the doctor.

"Only because you're *making* it a problem. We were fine. Before."

"We were *not* fine," Dani hissed. "We've *never* been fine."

Dr. Krusadian asked, "When was the last time you two had sex? Together?"

They turned to him, but neither spoke.

"I say *together* because it's quite obvious that Mr. Campbell has been sexually active for some time on his own. Not what *most* would think of as sex, but it's sex to you, isn't it?" He turned to Richard, still wearing that smile. "You drink heavily, so I would imagine you're impotent. Alcohol does that, you know. But you have found something *else*. Haven't you?"

Richard's face turned crimson, twisted painfully, and he turned away.

"And you," Krusadian went on, looking at Dani, "have closed your eyes to it all. Even joined in the fun."

"Wait, wait just a sec—"

"Do you still use a curling iron, Mrs. Campbell?"

She gasped and, seconds later, tears followed.

"I know what I've done," she sobbed. "At least I *admit* it! And I'm going to *stop!* Right now. Please. Let me go. I'll take Jason. I'll never let him near Richard again. I'll—"

"Like *hell* you will," Richard growled.

Dr. Krusadian lifted a hand. "Please. Let's not do this. Now, I believe, Mrs. Campbell, that you are *aware* of what you've done. I think both of you are, although one of you won't admit it. But I don't think either of you truly *know* what you've done." He pushed his chair back and stood, taking a key from his pocket. "Do you remember what I said earlier about removing the demons you have inflicted upon your son?"

Dani wanted to scream. She had never in her life wanted so desperately to empty her lungs into the air and run as fast and far as she could.

"Dr. Krusadian, puh-puh-please…"

He ignored her. "Well, I have done that. Even from you, Mrs. Campbell. You had a demon of your own that needed release."

"Please, duh-doctor, I-I-I don't… want to… duh-do this…"

"But you, Mr. Campbell, are a rock."

Richard did not even look at him.

"You refuse to let go of whatever monsters you have locked inside. And I *know* you have them. Your life, I suspect, has been a tragic one. Your father was a hard, cruel man, am I right?"

Richard's teeth crunched together dryly and tears sparkled in his eyes, unfallen.

"Your childhood was violent and cold. Did your mother look away, too? I suspect. Surely there had to be one moment in your life—one isolated redeeming moment—when you vowed that *your* children would never have to endure such cruelty. Hm?"

Richard clenched and released his fists between his knees again and again.

"I suspect. But you let it pass unheeded. Instead, you went on to kick and beat your son through the same hell from which you'd come, denying it all the while. In fact, you've wallowed in denial. For the past several hours, you've had the opportunity to break, to cleanse yourself, but even *now* you remain unmovable. That is unfortunate, Mr. Campbell. For your family… and you."

Dr. Krusadian went to the basement door and slipped his key into the upper padlock, releasing it with a loud, solid… *clitch.* He unlocked the lower one and placed them both on the table, then faced them and said, "Come. I've something to show you."

Dani felt herself coming unraveled. She stood, but her knees threatened collapse, making her wobble rather than walk backward away from the door.

"Please," she whimpered, finding little voice in her throat, "don't do this. I said I was sorry. I said I would stop. *Please.*"

"Not now. It's too late. Being sorry isn't enough," Dr. Krusadian said, offering his hand, "until you know precisely what you are sorry *for.* Come. I'll hold your hand. It will be all right. I promise. You, too, Mr. Campbell. What have you to lose? If you are so certain there is no problem, you have no worries. Do you?"

Richard looked around, blinking, as if coming awake, and sat up straight. Something dawned in his face as he turned to Dani. He seemed to be considering the possibility that her talk of punishment earlier had not been the ramblings of a drunk.

"Dr. Krusadian," Dani whispered, "*please* let me go. I-I'm sorry for what I've duh-done and I swear I'll make it all up to Jason, but please for Christ's sake let me—"

"*Enough!*" the doctor roared, then said with quiet threat, "if you do not comply, your son will be taken from you and all of this will be made public. If that appeals to you, then so be it. If not… then come let me show you something."

Dani watched the familiar anger creep into Richard's face, even into his posture. He stood, took a deep breath, and swallowed his fear.

"All right. You son of a bitch, all right," he whispered. "Come on, Dani, let's get this over with."

"No. No. Please."

"Goddammit, Dani, come on. How bad can it be, for Christ's sake? It's *our* basement."

Dr. Krusadian nodded, smiling, and said, "That is precisely the attitude I expected from you, Mr. Campbell. Now come." He pulled the door open and said, "After you."

Light from the kitchen spilled half way down the narrow wooden staircase, halting at a wall of darkness.

"Dani," Richard summoned.

"No."

"Dammit—" He grabbed her wrist and pulled her hard toward the open door, "—come *on*."

Dani shriveled up inside as he jerked her through the door, their feet clattering on the steps.

"Wait," she hissed, "wait, the *light*, it's dark, please get the li—"

The door slammed shut behind them.

The upper lock fell into place heavily and clicked.

Then the lower lock.

Blackness.

Dani screamed.

When he heard his mom's muffled scream, Jason hurried into the kitchen, frightened.

"What's-matter?"

Dr. Krusadian held up his palms in reassurance and said, "Nothing to worry about, Jason."

"But I heard Mom—" He stopped and looked around the kitchen. "Where are they?"

"They are in the basement."

"The basement? Why?"

Dr. Krusadian gently covered Jason's back with one hand and led him from the kitchen. "Come to the living room and I'll set up my camera, Jason. I want to take your picture. And don't worry about your parents. They will be fine, just fine. They have a lot of thinking to do. And when they have finished, things will be much different in this house." He patted Jason's back. "And much better."

Jason left the kitchen with Dr. Krusadian and the fearful shouting voices of his parents faded behind him.

26.

Dani flipped the light switch up and down a dozen times in rapid fire succession, sobbing uncontrollably, before she allowed herself to entertain the possibility that the light was not going to come on.

Richard's fists thundered uselessly against the door as he bellowed, "Open this fucking door, goddamn you, *open* it! This is kidnapping! I'll send you to prison for the rest of your fucking life, you son of a bitch!"

Pushing herself close to Richard, Dani clutched his arm and shook her whole body convulsively as if to toss the clinging darkness away from her.

"Get us out, Richard, please, you've gotta get us *out* of here!"

"Stop it, for Christ's sake."

"Don't you see why he put us down here? I tried to tell you he—"

Something moved down in the dark.

It was a wet sound. Bare feet stomping through a sewer. A silent baby crawling through pudding.

It was coming toward the stairs.

"Oh Guh-Guh-God," Dani breathed, then began pounding on the door, too, her elbow clubbing Richard's shoulder with each blow.

He ordered her to stop, but some of the fierceness had left his voice.

"The hell was that?" he muttered after a moment of still listening.

"That thing—I tried to *tell* you, Richard—that *thing!*"

It moved again.

Closer.

Richard took two steps down the stairs and Dani grabbed his shoulders, pulling him back and crying, "No, no, don't go down there, Richard, don't—"

He shook her off and snapped, "Will you leave me *alone?*" Two more steps.

Dani dug her fingernails into her palms and sucked her lips between her teeth, holding her breath.

"Who's there?" Richard shouted.

Silence.

Both were motionless for a moment and Dani found herself praying silently for the first time since she was a girl, when her grandmother told her again and again that Jesus was always waiting to help her whenever she needed him. Then Richard made a frustrated sound in his throat and muttered, "There's a flashlight here, somewhere."

She remembered the long black flashlight hanging from a hook on the wall over the stairs; Richard had hung it there years ago after the first time a fuse blew and Richard had to find his way down to the breaker box in total darkness. The thought of being able to see whatever was slopping around below made her insides wither and, when she heard his hand whispering over the wall in search of the flashlight, she reached out for him, groping until she found the top of his head.

271

"No, Richard, please."

He brushed her away, found the flashlight, and clicked it on.

The beam sliced through darkness and fell on the cement floor below, passing over boxes and bags and a few pieces of old dusty furniture. But beyond the bar of light, the darkness remained, heavy and fat.

"What's he done?" Richard whispered, sounding interested, perhaps even fascinated by the doctor's cleverness, then called, "Who's there?"

Dani clutched her own hair when he started down the stairs, unable to speak or even breathe.

Richard stopped, looked over his shoulder and said, "Well? Come *on.*"

"Richard, please, don't make me—"

His face stopped her; it curled into that mask of threat that had held her prisoner for so long.

"If you don't come down here right now," he said, so quietly she barely heard, "I'm gonna come up there and *drag* you down here by your *hair.*"

With her eyes only, she followed the beam of light downward again; she saw nothing, but she knew—as she knew the sun was coming up soon—that something awaited them down there, silent and with purpose.

"I-I-I'll just stay up here, Richard, really, I'm—"

"Get down here!"

Wiping a tear from her unswollen eye, Dani leaned heavily against the wooden handrail; she lowered her foot to the next step as if she were lowering it into boiling water. Then the next step… and the next… Then, under her feet, she felt something slick and sticky. She stopped, looked down at the step and, in the poor light, she saw a glistening strip of thick fluid that went all the way down the stairs, like the trail of a slug.

A very big slug.

With a dry, hoarse voice, she whispered, "Richard?"

Something slashed in a far corner of the basement and a stack of boxes toppled over. One box spilled Christmas ornaments and a bundle of sparkling red and green garland over the concrete floor; some of the ornaments shattered and tossed freckles of reflected light over the walls.

Richard hurried toward the corner muttering, "What the hell?" and kicked two boxes aside, searching for the cause of the disturbance.

Dani quickened her pace down the stairs, reached the floor and called, "Richard, I don't think you should do that."

He spun to her, holding the flashlight down at his side so it spilled a puddle of light around his feet, and barked, "Well, what the hell do you *want* me to—"

Something rose quickly in the shadows behind him— something that looked like a hill of pus—then fell forward, wrapping itself around the lower half of his body.

Richard dropped the flashlight and groped the air as he fell forward, sputtering helplessly.

The light flickered as it rolled over the floor, finally holding on the thing that was engulfing Richard. It sloshed forward up his body, stopped, opened a black cavernous maw, then closed it with another quivering forward motion, like a snake devouring a kicking rat. One glaring eye bulged atop the creature, black, dead, and unblinking, like a shark's; another was positioned lower and to the side.

Dani stumbled backward, groping for the handrail, trying to scream, but unable to take in a breath; her lungs had turned to stone.

The glistening shapeless mass bloated with each gulp until only Richard's arms, shoulders and head were visible. His mouth opened and closed, his hands clawed the concrete, and

273

when his helpless eyes finally met Dani's, he screamed like a child.

"Help meeee!"

Her heel caught the bottom step and she fell back on the stairs and began scrabbling backward up the steps because —

— the boxes in the corner were being pushed aside, scraping harshly over the floor, to make room for another, this one black, like a great clot of cancer dragging a tail of cheerful Christmas tree garland.

"Dani! For Chri—Dan—elp meeee!"

His arms waved and repeatedly slapped the floor until his hands left bloody smears on the concrete—

— until his arms had been swallowed up—

— until his head was gone.

But she could still hear him.

That was the worst of it—so far, anyway—hearing his muffled screams gargling from inside the creature as it bulged and constricted.

Finally discovering her breath again, Dani screamed, and once she started, she couldn't stop. The shrill cries came again and again, like unmanageable sobs convulsing her lungs, and she kept crawling backward up the stairs as—

— the creature that had swallowed Richard began to... *shrink.* The viscous snot-like mass began to take on a shape. *Richard's* shape. Even in her panic, Dani could make out the form of Richard's arm reaching upward inside the creature as it tightened around him, clinging to his body. She saw the curve of his shoulder, the lump that was his head, and the round indentation of his screaming mouth. The black eyes began to dissolve, run down the creature's sides like blood, and finally disappear as its size continued to decrease and Richard's body became more and more visible, writhing and groping for escape.

His clogged scream stopped.

Skin and tattered clothes became visible as the creamy slime began to disappear, as if evaporating.

Dani's back slammed against the locked basement door as Richard lay on his back down below, the middle of his body thrusting upward again and again, back arched, hands clawed; he stared blindly at the darkness above him, mouth yawning in a silent scream.

"Richard? Ri-*Richard?*" Her voice was raw meat and her fingernails were breaking loudly as she clawed the door behind her, trying to pull herself up.

With great effort, he rolled on his side toward her, the flashlight inches from his face, which was a deadly shade of gray and trying so hard to speak. He made only a rasping sound in his throat as he reached out a hand to her; his soggy, tattered shirtsleeve dangled in strips from his arm and his fingers quivered as they closed over nothing as—

—the creature behind him drew nearer, slopping over the concrete as lumps rose from its black gelatinous surface and—

—the lumps took the shapes of hands with four fingers and a thumb each and—

—the hands closed into powerful fists that lifted and poised to strike as the thing closed the space between itself and Richard.

"Get *up*, get *up*, Richard, for Christ's *sake*, get *up!*"

But he didn't seem to hear her, only kept reaching out, mouth twisting, throat squeezing out small pathetic sounds, eyes rolling in his head like loose marbles.

When the thing poured itself over Richard's feet and began to make its way up his legs, he turned toward it, sucked in a loud breath that sounded like metal shavings filling his lungs, and found his voice in a long, bone-scraping cry as—

—the darkness in the basement began to come alive with them and they moved forward slowly, wetly, different sizes, different shapes, but all moving in with steady, confident determination and—

—Dani's hand found the doorknob and clutched it, pulling until she was on her knees, turning toward the door and pounding desperately, pleading. Pleading...

They were screaming in the Campbell house again. But unless one listened very closely for them, the screams could not be heard from outside. They came from below. Had anyone heard, he or she would have known things were more unright than usual with the Campbells because these were not the screams with which the neighbors had become familiar.

But only Jason heard them.

He was in the living room with Dr. Krusadian, who had just finished setting up a camera on a tripod when the screams became words.

"I'm sorry!" Jason's mom cried. "I'm so sorry! I won't do it anymore, I *won't*, I *promise!*"

Jason froze and listened. At first, he'd thought it was just another fight between his parents, but now he knew better.

"Jason? *Jason!* Please help your mommy. *Please!* We'll go away! Well go away and you'll never be hurt again, I *promise!* Don't let them get me, Jason, *please don't let them get meeee!*"

He turned to Dr. Krusadian, a chill working its way over his body, and asked, "What's the matter with Mom?"

"Don't worry about it, Jason. Trust me. Now, I'd like to get a picture to remember you by."

"Jason, I *love* you! Your mommy *loves* you! Plee-h*ee-heeeze*, Jesus, get me out of here before, oh Jesus *Christ*, before they get me, *please!*"

He turned to the doctor with terrified eyes and whispered, "What's down there?"

Dr. Krusadian studied Jason's face as he spent a silent moment with his thoughts, then knelt down beside the boy and put an arm around his small shoulders, pressing his mouth close to Jason's ear.

"Listen to me carefully, Jason. You must promise you will listen carefully."

Jason nodded.

"Think back over the years, over your life. Have you been happy? Have you ever been truly happy?"

No reply.

"Listen to your mommy, Jason, *listen* to me! I'll take you away from him and he'll never hit you again, never, I promise just *get me out of here!*"

"You are smiling in none of the pictures," Dr. Krusadian went on. "You don't *look* happy. I don't think you've ever been. Have you?"

A slight shake of his head.

Screams—such terrified, desperate screams—drifted in from the kitchen like foul smells on the air.

"There have been times you've *wanted* to be happy, haven't there?" Dr. Krusadian asked. "Times when others around you were happy and enjoying themselves. But you could not. Because there was something inside you... something fat and suffocating that would not *let* you feel happiness. Am I right?"

Another tentative nod.

"Open this door, Jason, *right now!* You open this goddamned door for your mother or so help me God... oh Jesus, they're coming, they're *coming!* Jason, they're *coming!*"

The doctor gave him a gentle squeeze. "Well, Jason, that is gone. That thing inside you that kept you from being happy? I've taken it away. All this evening I've been taking it away a piece at a time. So you can be happy. Because I've taken it away.

And I've given it to the people who put it there. I've given it to your parents."

"*Ja*-son! *Ja*-son! *Jaaaaa*-soooon!"

"But," Jason whispered, "will… will they be okay? Will they be hurt?"

"They will be fine. Later. Things will be different. But they will be fine. Trust me."

Jason thought about that a while as the screams went on, growing into lung bursting wails, then diminishing into raspy sobs. He thought about it and the frown on his brow slowly relaxed.

Dr. Krusadian stood and said, "Now. Come." He adjusted something on the camera and led Jason to the hearth where he put his arm around the boy's shoulders. "Let's take a picture. Ready?"

He stood beside the enormous black man, expressionless and silent, still thinking about what he'd said. Then… slowly… Jason did something he hadn't done in a very long time.

With a click and a flash, it was recorded forever.

Dani wore her voice down to a hoarse croak as she pounded on the door, begging to be let out. The sounds coming from below were making her ill and she didn't want to look down the stairs, but when she felt she could scream no more, she looked over her shoulder against her better judgement and knew she was seeing her fate.

Richard was struggling in the grasp of the black creature that glistened like a big rotten peeled grape; the glutinous fists that protruded from it battered him relentlessly as it sucked him in, kicking and screaming Dani's name until her name was no more than a nonsense sound. And after it had devoured him whole, it, too, began to disappear around him like filthy water being sucked down a drain, until it left him lying alone on the floor, a sloppy quivering mess, naked now except for the gobs of fatty slime that clung to his body, as the others closed in. But before they reached him, Richard craned his head back until he was looking at her, his face upside down, hand reaching out again, lips battling with one another to form words as his body convulsed.

He hissed, "They're... inside me... now, Dani... puh-please..."

Then another was on him, this one purple as if engorged with blood, a long thick penis—tumorous and dripping fluids—jutting from its front, its throbbing head directed between Richard's trembling legs. He screamed again as it spilled itself over him, but his voice was losing its strength.

As Richard disappeared beneath it, Dani turned away, trying to pound on the door again, but was unable to clench a fist.

"I'm sorry," she rasped. "I'm sorry, I'm... so... sorry..."

Richard's weary screams were muffled, then swallowed, replaced by moist slurping sounds, then—

—silence.

A long silence.

Too long.

Her lungs clogged with dread, Dani turned her head slowly to look down the stairs again. Richard lay on the floor, the flashlight draping half his body in shadow, as another creature moved toward him silently, this one covered with long thin protuberances the size and shape of cigarettes, each with a glowing red ember at the end. It headed for him like an impossibly slow, malformed heat-seeking missile.

But there were three others, and they moved around Richard—

—coming toward the stairs.

With clumsy jerky movements, Dani turned her body toward them, pressing her back hard to the door and hugging her knees to her breasts. She ignored the others moving in the shadows at the far end of the basement as the three she watched oozed by Richard and into the glow of the flashlight. One came ahead of the others, the color of dead flesh, its bulk shifting this way and that as a hand—or the *shape* of a hand—reached out between the two bulbous eyes. Something grew out of the hand, something long and narrow, a familiar shape, with a long clamp running down one side. The clamp opened and closed as the fist squeezed the object's handle.

A curling iron.

The others advanced slightly behind, covered with eyes—*human* eyes—that were gouged and running with blood.

Blinded eyes.

Dani wanted to scream but didn't have the strength and saw no point to it anyway.

The creatures stopped at the bottom of the stairs. Waiting.

The most wonderful thought occurred to her then, as Richard began to stir again, surrounded by slime-fisted creatures with unfeeling eyes, his body clothed in slime. The thought made her so happy, so excited and hopeful, that she stood and grabbed the doorknob behind her, rattling the door as hard as she could.

"They can't come up the stairs," she muttered, then screamed it, pounding on the door again, her back to them, glancing over her shoulder every few seconds as she begged again for help—"They can't come up the stairs! Help me! They can't come up the stairs!"—until—

—the creature holding the curling iron out before it like a sword split open. Its enormous mouth gaped until it was a great black hole at the bottom of the stairs and Dani thought if she fell in she might never reach bottom. She stopped pounding, turned, and—

—a thick rope of slime shot from the mouth and up the stairs in a heartbeat, slapping around her ankle and pulling. Hard.

The world lurched and Dani found herself airborne, looking up at her feet until she hit the stairs and was bathed in sharp stabbing pain as the thing dragged her down over the hard wooden steps, closer and closer to the gaping cavern of a mouth that waited below, until she was plunged into the moist stale blackness and it closed around her and then —

—eternity began.

It was the first of three.

Jason stood in the kitchen doorway watching Dr. Krusadian. The big man stood at the rear of the kitchen, his ear inclined toward the basement door. The screaming downstairs had stopped some time ago, but the doctor listened carefully to the silence. Then he turned to Jason, stood straight and smiled, saying, "My work here is over." Jason followed him into the living room, where Dr. Krusadian picked up his bags and carried them to the front door.

"You're *leaving?*"

"I'm finished." He put his bags down, put on his coat and hat and faced Jason. "When your parents come up later, they will be... groggy. A little confused, perhaps. And quite messy. Pay them no mind. They will clean up, get some sleep, and be fine. Wait for them in your room. And don't go into the basement. Jason, my friend—" He held out his hand and they shook, "—it has been a pleasure. I'm happy to know you."

"But... will I see you again? Can I call you? I mean, if I ever need you again?"

"You won't."

He touched Jason's head gently, then left.

27.

Jason awoke on the sofa to the light coming from outside. He went to the window and watched the sun climbing into a cloudless sky. The storm was over.

A sound from the kitchen startled him and he spun around, watching the doorway anxiously. He heard their voices first as they came out of the basement.

"What time is it?" his mom mumbled.

Someone stumbled.

"Richard? Are you all right?"

"I'm… yeah, I'm… I think I'm… gonna be sick."

"Where's Jason? *Jason?*"

"Yeah, Mom?"

"Are you okay?"

He started toward the kitchen, calling, "Yeah, I'm okay."

"Don't come in here!" she blurted weakly, but firmly. "Just… why don't you just… go upstairs for a while. 'Kay?"

"Yeah. Sure, Mom."

But he didn't. As they continued muttering to one another, Jason crept to the kitchen doorway hoping to peer around the doorjamb without being caught. Then he heard a sound that he couldn't at first identify; it was like a wet, ragged cough.

No, not a cough. A sob.

His dad was crying.

"Richard," his mom soothed, "Richard… c'mon, Richard…"

Jason no longer wanted to look. He hurried upstairs to his room.

Dani stared at Richard, horrified and weakened by the sight of him. Naked and shivering, his body dripping slime, he appeared, for the first time she could remember, cowed and broken. He leaned heavily on the table, shoulders hitching as he cried quietly and fought to hold down his gorge. Beneath the dark wet streaks that striped his head, Richard's brown hair was completely white.

"My God, Richard," Dani breathed, "look at you. Did... did that really happen? What did he do to us?"

"Stupid question, Dani," he muttered, padding across the kitchen. "Stupid question." He leaned forward and vomited into the sink.

When she heard Jason's bedroom door close, Dani left the kitchen and carefully scaled the stairs, her body aching from head to foot. More than anything she wanted a hot shower, then crisp sheets and a long dreamless sleep. But as she trudged through her bedroom and into the bathroom on watery knees, she had a feeling there would be no more dreamless sleeps.

The rectangular mirror over the sink, framed by strips of glaring white lightbulbs, was unmercifully cruel. She stared at the stranger trapped in the flat glass and wanted to cry, but was too exhausted to shed any more tears.

The substance clinging to her made her look old and lumpy. Lumpier than usual. Clots of it dribbled from her breasts, down her belly and over her face, and a string of it dangled from her chin. And her hair...

Mingling with the honey blond were broad streaks of white. Old lady white. Aged, decaying white.

She watched the reflection closely, half hoping it would change, or better yet, go away. When it didn't, she reached up, wiped the slime from her face and slopped it into the sink, revealing the deep lines that were carved into the flesh beneath her eyes.

Dani backed up three steps and sat on the edge of the bathtub, silently asking herself questions she couldn't answer.

What happened?

How much time has passed?

What were those things?

Closing her eyes, she tried to recall it all—

They're... inside... me now...

—but it was murky. She went back farther to their conversation with Dr. Krusadian—

My job is to remove from Jason all the demons you have inflicted upon him...

—to the hint of smug threat in his voice before he sent them down into the basement—

It is time to face up to what you have done to your boy...

—and back farther still to the fall that broke Jason's arm and brought the huge black doctor into their house—

No, she thought, feeling ill...

—and before that to the evenings full of screams and cries and the sounds of fists beating flesh—

... no, no...

—but the memories that stretched back almost a full nine years were somehow different, changed, as if someone had rummaged through her mind and rearranged them, and—

... please God no, he couldn't have...

—no matter how hard Dani tried to shift those memories in her mind, no matter how hard she tried to turn them this way and that and look at them from several different angles—

... they're inside me now, sweet Jesus, they're inside me now!

—those scalding memories of violent nights and scab covered mornings would not return as the safe, padded memories they had once been and Dani slid down off the tub and curled into a sobbing, retching ball on the tile floor.

The memories were not hers. They were no longer viewed through *her* eyes, tinted by the filter of her own thoughts and perspectives.

They were the memories of a victim, not of an observer.

The memories were Jason's.

And they were there to stay.

Dani screamed into her hands until she lost consciousness.

28.

They didn't scream in the Campbell house anymore. And things *did* change, just as Dr. Krusadian had promised.

Jason's parents stopped drinking. They didn't mention it, didn't even act as if they'd ever *touched* alcohol. The bottles that had been emptied at Dr. Krusadian's insistence had simply not been replaced.

Jason's mom kept busy around the house; she began to cook large delicious meals on the weekends and, during the week, they ate out more often than before, frequently at the restaurant of Jason's choice. His favorite was Chuck E. Cheese, where his dad always filled Jason's pockets with tokens and let him roam the game room while Mom and Dad sat quietly at their table.

Dad stopped reading the paper so much and spent more time with Jason in the evenings. In fact, they *both* spent more time with Jason.

Yes, there was definitely something different about them, but—except for the way they *looked*—they were different in a good way. They were quiet and nice and they touched him softly, sometimes staring at him silently for a long time with a sad look in their eyes. But they looked tired and... older. Their voices were thinner; they spoke slower and walked slower, shoulders heavy and brows furrowed. And in the bathrooms, Jason noticed bottles of coloring with labels that promised to hide gray hair.

But that wasn't so bad, because things were better.

They traveled. Disneyland was much more fun the second time around, and at Marine World and Safariland, Jason had his picture taken with animals he hadn't even known existed.

They took lots of new pictures to replace the old. Jason laughed and waved from the back of an elephant; he and his parents stood with Goofy and Donald Duck; he smiled as he hugged his mom on the beach and laughed on his dad's lap on a picnic in the Redwoods.

The new pictures were all very different from the ones they replaced because, in each of them, Jason looked happy. Very happy.

His parents didn't, though. They never smiled for the camera anymore.

Mom had arranged them all on the mantle in the living room, putting two on each side of Jason's favorite picture.

It was an eight-by-ten, framed in brass, and had arrived in the mail in a plain brown envelope addressed to Master Jason Campbell. There was no return address.

It was the picture that had been snapped immediately after Jason learned what had been done to his parents in the basement.

Jason stood next to the mountainous Dr. Krusadian in front of the fireplace.

And Jason was grinning joyously…

About the Author

Ray Garton has been writing novels, novellas, short stories, and essays for more than 30 years. His work spans the genres of horror, crime, suspense, and even comedy. *Live Girls* was nominated for the Bram Stoker Award in 1988, and Garton received the Grand Master of Horror Award at the 2006 World Horror Convention. He lives in northern California with his wife Dawn, where he is at work on a new novel.

BIBLIOGRAPHY

NOVELS AND NOVELLAS

411
Bestial
Biofire
Crawlers
Crucifax
Dark Channel

Darklings
Live Girls
Lot Lizards
Loveless
Night Life
Meds
Murder Was My Alibi
Ravenous
Scissors
Seductions
Serpent Girl
Sex and Violence in Hollywood
Shackled
The Folks
The Folks 2
The Loveliest Dead
The Man in the Palace Theater
The New Neighbor
Trade Secrets
Trailer Park Noir
Vortex
Zombie Love

COLLECTIONS
Methods of Madness
'Nids And Other Stories
Pieces of Hate
Slivers of Bone
The Disappeared and Other Stories
The Girl in the Basement and Other Stories
Wailing and Gnashing of Teeth

Curious about other Crossroad Press books? Stop by our
website: http://crossroadpress.com
We offer quality writing
in digital, audio, and print formats.

Subscribe to our newsletter on the website homepage and
receive a free eBook.

www.ingramcontent.com/pod-product-compliance
Lightning Source LLC
Chambersburg PA
CBHW030318200626
46816CB00006BA/1834